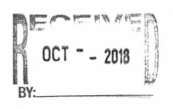

TRUST BUT VERIFY

Karna Small Bodman

Bodman

TRUST BUT VERIFY

REGNERY FICTION

Regnery Fiction™ is a trademark of Salem Communications Holding Corporation; Regnery® is a registered trademark of Salem Communications Holding Corporation

Cataloging-in-Publication data on file with the Library of Congress

ISBN 978-1-62157-779-9
e-book ISBN 978-1-62157-854-3

Published in the United States by
Regnery Fiction, an imprint of
Regnery Publishing
A Division of Salem Media Group
300 New Jersey Ave NW
Washington, DC 20001
www.RegneryFiction.com

Manufactured in the United States of America

10 9 8 7 6 5 4 3 2 1

Books are available in quantity for promotional or premium use. For information on discounts and terms, please visit our website: www.Regnery.com.

A man is usually more careful of his money than he is of his principles.

—Ralph Waldo Emerson

CHARACTERS

THE PRINCIPALS

Samantha Reid, Director of the White House Office of Homeland Security

Brett Keating, Special Agent, FBI

GOVERNMENT STAFF

Homer Belford, Assistant Secretary of the Treasury for Financial Crimes Enforcement

Ken Cosgrove, National Security Advisor

Nori Hotta, FBI Field Agent

Trevor Mason, Supervisor, Washington, D.C., FBI Field Office

Angela Marconi, Deputy Director, Presidential Scheduling

Philip Pickering, Secretary of the Treasury

Jim Shilling, Principal Deputy to Samantha Reid

Joan Tillman, Administrative Assistant to Samantha Reid

Dominic "Dom" Turiano, Special Agent, FBI

CIVILIANS
Tripp Adams, Friend of Samantha Reid
Eleanor Clay, Washington Real Estate Agent
Joleen, Georgetown University Student
Wilkinson, Friend of Samantha Reid

RUSSIANS
Vadim Baltiev, Oligarch
Maksim "Misha" Baltiev, Vadim's Brother and Business
Partner
Otto Baltiev, Vadim and Maksim's Nephew
Stas, Member of the Russian Mafia
Lubov, Member of the Russian Mafia
Alexander Tepanov, Officer of the Central Bank of Russia

ONE

WHAT AM I DOING HERE?

Samantha Reid fought the impulse to pull her cell out of her evening bag and check for any updates from the Situation Room. She felt anxious about slipping out of D.C. when there were so many threat scenarios crowding her inbox.

Sure, senior officials were entitled to a little time off once in a while, and her boss had okayed this short weekend trip. But as director of the White House Office of Homeland Security, she felt guilty about leaving a stack of problems on her deputy's desk.

In spite of her apprehension, she had to smile when a valet opened the car door and she heard him mutter, "If she were any better looking, she'd need a bodyguard."

The invitation from Tripp Adams to fly down to Naples, Florida, to visit his parents and attend a charity ball had been a welcome, if unexpected, diversion after a particularly hectic

1

week. She had been dating him off and on for a while, but his travel schedule coupled with her long hours and increased responsibilities meant they weren't able to see each other often. Yet, now he wanted her to spend time with his folks. Did that mean he was finally getting serious? She had no idea.

Tripp took her arm, and they followed his parents to the front entrance of the Ritz Carlton. Surrounded by mangroves and palm trees, the beige stone structure formed a U-shape with the tallest building in the center, flanked by low wings on either side, each topped with a tawny Spanish tile roof. Behind the wall to the right was a large ballroom.

Samantha brushed a strand of long brown hair off her forehead as a warm breeze blew in from the gulf. But she couldn't brush away her worries about the intel she and the national security advisor had received. A new deluge of arms had been delivered to militant groups by what she and the advisor suspected were Russian sellers. Not corrupt government officials, though there were plenty of those.

She had been tracking a group of oligarchs who might be involved in the illicit and dangerous trade, and she knew there was a bevy of analysts back at the White House, Treasury, and CIA following the same threads. She sighed inwardly and resolved to check in with the Sit Room to get the latest when this event was over.

When Samantha approached the door, a flash went off, and a reporter for the Neapolitan Section of the *Naples Daily News* shouted, "How are you enjoying Naples?"

Another yelled, "Any national security problems down here, Ms. Reid?"

"What about those arms dealers you're tracking?" a TV news anchor inquired.

Samantha and Tripp sidestepped the questions and ducked inside without making a comment. They were greeted by strands of a Cole Porter song, played by a musician seated at an ornate piano under crystal chandeliers, which bathed the coffered ceiling and paneled walls in a golden glow. Several volunteers directed the guests down a hallway to the dinner check-in tables.

Tripp leaned toward her and asked, "Don't you ever get tired of dealing with the media?"

"I usually refer their questions to the press office, but we all get ambushed occasionally. There was a leak a while ago about our latest investigation, and my boss thought I should try to respond. I didn't think there would be reporters here tonight, though."

Tripp's mother stepped closer and said, "Oh, my dear, in Naples we try to get news coverage, especially for our charities. The more the merrier I'd say." She appraised Samantha's short, green, silk dress. "You look nice tonight, dear. That color matches your eyes."

"Thanks," Samantha replied, giving the older woman a warm smile.

"By the way, Mom," Tripp interjected, "you've got a pretty good crowd here. What are they going to do with all the money from this dinner?"

"Oh, we have so many projects in the Everglades. Saving all the creatures—that sort of thing."

"I think they should just gather up the alligators and make belts. They'd probably make more money that way," Tripp whispered to Samantha. She chuckled and gave him a wry grin. She was starting to relax. This might be a pleasant weekend after all.

Walking into the crowded ballroom lit by shimmering chandeliers and small candles on white tablecloths, she took a glass of chardonnay from a passing waiter and looked around the room. "This is amazing. Look at the orchid centerpieces, the votives, the dance floor. It's just like the events they have in Washington. The only thing missing is the Marine Band."

Samantha noticed a group of people gathering around a tall man shaking hands with everyone in the circle. When she spotted several security guards standing at a discrete distance, she immediately recognized the governor.

Tripp took her arm. "I hear those little chimes. I think we're supposed to find our table. Oh, and I have something important I need to talk to you about when we're seated."

TWO

SATURDAY EVENING;
NAPLES, FLORIDA

THE YOUNG MAN ADJUSTED A HOTEL UNIFORM jacket that was a shade too large for his thin frame. He was glad the catering manager had finally found one in the stockroom that fit him well enough. Blending in with the rest of the staff was crucial, and, thankfully, he looked the part. Though the others probably hadn't used fake IDs to get their jobs.

Finding the online application for a temporary hire for this event was a stroke of sheer luck. He had shown up, phony resume in hand, and talked his way into a wait staff position for one night only. The HR person was busy and seemed relieved to find someone she said was "presentable." She had hurriedly checked off a few boxes and told him when and where to show up on the appointed night. She also promised to keep his resume on file for future events, but he knew that wouldn't be necessary.

He had never done anything like this before, and he was nervous. He knew he was being tested the way guys back home

5

were tested during gang initiations. Straightening his tie again, he moved to the back of a line of servers and checked his watch. He still had time to find her and verify she was in the ballroom, just like the press reports said she would be.

A few feet away, the pastry chef fussed with a torch he was using to burn the sugar atop the crème brûlée they would serve for dessert along with raspberries and miniature chocolate truffles.

"What's the matter with it?" the sous chef asked with a look of concern.

"I don't know. It keeps flaming out and cutting off."

"Well, hurry up and fix it."

There was a menacing tone in the sous chef's voice as the pastry chef cursed the blow torch and concentrated on arranging the berries and little chocolates on the myriad plates along his counter. A dishwasher put a stack of towels down and stared at the torch. "Not working, right?"

The wine steward stepped forward and shouted, "Circulate. Circulate. Offer the Sauvignon Blanc first then the Cabernet. Move. Move. You have your table assignments, but keep your eyes open for overlooked guests with empty wine glasses."

Keeping his eyes open was exactly what the young waiter intended to do. He pressed forward, grabbed two bottles, and entered the ballroom. His tables were between the kitchen door and the dance floor. He scrutinized the guests in that area.

Ah, there you are.

He quickly walked to her table and offered wine to those seated on the opposite side so that he could look across and be certain it was her. "Red or white?" he asked a distinguished look-ing gentleman.

"Red please. Thank you," the older man replied without looking up.

The waiter poured a proper half glass. He paused and took a mental picture of the attractive, young woman with long, dark hair. He worked his way around the table, eventually standing just to her right. "Red or white?" When she didn't respond, he repeated, "Red or white?"

Finally, she paused mid-sentence, looked over her shoulder, and murmured, "Oh, sorry. White, please."

The waiter leaned toward her. He poured the wine into her glass, wishing he could simply slip poison into her drink instead of targeting an entire room. But he didn't have any poison, and he couldn't have known that he would be assigned to serve her table. Besides, his instructions were pretty specific: get rid of an enemy and test the components of this project for prospective use later.

When he had filled her glass, she said, "Thank you," in a lilting voice. He didn't want to leave just yet. He wanted to study her for another moment.

She started talking to the man next to her, who looked uncomfortable as he said, "I wanted to tell you that I've been transferred to our Dallas office."

"You're leaving? When?" she asked, sounding upset.

"I head out next week. Sorry, hon, but with my job on the road and your hours at the White House, we hardly ever see each other. But we can keep in touch."

The server took his now empty bottles back to the kitchen, put them into a crate, checked his watch, quietly slipped out a rear kitchen door, and headed to a maintenance area. He moved quickly, glancing back down the corridor every few seconds. No one else was around. He pulled on a pair of gloves he had stashed in his pocket, opened an electrical box, and reached inside to examine his handiwork. He set the timer and then slipped out the back exit.

THREE

SAMANTHA GLANCED TO THE SIDE AND SAW A banquet manager holding the service doors open for a parade of waiters carrying dinner entrees. She heard someone inside the kitchen shout, "It's burning again!" Craning her neck, she saw a chef drop a blow torch onto a set of towels that immediately ignited, sending flames shooting toward the ceiling. The fire rose higher. Suddenly, the blaring scream of an alarm sounded throughout the complex.

"No, no, no!" the head chef screamed.

The fire alarm continued to wail as the Adamses and their tablemates pointed toward the kitchen where layers of smoke filtered out through the swinging doors. An assistant manager raced to the band stand to grab a microphone.

"Ladies and gentlemen. Ladies and gentlemen." His voice could barely be heard over the blaring siren and din in the room. "We have a small emergency in the kitchen. Nothing serious, I'm sure. If you could leave the room and walk toward the front of

9

the hotel, the staff will escort you to a series of exits. I'm sure we will have everything back in order quite soon."

Mr. Adams took his wife's arm, and Samantha saw him try to loosen his black tie. Then she heard him mumble, "Can we go home now?"

Samantha stood up and then stopped to adjust the strap on one of her high heels.

"C'mon, Samantha," Tripp demanded, reaching for her hand to pull her along. "We need to get out of here."

"Okay, okay. I'm coming," she said, feeling for the first time that she wanted to keep her hands to herself. Once outside, some of the guests stood under the portico while others moved down the driveway. The governor was hustled away by his security detail, and the valets were standing in a huddle, waiting to see if anyone would turn in a chit to get his car back.

Samantha glanced around and heard a few people saying that it wasn't bad being out in the lovely night air and that they hoped they wouldn't have to leave the beautiful dinner. Then she thought about Tripp leaving. This time for good. Then again, since they rarely saw each other, what did she expect? She should have stayed in Washington this weekend after all.

Suddenly, the fire alarm was drowned out by an explosion that shattered the side doors they had just used to leave the building. Part of a ballroom wall disintegrated right in front of them. Everyone started screaming. People grabbed loved ones and dragged them down the drive, away from the building. Samantha stood transfixed as Tripp tried to yank her back.

Staring at the flames, the smoke, and the rubble, she trembled. *Could this be a terrorist attack?*

She shook off Tripp's grip and fumbled in her purse. Finally, she shouted, "I have to call this in." With a shaking hand, she grabbed her phone and dialed the direct line to the NSC advisor. Using halting phrases and trying to think past the clamor all around her, she described the awful scene. After listening to her story, he promised to brief the FBI right away, but he also told her to try to gather more details and get back to him ASAP. As she clicked off, she heard fire engines in the distance, summoned by the initial alarm.

She spotted two hotel security guards pushing employees out the front door. The young uniformed people were coughing. She ran toward them, still clutching her cell.

"Samantha, come back!" Tripp yelled.

She ignored him and rushed toward the front entrance. A guard held up his hand to stop her.

"I'm Samantha Reid. White House. Homeland Security. Can you tell me what happened here?"

"Don't know yet, lady. Manager just said something about a gas explosion. Gotta get more people out."

"Out of the way," another guard yelled.

The first fire truck careened up the driveway. A dozen men jumped out, grabbed hoses, and ran toward the flames. The fire chief hurried to the entrance, pushing Samantha aside.

"There might be casualties in the kitchen," a guard shouted as an EMT crew jogged by carrying stretchers.

Holding her hand over her mouth, trying to breathe through the smoke and soot, Samantha stared into the inferno. She dealt with terrorist threats and crises every day, and now she was in the center of one. And she, along with the others, could have been killed.

FOUR

MONDAY MORNING:
SAN FRANCISCO, CALIFORNIA

"DURAK! STUPID IDIOT." VADIM BALTIEV shouted, wiping the perspiration from his bald head with a cocktail napkin. He tossed back a shot of vodka, almost spilling the last of it on his black shirt. He waved his empty glass at the young man standing mute in front of him. "What were you thinking?"

Otto paused for a long time, studying the floor.

"Well?" Vadim asked. "Would you care to explain how you managed to destroy part of a landmark hotel and how our target lived to tell about it?"

"I—the fire alarm went off before the timer, and they all…" Otto refused to look up.

Vadim turned to his younger brother who was mixing another round at the bar in the corner of the Russian Hill penthouse. "Misha. What do we do with this moron?"

"Relax," the swarthy Maksim Baltiev said in a calming tone. "So somebody set off the fire alarm. The bomb didn't do the job we needed, but it was more than just a weapon. Now we can do

13

a better job next time. Whenever that is," he spoke his last sentence under his breath. "And we also learned that timers aren't the best triggers. We may have to go back to cell phones. It's not Otto's fault there was a fire in the kitchen. I'm just glad he got out clean." He paused and turned to Otto. "Driving to Miami and flying back from there was smart." Misha turned back to Vadim. "No one knows his real name or where he is now. We can use him again."

"We can use him again," Vadim mimicked. "We may have to. But this nephew of ours better put in a winning performance next time." He raised his arm. Otto cringed then relaxed when he saw Vadim simply checking the time on his new Rolex.

Maksim interjected a more positive note. "Don't forget the kid is great online. He's the one who set up our *Google Alert* and *Mention* systems. Without those, we wouldn't have known she'd be going to the Naples dinner. And we never would have seen the staff opening for that event. Think about it. He got past their HR people, played his role well, placed the C-4, set the timer—"

"And then completely screwed it up." Vadim raised his voice again.

Maksim Baltiev was used to his older brother's mood swings. Dealing with the man's temper was a daily challenge. One he endured because Vadim was a genius when it came to making money.

Being two of the nearly one hundred oligarchs in Russia, the brothers started out by snagging a state-owned coal company. They fired some workers, cut costs, sold it, and then migrated to the illicit arms business. Now they were desperate to maintain the wealth and status they had built.

Glancing around the spacious penthouse with its cream carpets and black leather couches, Maksim was drawn to the floor-to-ceiling windows. They looked out onto the Golden Gate Bridge, now highlighted in the morning sun.

When they first looked at property, they had enjoyed the irony of relocating to an area called Russian Hill. Now they enjoyed an unrestricted panorama that included Alcatraz, Tiburon, Angel Island, and Belvedere to the north and Treasure Island halfway across the Bay Bridge to the east. A great piece of real estate. All paid for by Vadim's mind and its terrifying moods.

As he poured another drink and tried to ignore his brother's rants, Maksim thought back to their days growing up in Moscow when Vadim had looked after him, called him "Misha," and taught him all sorts of clever ways to gather rubles. Back then, they stole toy guns from GUM, the famous, state shopping mall on the eastern side of Red Square, and sold them to kids in their neighborhood.

Now they sold (many more) real guns and rockets to virtually any militant group that found their cell numbers. Vadim knew how to pay off certain Russian officers to loot weapons from their stock-piles, send shipments to international clients, and stash the payments in various banks with lax record-keeping. It helped when Maksim found bank clerks willing to set up their numbered accounts and then bury the paperwork. For the right price.

Their well-oiled business model back home allowed them to conduct some of their best business abroad. They sold arms to FARC in South America and Lashkar-e-Taiba in Kashmir. And when Hamas and Hezbollah became major buyers, it just added more intrigue and profit to the mix. They never sold to ISIS in Syria or Iraq, though. They wanted to sell guns to rogue armies, not machetes to militants who had a penchant for decapitating Christians. After all, they had standards.

While Vadim could manipulate the numbers, shipments, and pay-offs, he couldn't predict politicians. They lost a fortune when their accounts in Malta and Cyprus were raided by governments trying to manage deficits by confiscating deposits. And when Putin made his first moves in Crimea and sanctions kicked in, they lost a lot more. Additional sanctions related to election tampering almost wiped them out, but not entirely. Maksim realized these developments just added fuel to his brother's fiery temper. As he gazed around their expensive condo, he knew it was time for another idea.

As if reading his mind, Vadim called out, "Come over here, and I'll tell you about our next moves."

"You've come up with a Plan B already?" Maksim said, handing his brother a refill. Otto quietly crept over to a side chair to listen.

"I always have a Plan B, even a Plan C." Vadim glanced at his nephew and continued, "Plan B is to send Otto to Washington to deal with the woman again. With her out of the way, some of their tracking schemes will slow down. At least for a while. We can work out those details later. Now Plan C is about our cash. I've been thinking about how to replace the money we've lost. Our sales are one thing, but I'm talking about a hit. I just sent word to our favorite *mafya* comrades in Moscow. Stas and Lubov are coming over to execute it," Vadim said with a confident smile, taking another drink.

"I don't get it. What kind of hit are you talking about?" Maksim said.

"Not just one hit. A major hit," Vadim said, waving his hand. "It's going to be where no one would ever expect."

"Where?" Otto ventured from across the room.

Vadim took a deep breath and announced, "A place called Jackson Hole."

FIVE

MONDAY MORNING: WASHINGTON, D.C.

BRETT KEATING FLASHED HIS BADGE AT THE security guard at the entrance to the underground parking garage. The hard, plastic ID was blue with the letters "LE" in red on the lower right-hand corner, indicating he carried a gun. He drove to a low level, parked the car, and took the elevator to his floor at 601 Fourth Street NW in downtown Washington. He sprinted down the hall of the FBI's Field Office, his new home of one whole week.

He was transferred from the Chicago bureau where he gained an impressive reputation as a special agent by ferreting out the connections of crime bosses.

Now, with a promotion and a decent cubicle in the new place, Brett thought he could spend some time assessing the D.C. scene. No such luck. He was right back in the midst of a major investigation. A possible terrorist attack in Naples of all places. Who attacks a vacation town in Florida?

A step away from his cubicle, he sloughed off his jacket and removed his coffee thermos from his briefcase, having learned on his first day that what he made in his condo was gourmet compared to the Turkish tasting stuff in the office pot.

"Brett, get in here." The order came from a conference room at the end of the hall.

He tossed his briefcase and jacket on his chair, poured the steaming brew into the mug he kept on his desk, and headed to the supervisor's command center where two other agents were already seated at a long table flanked by American and FBI flags.

"Nice of you to grace us with your presence," Trevor Mason said in a raspy voice. "We just received an update from the Collier County sheriff in Florida on that explosion." He passed out copies of a report. Brett pulled out a chair, sat down, and quickly scanned the memo.

"So, you'll see that he agrees with our guys on the ground that there was some sort of timing device hidden in an electrical cabinet," the boss continued. "No prints, no fibers, nothing we can trace. They're saying it was C-4. Our team in Tallahassee is all over it, and DHS sent a team down overnight. They've been interviewing every single employee in the hotel, along with management, of course.

"The governor's security detail has been helping," Trevor went on. "His social staff went over the guest list. Nothing suspicious there. No unusual foreign names. Just a few Germans who live in Naples with no motive to blow up their own playground. Only problem is that the hotel people say they first thought it might be some sort of gas leak. Not an attack. They're used to tourists in Naples, not terrorists."

Brett flipped a page of the report and locked eyes with his boss, an aging man with the eyes of a basset hound. The guy was ready to retire, yet he kept going at all hours. He'd been working to wrap up a whole raft of cases and didn't look like he planned to call it quits any time soon. Brett had heard he often got hung up on bureaucratic procedure and could be pretty cantankerous when the coffee ran out. He took a sip from his mug and asked, "What about injuries? Says here that a pastry chef got some burns, but it was from a blowtorch, not the explosion. Looks like he got out before the blast. If he were the only one hurt, that would be amazing considering the damage."

"They say they're all accounted for except for one guy," Trevor said.

"A new hire," Agent Dom Turiano said. "Temporary for that shindig. Management says they were in a hurry to line up some extra servers when the attendance list expanded. They took on several applicants who could speak English. Guess they didn't take time to vet them too closely. Name they've got here is Otto Kukk. What kind of name is that?"

"Could be Estonian," said the one female analyst at the table. Nori Hotta was the office linguist who spoke half a dozen languages.

Brett turned to the petite woman with black hair and round, wire-rimmed glasses. "We haven't had that much trouble with Estonians, except for those hackers who steal credit cards. Probably an alias anyway." He glanced down and continued, "I see that nobody with that name has a Facebook or Twitter account."

"Point is we need to find this person." Trevor said. "We've got a BOLO for the guy," he continued, referring to their be-on-the-lookout order. "Not ready for an All-points just yet. Go to the last page of the report. Our artist did a mock-up. Got descriptions from HR, a chef, and a bunch of others in the kitchen."

Brett studied the drawing. "A lot of dark hair, pretty thin. Does look Eastern European. Or maybe Russian. Nori, what do you think?"

She scanned the page. "Yes, I agree. Looks young too. A student maybe."

"Most of the terrorists we've ID'd are young," Trevor said. "ISIS recruits teenagers. What the hell are they thinking?" he muttered as he shook his head and pointed to the image. "If he is Estonian or Russian, we haven't seen any ISIS types from those countries. This could be entirely different. We're circulating this picture everywhere, checking all our databases. Just for questioning since we've got no proof and no connection to anything yet. Now, let's see what else." He shuffled the pages and went on. "Our guys on the scene are briefing the media, asking anyone who might know the kid to call it in on the usual FBI number. Wish we had video. The Ritz doesn't have surveillance in its kitchens or back hallways. Then again, if this waiter *is* involved, I figure he's either long gone or long dead."

"On the other hand," Nori said, "maybe he's an illegal who was just looking for work. Maybe he had false papers and just got scared when the fire started and ran away. They have thousands of undocumented immigrants working everywhere in Florida. Maybe it was put together by someone else on the staff, or even a hotel guest."

"Could be. Whoever it is, this doesn't look like the work of some lone nutcase or a single terrorist," Trevor said. "That was a damn big explosion. It had to be pretty well planned. And if it wasn't a terrorist, it could have been some crazy plot to wipe out the governor. He had the highest profile in the place, except for a bunch of CEOs. Oh, and Samantha Reid from the White House. In any event, the blast didn't nail any of the important types, or anyone else, because the fire alarm kicked off first."

Brett studied the memo again and murmured, "I wonder."

"What?" Trevor barked.

"The waiter, Otto. The idea that he was trying to nail the governor. Reminds me of Occam's razor."

"Whose razor?" Dom asked.

"Occam's razor," Brett repeated. "The theory that a simpler hypothesis is generally better than a complex one. But in this case..." He shook his head. "Something doesn't compute."

"Smart-ass," Trevor mumbled.

"I see what he means," Nori said, pointing to the paper. "Too many loose ends here. The governor, the Reid woman, this Otto person. I know the police are working on this, but it could be a lot more complicated than this summary from the sheriff or anything we've received from our Florida agents."

"So, what now? Besides the bureau, the sheriff, and DHS, what's the latest on briefing the president? Has the FBI done that yet?" Brett asked, addressing the question to his boss. He took another sip from his mug and waited for the answer.

"Director was notified within minutes of Samantha Reid's call to the White House, along with the attorney general. The president is being kept up to speed. He usually likes to sound all in the know about these things, but my hunch is that he'll wait until the director gives him something substantial. Which could take a while. No one knows who did this, who, if anybody, was the target, and why the hell they picked Naples."

Trevor pointed to Brett and continued, "Head over to the White House and get an appointment with this Samantha Reid. She works on a whole raft of issues with the DHS, CIA, DOD, and treasury. Seems some part of almost every threat or attack makes its way to her office. I need more from her on this whole scenario. We already have her statement, but they took it right after the blast. Check if she's back in town. Maybe she's had a chance to remember more details. Show her the drawing. See if it registers. And when you get back, come talk to me. I've got another assignment for you."

Brett shoved his chair back, grabbing it before it hit the tile floor. "I'm on it," he said and hurried back to his office to make the call.

SIX

"BRETT KEATING, FBI, TO SEE SAMANTHA Reid," he said, showing his ID for the second time. His white visitor badge signaled that he had already passed through gate security at the northwest entrance to the White House. A nod allowed him to proceed down a long walkway toward the West Wing. As he walked, he noticed scores of reporters doing stand-ups on the north lawn. Finally, he was ushered into the West Wing lobby by a marine who nodded and opened the door for him.

A guard inside compared the ID to a list on his desk and reached for the phone. "If you'll take a seat, Agent Keating, I'll let her assistant know you're here."

"Thanks." Brett stepped over to look at a painting hanging on the west wall. It was Emanuel Leutze and Eastman Johnson's *Washington Crossing the Delaware*. There seemed to be a woman in the (president's) boat along with several others, including a fellow holding an American flag. Brett frowned and shook his head. He vaguely remembered learning in an old American history class that the flag was designed after Washington made that crossing.

It's still a pretty good picture even if they sort of got it wrong.

On the other side of a tall, mahogany bookcase was another painting. This one was titled *Old Faithful* by Albert Bierstadt. The national park looked like a great place to explore someday. That is, if he ever got some time off, which he knew wouldn't be any time soon.

"Mr. Keating?" a short, trim, young woman with a welcoming smile motioned to Brett.

"Yes?" he answered, walking over to display his ID again.

"That won't be necessary. I'm Joan Tillman, Miss Reid's administrative assistant. Right this way, please." She walked past two blue camelback sofas and headed down a hallway. He followed as she climbed a narrow staircase leading to a small office on the second floor. The door was open. She knocked on the doorframe. "Samantha, Special Agent Brett Keating to see you. And by the way, anyone want coffee? We have a fresh pot."

Brett nodded to Joan. "That would be terrific. Just black please."

"I'll have my usual," a well-modulated voice called from inside.

So, this is the White House Homeland Security Director, Brett thought.

Samantha, clad in a narrow, navy skirt and beige, silk blouse, walked around her desk to give him a firm handshake. He had seen a few pictures of her in recent news reports about how she was leading a task force to crack down on illicit arms sales. The photos didn't do her justice. "Pleased to meet you," he said. "I'm sure you're swamped. Glad you could fit me in."

"I have another meeting shortly, but you said you were working on the Naples explosion. So, how can I help?" She returned to her desk and motioned to Brett as she sat down.

He pulled up a scarlet, leather side chair, yanked the Collier County sheriff's report out of his briefcase, and handed it to her. "You may have seen most of this already, but we just got a drawing of a possible suspect. A waiter, Otto Kukk, which probably isn't his real name. I wanted to see if it jogged your memory. Maybe you saw him or heard something while you were there."

She studied the report for a minute. "Rather long, isn't it?"

"Yeah, sometimes those things are a waste of toner. But this one includes some interesting facts about what they found," Brett said.

"Here's your coffee," Joan said from the open door. After she circulated the room, Brett and Samantha held matching mugs. Each had a golden White House seal on one side.

Brett took a sip and said, "Thanks a lot. Much better than what the FBI has these days."

"We aim to please," Joan said and quickly left the room.

Samantha flipped through the report until she found the drawing. She paused and closed her eyes, trying to visualize the scene. "It was all so weird and violent," she said with a slight shudder. "Here we were at a fundraiser with, as my dad used to say, 'the great and the near great.' And a waiter came around with red and white wine." She looked up at the ceiling, hesitated, and said, "Yes, that's it."

"What's it?" Brett asked, leaning forward.

"I think this is the waiter who offered us wine," she pointed to the picture. "He was right over my shoulder."

"Watching you?"

"Perhaps. He kept saying, 'Red or white?' When I stopped talking and looked up, I sensed he'd been there a while."

"Then that's him. He spotted you," Brett said. "Did you see him again?"

"I don't think so because the fire alarm went off after that. Then we were all ushered outside right before the explosion. It was incredible. Part of one wall kind of disintegrated in front of us. People were yelling, running, covering their ears. I couldn't move.

"In the midst of all the chaos," she explained, "all I could think about was whether anyone had been killed and if it was some kind of terrorist attack."

She took a drink of her coffee, set the mug down, leaned forward, and then handed the report back to Brett. "I saw in the report that they found a timer. Who set it and why? Do you think it was that waiter? I've often thought the bomber could have been targeting the governor, but that theory never adds up perfectly. If someone were trying to kill him, it would be much easier to do it in Tallahassee even with his security detail. And why take out an entire room of innocent people if you're trying to get one guy? Why not just put something in his drink?"

"Interesting idea," Brett said. "On the other hand, if this waiter was someone's errand boy, maybe he was told to use C-4 so that he wouldn't miss his target in a big ballroom."

"I guess," she said.

"There's also the possibility that *you* were the target," Brett said. "As you saw in the report, they've been interviewing everyone on the hotel staff, and the only guy they can't locate is your waiter. They're going through every staff resume looking for connections even though he was a temporary hire. No one wants to rule out the possibility that someone they fired was crazy enough to do it for revenge."

He glanced down at the memo again. "Back to this Otto Kukk. He was hired just for the event. HR said they were desperate for extra help when the charity's guest list multiplied at the last minute."

"They must have had some references for him. An address, phone number, something," she ventured.

"That's what they're checking now, although most of it has turned out to be fake. They must have been in a hell of a hurry to get him on board. Anyway, our people figure that whoever he is, he's long gone. Must have slipped by the road blocks. The governor ordered the Fort Myers Airport shut down too. Of course, he could have taken a back road and flown out of Miami. No one considered closing that airport. At first the hotel people were talking about gas leaks, not terrorists. So, there was a slight lag in the time frame."

Brett took another swig of coffee and went on. "Let's focus on motive for a minute. What if you *were* the target? What if it was personal? After all, the news has linked you to this trafficking issue and a whole list of threats you're working on. Maybe someone is trying to stop you in your tracks." He paused and eyed her. "How in the world do you stay so calm when you're dealing with all of this?"

"I work in the most guarded eighteen acres on the planet," she said with a rueful look. "And why would anyone think he or she could stop the efforts of the whole government by eliminating me? I mean, whenever our people are attacked—government or civilian—that's when we really get serious. After 9/11, we geared up so much that it's almost impossible to keep track of who heads what bureau at any one time. And last I heard, the FBI had over thirteen thousand special agents and even more analysts. Is that about right?"

He nodded. "Combined," she said, "there are hundreds of thousands of people with various clearances protecting the country." She hesitated a moment and added, "Of course, sometimes someone gets a top secret clearance who should never have been hired in the first place."

Brett smiled.

She gave him a slight smile in return and said, "I know none of this is news to the FBI. As for the person or group responsible for this attack, they can't kill us all. So, what about you? You probably deal with the same thing or worse."

Brett shifted in his seat. "I guess." He gingerly fingered a small scar on the side of his cheek, a reminder of a fight with a crime boss. It wasn't his only scar. Just the most obvious one. "But I'm here to jog your memory. If you *were* a target, why were you attacked there? Did you notice anyone tailing you around Naples? Anyone who seemed out of place at the dinner or before you got there? Do you remember anything at all that could help us?"

Samantha sat back for a long moment. "I remember arriving Saturday morning at the Fort Myers airport," she finally said. "It was crowded, and it seemed like more people were leaving than arriving. Probably all the snowbirds heading north for the summer. I didn't notice anyone following me at the airport."

She hesitated before continuing. "My friend picked me up. We drove down I-75 to Naples and had lunch at the Port Royal Club. Nothing strange there. Later we drove to the Ritz. Can't say we were followed. I wasn't looking out the back window. When we got to the hotel entrance, I saw the governor's limo pull up. He was surrounded by his security people. Nothing odd about that."

"What about the others you were with that night? We have a guest list, but we don't know who was in what group," Brett said.

"I was with Tripp Adams. He works in the private sector, VP of GeoGlobal Oil & Gas. And his parents. His dad is a retired CEO. His mother is the one who's on the board of the Everglades charity group. That's why we were there."

Brett grabbed a leather folder from his briefcase, opened it, and scanned a long list. "So, Tripp Adams. Would that be Hamilton Bainbridge Adams III?" He asked, raising his eyebrows.

"Well, yes," Samantha admitted with a slight sigh. "He hates the long name. That's why he goes by Tripp. I doubt he was a target, though. He negotiates oil leases around the world."

"I agree," Brett said, jotting down some notes. "Let's get back to you. How would anyone know you had left Washington and were going to Florida? And how would any potential enemies know you were going to a fundraiser on a Saturday night? I know top White House officials are often watched, shall we say, by foreign operatives, but in Naples?"

"I know, I've thought about that too. All I can think of is a clipping Mrs. Adams showed me from a social column in her local newspaper about the dinner. It listed a number of people who were on the guest list, like the governor, the board members. And yes, my name was also there. It was all in a press release the Everglades committee compiled to get publicity for the event. It was on their website too."

"Was that smart?" Brett asked.

"Obviously not," Samantha said. "But I wasn't in charge of that one."

"You do get a lot of publicity on your own, though."

She nodded. "It all started with a leak to a New York paper about our efforts to track weapon shipments," she said. "I was really upset and started to feel like a piñata for the White House Press Corps during the follow up stories and all that. So, you're right. There's been more coverage about what we're doing to shut down certain accounts that end up in the hands of the worst players. Agent Keating—"

"Why don't you call me Brett?" he interrupted. "I assume you'll want updates, so we'll probably be in touch."

"Absolutely. I know a lot of people are working on the investigation, but I really appreciate your coming over and keeping me up to speed on this."

"And on that up-to-speed note," Brett said, "here's my card with my cell number." He handed it to her. "If you think of anything, anything at all, please call me. Day or night."

She studied the number and looked like she was committing it to memory. "Here I am working on all sorts of threats. But this is the first time I've felt I might have been…a target. And perhaps it was personal."

SEVEN

SAMANTHA GRABBED THE CLOCK AND punched the alarm to stop the dreaded buzzing that always reminded her of a swarm of bumble bees. 5:45 a.m. The first rays of light were seeping through her plantation shutters. As she threw back the covers on her standard double bed, the largest that would fit into her miniscule bedroom, she made a mental note to buy a new clock the next time she had a chance to go shopping, which was never these days.

She didn't mind the tight quarters too much, though. Perched on the second floor, she had a decent view of the park across lower K Street where she could jog along the Potomac River. The park was a stone's throw from the shops and restaurants at Washington Harbour and a few blocks from the very heart of Georgetown.

Samantha pushed her hair out of her eyes, grabbed her robe, and began her morning routine, one that would get her to the office by 6:30 a.m. As she walked to her galley kitchen, a small

31

yawn reminded her why she had moved to this red-brick complex with underground parking. With a condo overlooking the White-hurst Freeway—which wasn't a real freeway, just a shortcut to downtown—she was close to the White House. Unfairly close. Her seven-minute commute was unheard of in D.C. And she had her supervisor at the Department of Energy to thank for it.

When he was named White House Director of Homeland Security, he brought her with him to the West Wing as his deputy. Moving closer to the White House had helped her put in the long hours necessary to perform well in her new role. Her ability to analyze and synthesize complicated issues hadn't hurt either. At first she focused on energy and nuclear threats, but she quickly shifted to issues in all six directorates dealing with chemical, biological, and transportation threats and other threatened sectors. It wasn't long before the chief of staff started asking her to prepare briefing papers for presidential news conferences. But after a few years, her boss was charged with a hit-and-run assault and had to resign. That's when the chief of staff promoted her to the top job with a direct report to the head of the NSC, Ken Cosgrove.

When she padded into the kitchen, Samantha made a small pot of coffee, forked open an English muffin, and started the toaster. She flicked on a small TV on the counter and clicked to Fox News to catch the latest. The anchor summarized the investigation in Naples, saying no suspects were in custody. Nothing new there. Samantha often knew the biggest news stories long before Fox or CNN or any other network. Yet she always found herself tuning in and switching between channels to see how developments were reported and analyzed. It was also interesting to try and guess who had leaked what to which reporter.

She frowned as the anchor estimated the damages caused by the explosion. For the first time in her life, she felt slightly vulnerable and off-kilter. Samantha switched the feed to CNN and checked the toaster as the new anchor introduced CNN's White House correspondent.

"We're expecting an announcement later this morning regarding the state visit by the Prime Minister of Great Britain. CNN has learned that the two leaders will be discussing upheavals in Pakistan amid worries over future control and proliferation of their nuclear arsenal, efforts by NATO and the European Union to contain further moves by Russia, and coordination to combat new types of cyber-crimes believed to be emanating from Bulgaria as well as China and North Korea. We will have more details after the noon briefing by the press secretary. Reporting from the White House, this is Luzelle Malanghu for CNN."

How did she find out about the topics of discussion? We haven't announced those yet. Some of the subjects are classified.

Samantha frowned more deeply.

We don't just have leaks, we have a colander.

She grabbed the muffin as it popped up, spread a bit of butter and strawberry jam on it, poured a cup of coffee, and added cream and sugar to it. She carried her breakfast to the small, square table in her living room that served as a combination desk and dining spot. It was the only space that allowed her to eat while checking her two email accounts in the morning before heading to the White House. She took a sip from her mug, entered a password on her secure computer, and quickly scrolled down the official list of messages.

She saw a dozen notices from DHS and the Treasury, though nothing new on Naples. There was one from her friend Angela Marconi, now the number two in presidential scheduling, saying she was coordinating the president's meeting with the Brits but might be free for lunch tomorrow. Then she switched to her personal email and stopped to read a note from Tripp.

Hi, Hon. Getting settled into my new place. Dallas is a lot hotter than DC, but the condo is great...not far from SMU. It's about the same size as my place at Turnberry Tower. You'll have to see it sometime. Heading down to South America day after tomorrow to negotiate another deal. Back to you later.... T.

As she reread his email, it reminded her of a piece of modern art—something open to interpretation.

See it some time? He's probably never there. Just like he was never in D.C. when he had an office on K Street. And what is with that sign off? No "Love you, babe" or anything even close.

She gazed out her living room window toward Key Bridge. Ribbons of headlights streamed into the city and passed the tall outline of Turnberry Tower in Arlington. She remembered many evenings on its eighteenth floor, though she rarely enjoyed its view. Her fear of heights always kept her off the balcony, but that had never seemed to matter.

Samantha glanced at her watch and realized it was getting late. She quickly finished her muffin and reached for a final sip of coffee when her computer signaled a new government email. It was from the Situation Room. She scanned it, replied, "On my way, thanks," and raced to her closet.

———

"Good morning, Ms. Reid," the Secret Service agent said. She turned and hit a button that gave Samantha access to the Situation Room complex in the basement of the West Wing. The rooms were redone a few years ago. They had little resemblance to the original command center President Kennedy had set up to monitor the Cuban situation. Since that time, presidents frequently headed downstairs to check on the latest developments around the world, monitored 24/7 by dedicated staff. So dedicated that they refused to leave their posts when the rest of the White House was evacuated on 9/11.

Samantha headed into the Sit Room, as everyone called the area. The elaborate Sensitive Compartmented Information Facility, or SCIF, was one of many throughout the White House and Executive Office Building. This one, equipped with secure video and phone lines, also had clocks set to the time zone of wherever the president happened to be. Right now, the clocks indicated that he was in D.C. Just upstairs, in fact.

When she started attending staff meetings and conferences in this Sit Room, she couldn't help but compare it to Hollywood sets in movies, which often dreamed up a thrilling mélange of flashing lights, huge screens, and clattering banks of computer keys. She doubted if film producers would ever think the actual Sit Room was exciting enough to replicate realistically.

Samantha settled her cell phone into a special box at the entry. They were verboten inside. No flash drives or any other devices were permitted. She hurried to the back where the staff was compiling data and analyzing satellite images.

"Look at these, Ms. Reid," an officer said, handing her several photos. "They were taken by our birds covering Pakistan and Kashmir."

She studied the grainy blow-ups. "Looks like Russian markings on those big crates."

"We think so. Same with this second set we took along the Colombian border. First one could be for that terrorist group, Lashkar-e-Taiba. Ever since their main cell was taken down by

Indian forces, their remaining members have been recruiting again."

"Yes, that's the same group that stole cruise missiles. But they were stopped by Cameron Talbot's new missile defense system," Samantha observed.

"But now we've seen some reports speculating they might try to attack India again," the officer said.

"Thus the new shipments," Samantha said.

"As for the Colombia pics, they're undoubtedly meant for FARC. Same markings. They keep signing various agreements with the government, but they all seem to fall through." The staffer pulled another set of photos to the center of his desk and pointed to the top one. "I don't know if you saw this particular picture we captured a while ago of the Jewish school that was hit by Hamas."

Samantha stared at the enlargement showing relief workers carrying bloodied kids away from a burning building. The picture of little children surrounded by what could only be anguished parents hit Samantha so hard, she caught her breath. "I heard about the attack but never saw close-ups like these. Those poor kids."

The officer put another photo on top of the pile. "This shows a shipment that Hamas received right before that attack."

Samantha peered at the second shot. "Same Russian markings as the new ones. We have to stop these shipments," Samantha said, grabbing photos from the two piles and shoving them into a folder with her meeting notes. "Thank you for this," she said. As she headed toward the conference room, she muttered under her breath, "Whatever it takes, I will find a way to stop those bastards."

"Hope you can track those shipments," the staff member called after her, and then turned back to his console.

Samantha walked down a short hall, stepped onto navy carpeting, and took a seat at a long, polished, wood table. She checked her watch and waited for Ken Cosgrove and Homer Belford to get there. She always tried to arrive early so that she could quickly review her talking points and never keep the boss waiting.

"Hey, Samantha, good to see you. Got a few updates for you today," Homer said, ambling in and settling into a charcoal gray leather chair. He pulled some papers out of his briefcase. "Is Ken coming to this one?"

Samantha glanced up at the brilliant head of FinCen, the Financial Crimes Enforcement Network at the Treasury Department. In his slightly rumpled suit, he didn't exactly resemble the super detail-oriented math whiz she knew he was. She guessed that he was so focused on his research and spread sheets that he didn't have much time to shop at Brooks Brothers. Not that she cared. Samantha was glad to be working with the slightly unkempt accounting guru on her latest project.

"Hi, Homer. Yes, Ken should be here in a few minutes," she said. "Thanks for driving over from Virginia. Must be a drag with all the traffic."

"It was terrible. I usually like working at our McLean office, but it took me forty-five minutes to get across Chain Bridge and into town this morning."

"Well, you know we only have two seasons in Washington: winter and construction."

Homer chuckled.

"When he gets here, I want to show him some new satellite photos that could indicate a whole slew of arms shipments to Lashkar and FARC," she said. "At least those would be high on our list of suspects. They're also from the same syndicate that sells to Hamas."

"About Lashkar, didn't the shoe bomber, Richard Reid, belong to that crowd at some point?" Homer asked.

"Sure did," she said. "That's why we still have to take our shoes off at the airport."

"Unless you're about seventy-five," Homer said. "The Reid terrorist? Guess you're not related," he added with a grin.

"Get serious," she said and smiled.

The national security advisor strode into the room. "Sorry to keep you waiting. First, have you picked up anything new on the Naples explosion?"

Samantha shook her head. "Not really. I met with an FBI agent yesterday. They have a sketch of a possible suspect, but they have no clue who he is or where he is."

"We'll let those experts handle that investigation," Ken said. "We're all just relieved you got out of there when you did." Samantha smiled weakly as her boss continued. "I've talked to the president about our priorities for the British visit. Are they helping us enough on your projects, Homer?"

The Treasury aide looked up and said, "Actually, they've been terrific lately. We're working with them and the Portuguese on transfers in and out of a bank in Macau. When the Cyprus banks imploded several years ago, a lot of those customers moved their business to Macau and other places like Malta. The Russians still lost a bundle, though. They had five times more money deposited in Cyprus than that country's whole GDP. So, now we have to figure out where they've parked what's left."

Homer paused and handed some papers to Ken and Samantha. He added, "We're monitoring and enforcing the latest sanctions, of course. Since the beginning when everyone thought they'd just hurt a few of the top guys in the Kremlin, there's been an incredible ripple effect. But with all the corruption over there, most of the targets have figured out ways to get around them."

"And Ken," Samantha said, "this all ties in with some new intel on possible Russian arms shipments. Not government to government." She passed him the satellite photos. "These shipments could be from some of the syndicates that lost all that money. We think they're still trying to make some of it back by selling to FARC, Hamas, and a few others."

The advisor studied the pictures. "Damn! They look just like the shipments the terrorists used on those innocent kids." He turned to Homer. "More fuel for your fire. I'll get these over to DOD and see if they can do some intercepts on the latest trove here."

Homer grabbed a silver pitcher from the table's center and poured three glasses of water. He passed the drinks around and said, "The Russians are going to need a lot more than a few arms sales to make up their losses. Still, the more deals like this we can stop, the more violence we can tamp down. Trouble is, there are so many of them. We think the Russian mafia now controls four out of every ten businesses and sixty percent of state-owned companies. Could be more."

The NSC advisor turned to Samantha. "The president appreciates your efforts to connect those groups and their money to illicit arms sales, but we could use more international cooperation. And that brings me to a new idea. Well, not exactly an idea. It's an assignment."

"Another assignment?" Samantha asked with a worried look.

"This one could reap some very important results and get us even more support from the world-wide financial community." He motioned to Homer, "Not that you all aren't doing a great job at the Treasury." Homer gave a slight nod as Ken took a little booklet out of his ever-present leather folder and handed it to Samantha. It had a picture of a lake surrounded by mountains on the cover.

She studied it, hesitated, and read out loud, "The Federal Reserve Bank of Kansas City's Jackson Hole Economic Policy Symposium? What does this have to do with me?"

"That's where you're going," Ken replied.

"Why?" Samantha asked, sounding somewhat agitated. "This is a conference for members of the Federal Reserve."

"Yes, it's next week. But it's not *just* the Federal Reserve. It attracts over one hundred top financiers from all over the world. There'll be central bankers, finance ministers, chairmen of banks like JP Morgan Chase, economists from places like Goldman Sachs, the head of the International Monetary Fund—you get the idea. Can you imagine a better place to highlight *your* strategies and get their cooperation to tighten up on money laundering and secret accounts? Before my meeting with the president, I talked this over with Phil Pickering. The Treasury secretary is in complete agreement."

He glanced at Homer again. "I wanted to give you a read-out on this as well because we want to send you too." He turned back to Samantha and continued. "We've already had a preliminary discussion with the chairman of the host committee who's organizing the conference. He was very enthusiastic about offering you an invitation to talk at one of their special sessions."

"I see the connection but—" She halted, trying to gather her thoughts.

"What is it?" Ken asked.

She sat back and took a deep breath. "Look, Ken, I know we can't put personal situations before our responsibilities here—"

"Personal situations?" Ken asked. "What are you talking about? This is one of the most important conferences you could attend. What *personal situation* could keep you from accepting their invitation?"

She rubbed her forehead and tried to hold back the tension building there. "Uh, Ken, I don't know if you've heard about my background."

"Of course, I know your background. Princeton, private sector, Department of Energy, White House. There are a lot of experts floating around the government, but we didn't just promote you to the director's job because you're qualified and a quick study. We also promoted you because you're a very competent spokesperson. And that's what we want you to be in Jackson. Have you ever been there?"

She had a momentary flash back to her experience in Naples a few days ago. She had escaped that disaster unscathed. Several years ago, she hadn't been so lucky.

Samantha stared at Ken and finally replied in a soft voice, "Yes, I've been there. That's where I almost died."

EIGHT

TUESDAY EARLY MORNING:
WASHINGTON, D.C.

"GET ANYTHING AT THE WHITE HOUSE
yesterday?" Trevor Mason called to Brett as he came into
the office.

"An ID on Otto Kukk. Samantha Reid remembered the
waiter. He actually poured her wine," Brett said, hanging up his
navy suit coat on a hook in his cubicle's wall.

"So, he could have been looking for her?" the boss said, leaning against the wall near Brett's coat.

"Could be. She remembered him hanging around longer than
the other staff. And in a large ballroom, this one guy waits on
her," Brett said.

"Yeah. Could be significant. Or not. Anything else?"

"She gave a detailed report to the Florida field agent," Brett
said. "Even though we don't know who the real target was, I have
a strong suspicion it was her." He started to pour coffee from his
thermos.

"Anything else?" Trevor demanded.

43

Brett paused and then said, "It must have been pure chaos down there." He was reminded of the way the Chicago agents used to define the word "CHAOS": Chief Has Arrived On Scene. Dealing with Trevor was going to be a bit challenging, and sure enough the man immediately barked out another order.

"Well, stay on it. I want our agents to solve this before DHS or the locals." He walked over, yanked a metal chair in front of Brett's desk, and sat down. "Now, we've got another problem. Our agent assigned to embassy penetration is sick. Out for a while. Can't pull anyone else off other assignments right now. You're new. That means you're taking it over. I saw in your file that you dealt with listening devices when you worked on that human trafficking case back in LaGrange."

"We got lucky on that one," Brett said. "We heard they were going to move some women from El Salvador up north for their prostitution trade. Not the usual kind. This was much bigger. It was more like a slave trade operation. We nailed the bastards."

"We do things differently in the capital," his boss said. "We're not tracking slave traders, but we *are* tracking certain diplomatic types from China, Russia, Somalia, Egypt, Colombia, and elsewhere. They spy on us. We spy on them."

"They get pretty vocal about that when NSA gets publicity," Brett said. "Remember when we built our embassy in Moscow way back?"

"Sure," Trevor said, "I was just going through my FBI training. We found so many bugs in the building, even inside the concrete columns, all built by Russian contractors, of course, we had to tear the whole thing down and start over with our own people."

"Jeez," Brett said. "Reminds me of the Russian diplomat we kicked out for planting a bug inside our state department."

Trevor nodded. "The Russians are experts at that kind of thing. They even planted bugs in the pen gift sets they gave to our ambassadors when they arrived in Moscow. We don't fall for that bullshit any more. Anyway, back to our current problem. When a foreign property changes hands in Washington, we need to know in advance so we can plant our own listening devices or refresh the ones already there."

"Figures," Brett said, slowly sipping his coffee. "How do we keep them from finding our bugs? They sweep all the rooms before they move in."

"We have some new equipment coming in. It's pretty sophisticated. When we think they're doing their initial sweeps, we turn it off and then turn it back on the next day. They still suspect we're listening, but you'd be amazed by what our guys have picked up lately. Someone on staff slips up on the phone, another mentions the name of a suspected militant group—it goes on and on."

"Okay. So, what's next?"

"You're gonna have to clean up the mess the other agent left. He missed one. A house over on California Street was bought by the Chinese."

"Didn't he coordinate with State?"

"State has its Office of Foreign Missions helping them find properties, but a real estate agent evidently made a contact on her own. Obviously, she didn't go through State or here. Usually, our agent stays on top of real estate deals between countries and certain local real estate agents, but she wasn't on his radar and slipped through the cracks. Here's the file."

He handed Brett a blue folder. "Go. Find her. Turn her into a CHS like some of the other good ones." He got up, turned on his heel, and shuffled back to his office at the end of the hall.

CHS. Clandestine Human Source, Brett translated mentally.

He sat down at his desk and opened the folder. Her name was Eleanor Clay, and she worked for Washington Luxury Properties. A photo showed a short, rail-thin woman. As he examined it, he tried to place her age.

Maybe thirty-five? Could be forty-five or fifty if she's had some work done.

He glanced back at the file. Her age was not listed. As he resumed his scrutiny of the photo, he realized she might be kind of attractive to some people. If they liked the skin-and-bones type, which had never appealed to him. The file said she was divorced and had moved here from New York.

Makes sense.

All the women he'd met up there were obsessed with salads and Pilates.

What did they used to call them? X-rays?

He turned a page. She had made many high-end sales in Kalorama, an area off Massachusetts Avenue where a lot of embassies were located. And there it was: a sale to a Chinese cultural minister. "Cultural, my ass," he muttered to himself. "Station chiefs often use that cover when they head their spy operations abroad. No wonder Trevor is fuming over this."

Brett turned to the next page. She had several listings for other properties, and he wondered which foreigners were looking to buy what. Her office was in Foggy Bottom, not far from the State Department. He made a note of her number and picked up the phone.

NINE

SAMANTHA'S HEAD WAS POUNDING. SHE HAD to stop thinking about the Tetons and focus on current threats to the country, along with terrorist organizations attacking children. She had seen bombing scenarios on TV news reports, but she knew the producers often edited out the most gruesome scenes. The unadulterated close-ups she had seen that morning kept invading her mind's eye. She glanced around the small conference table at Joan and the heads of her six directorates as her deputy continued speaking.

"Just got word of a possible threat at Wrigley Field," Jim Shilling said, passing around copies of a memo. "NSA picked up a conversation between an operative in Yemen and some dude in Chicago. It's a new connection, okayed by the FISA Court. FBI is all over it."

Samantha looked at the forty-five-year-old terrorism specialist she had recruited. When Jim worked for the Director of National Intelligence, he had proved to be a top-rate analyst.

47

Having him detailed from the DNI's staff had made her quite happy. Jim was by far the most irreverent, wise-cracking member of her staff. But considering the gravity of their issues, she figured his attempts to lighten the office mood weren't all bad.

They studied the memos and made some notes. "Speaking of the FBI, anything new on the Naples explosion?" another staffer asked.

Samantha shook her head. "I met with the D.C. special agent assigned to it. Brett Keating. Nice enough. Pretty professional. Doesn't waste your time. Evidently, there's only one hotel employee they can't find. A waiter named Otto Kukk. Must have run out."

"Can't blame him for that," Jim said.

"When they went over his application, most of the information turned out to be bogus. Apparently, they were in such a hurry to find extra servers for the event, he just slipped through. They have a mock-up of him. I'm pretty sure I saw him there. Serving right at my table."

"Serving you?" an assistant asked. "Do you think he was scoping you out?"

"That's what the FBI agent thought. That maybe he was targeting me instead of the governor who was there. But I can't imagine why someone would bother with an explosion just to deal with me," Samantha said with a sigh.

"But if wasn't aimed at you or the governor, what could be the motive for bombing a fund-raiser for the Everglades?" another asked.

"Someone who hates crocodiles and egrets," Jim murmured.

"Nobody has taken responsibility," Samantha said.

"Let's go back to the idea that you *were* the target. They would have to be willing to kill hundreds of innocents at the same time. It would take a really crazy type to try that," Joan said.

"Same kind of crazy type that plans *all* of these attacks," Jim said, waving his memo in the air.

After exhausting the subject, Samantha went on to summarize a litany of threats she had gleaned from emails and conference calls in the last hour. Her team went over the list and suggested which ones could be handled best by DHS, the CIA, or the FBI and which ones should be elevated to the national security advisor.

Once they finished, the head of her department's secretariat division pulled out a sheet of paper from her notes and said, "Just got an update on how many other plots they've tracked down." The staffer started to read. "There have been 137 terrorist plots identified by the FBI with 386 arrests or indictments. Well, that's going back several years. But they were able to pinpoint, infiltrate, and stop each one. Kind of amazing, isn't it?" She held up her hand and Jim slapped it.

"Like the old Wayne Gretzky line, 'You don't skate to the puck. You skate to where the puck is going to be,'" he said.

Samantha nodded. "By the way, I need to tell you where I'm going to be next week."

"I know," Joan said. "It's the Fed meeting. I just saw your invitation to speak to that group."

Jim gave a low whistle. "Speak to the Federal Reserve? Sounds like a pretty big deal. What's the story?"

"It's their annual meeting in Jackson Hole." She turned to Joan. "Please see what you can dig up on the conference agenda, hotel, and flights."

"Got it," Joan said, making a note on a legal pad.

"Okay, that's it for now. Thanks, everyone," Samantha said.

As she got up from the table, Joan leaned over and whispered, "I can't believe you're going out there again. I mean after everything. . ."

Samantha rubbed her forehead and muttered, "Believe me. Neither can I."

TEN

"VINTAGE MODERN. ISN'T THAT AN OXYMORON?"
Brett asked, getting out of the Jaguar the real estate agent had
parked in front of a classic Georgian townhouse on Prospect Street.
It was just down the block from Café Milano, a trendy hangout for
high-powered politicians and the aspiring social set.

He was following Trevor's orders to determine if Eleanor
could become a valuable source, but he resented the time he had
to waste looking at property when he had a perfectly decent
rental downtown. Still, asking to see a few of her listings was the
easiest way to meet the woman.

"Well, I guess you could say that." She reached into her
shoulder bag, fished out a key, and opened the door to a small
foyer where a steep stairway dominated the area. "It has some
historic features, but it's been completely redone. It's not terribly
big. In fact, you could call it cozy," she commented as Brett came
inside and closed the door.

51

"By cozy, does that mean a lamp couldn't fit in the bed-rooms?" he said, looking around.

Eleanor gazed up into his eyes and gave him a big smile. "Well, I wouldn't go that far. Let me show you the kitchen. It's all been upgraded. Stainless steel appliances, the latest quartz countertops, and new floors." Pointing down, she gushed, "I just love this Mazama South American hardwood made of Cumaru. They call this color 'espresso.'" She spread her arms, inviting him to take in the whole scene.

Brett followed her up the narrow staircase, noting that her skirt was also quite narrow. And rather tight. As they climbed, she kept looking over her shoulder. From the way she had been sizing him up, it felt like she was on the prowl. Trolling might be a better description.

When he called to make the appointment, he had told her he might buy a place of his own and that he was just renting for a while to get the lay of the land. After sensing her reaction, he regretted his choice of words. He hadn't told her where he worked. He would do that later. For now, he'd play along with the house tour.

"Nice living room," he said. "Does this place come furnished?" He examined a pair of love seats covered in purple fabric with flowers all over it.

Hope not, he thought.

"That could be negotiable. You probably have your own things anyway. Most people do, unless they're diplomats and move around a lot."

This could be useful.

"Do you work with a lot of those?" he asked.

"Occasionally. I'm just building my clientele, but I've made a point of meeting several of them. Pays to have the right contacts in this town."

"So I've heard," he said. He walked around a glass coffee table resting on a brass base in the shape of a swan. "So, who's buying right now?"

"Lots of people. Any time there's a mid-term election or change of administration, a slew of people come to Washington. Sometimes it's hard to find the right properties for them because the displaced people never want to leave town or be separated from the power, even by a few blocks. They end up taking jobs as lobbyists or working for a think tank or a nonprofit if they can afford it. You'd be amazed by how many people come here saying they're going to take a position for a year or two and then stay on for life."

"Yes, I've heard that. But what about the foreigners? They're only here for a couple of years. Do they still buy houses?" Brett asked, trying to steer the conversation back on track.

"Many of them do. And the embassies, some of the larger ones, are always trying to increase their presence here."

"Oh yeah? Which ones?"

"Let's see...the Canadians. They're our biggest trading partners, of course."

"Anyone else?" Brett asked, pretending to examine an impressionist painting.

"Oh, the Chinese, the Russians, Abu Dhabi. I try to meet them all," she said with another appraising grin.

If he could keep this line of communication going, he just might learn something to keep Trevor placated. "I figure prices are pretty steep for houses, so I was wondering...what about a high-rise? Are there any better deals that are also close in?"

"As you've noticed, we don't have real high-rises in D.C. They build those over in Virginia," she said somewhat disparagingly. "Here we have strict height limits. The rule used to be nothing taller than the Capitol. It was adjusted a little, but not by much. I'll go ahead and research some of the larger low-rise apartment buildings for you," she said.

She led the way back down the stairs. When they got to the front door, she was already scrolling through her iPhone. "Of course, we have tons of listings. Have to watch out, though. Here's one described as 'historic.' That means, 'Good luck on maintenance,'" she said with a laugh. "If it says, 'close to attractions,' that can mean it's wedged between a grocer and a liquor store. I have to be careful about single family homes too. I had one client who fell in love with a darling house on Q Street, but his neighbor turned out to be a bee keeper."

Brett chuckled and said, "There must be something else—perhaps a bit more modest—that we could look at." He wasn't sure how long it would take to turn her into an informant, but he had a feeling it wouldn't be soon. Which agitated him. He wanted to find the low-life who triggered the Naples blast that could have killed Samantha Reid. Even though scores of agents were working on the investigation, he kept wondering if she really was in danger. No one could get to her inside the West Wing, but what about the rest of the time? He shook his head slightly to clear away the image of her calm face and tried to refocus on the realtor who was answering his question about cheaper digs.

"Oh certainly," Eleanor said. She glanced at the espresso-colored floors and laughed. "I completely forgot there's a Starbucks around the corner. Why don't we stop there and go through some listings over a caramel macchiato or a café mocha cinnamon? Personally, I like the skinny flavored lattes."

That tracks.

Brett glanced at her body. It reminded him of the hollow-cheeked model he saw on the front of a magazine in the checkout line at a Seven-Eleven. Then his attention snapped back to the Naples investigation.

He wondered if the Florida sheriff had any more details about the explosion. He stole a glance at his cell, but no new texts had come in since he left the office. He would double-check the sheriff's report as soon as he was finished with the skinny latte woman. Right now, Starbucks sounded like the perfect tonic. And a simple cup of black coffee would be just fine.

ELEVEN

"RULE NUMBER ONE: NEVER LOSE MONEY.
Rule Number Two: never forget Rule Number One," Vadim said, gazing out the passenger car window toward the bay. There, a dozen sailboats were unfurling their spinnakers to catch the afternoon wind. Some were bright blue. Others were red and yellow as they raced to an imaginary finish line.

Maksim turned in the driver's seat and glanced at the rippling sails. "Didn't that American investor make those rules? Name's Buffett, I think," he said.

"Yes," Vadim agreed. "Makes a good point. Unfortunately, we haven't been following his rules. But we'll take care of that soon." He looked at the rearview mirror and eyed Otto sitting in the back seat. "Did you take care of the toll on the Golden Gate Bridge?"

"Sure did. They closed all the toll booths, so you have to use a pass or pay electronically. I did a one-time payment online." He started swiping his iPhone. When he looked up again, he said,

"Uncle Vadim, I have an idea about how to protect our money and make more."

"You have an idea? An idea for our business? This I gotta hear," Vadim said.

"Why don't we get into crypto-currencies? We can set up a virtual account and trade without the authorities tracking us."

"Why should we transfer our good money into those crazy Bitcoins? They go up. They go down. Way too volatile," Vadim said.

"Sure, but they're already worth billions," Otto said. "I've been studying them. You can buy them with credit cards or wire transfers—lots of ways. And we can take them as payment for some of our shipments. When they first came out, money-launderers, mostly drug people, started to use them so nobody could trace where their money came from."

"We don't deal in drugs," Vadim said.

"But we could still use crypto-currencies to eliminate our business's paper trail. Nobody could find our money." He paused and mumbled, "I mean, your business's money."

"Wait a minute," Maksim said, accelerating up the hill just beyond the turnoff to Sausalito. "Who sets the value? How do you know they're safe?"

"They're sort of like gold. The market sets the value," Otto said. He held up his iPhone to show his uncle a website. "See, here's one of the sites with a trading platform."

Vadim leaned over, grabbed the phone, and stared at the little screen. "I still say the price could tank. How would that be good for us?"

"You just hold on through the ups and downs. Besides, it's spreading fast. They're using it to pay for dowries in Sudan, make bets on soccer games in Kenya—all kinds of stuff," Otto said.

"Sounds like a Ponzi scheme," Maksim said. They were driving over a ridge and had a clear view of the Tiburon Peninsula where multi-million dollar homes dotted the hillside.

"So, these coin things aren't backed by a central bank. Right?" Vadim asked.

"No," Otto said. "That's what's so neat about them. No banker looking at your accounts."

"Speaking of banks," Maksim said, "I've been studying which ones might welcome what cash we have left and forget to file the CTRs."

"CTRs?" Otto said.

"Currency Transaction Reports," Maksim explained. "Whenever anyone tries to deposit more than $10,000 in cash, they have to fill out a form."

"You have a lot more than that coming in," Otto said. "What do they do with CTRs?"

"They go to the back office. Nobody pays attention to them unless there are patterns. Lots of smaller deposits of $9,000 would raise a red flag," Maksim said with a smile.

"But you've talked about millions," Otto pressed.

"Right. But we split it up in a bunch of numbered accounts and look for offshore banks that don't get hung up on paperwork. For a small fee, of course."

"Sounds like a lot of work. Dealing with electronic money could be easier. No forms either," Otto said.

"We'll see," Vadim said cautiously. He handed the iPhone back over the seat. "At least you're thinking these days. What I've got in mind is huge, though. We need a central banker to help us out. Misha, remember our old friend Alexander Tepanov?"

"Sure. He set up the accounts that ran the money we got from those sales in Sierra Leone. He laundered it through the car dealers we set up, and he only took 20 percent as I recall."

"That's the one," Vadim said. "You'll never guess what his new job is."

"He's still in Moscow, isn't he?"

"Yes. In a brand new position. He was never listed for any sanctions because he operated under the radar. Now he's been named one of the central bankers."

"So, he can help us with almost anything," Maksim said.

"Precisely. His official salary isn't that much, so I'm sure he'll be happy to do things for us on the side," Vadim said. He glanced at the road and then looked at Maksim. "You sure you've got the right directions to the gun range in San Rafael?"

"Got 'em," Maksim said.

"Good. I don't want to be late. I want plenty of time to make sure Otto knows what he's doing with a Glock."

"I don't think you have to worry. He's had plenty of practice."

"That was back home and a while ago. He's here now. Needs new training," Vadim said. "We'll practice too now that we carry at all times." When Maksim sighed, Vadim turned to him and said, "A gun is like a parachute. If you need one and don't have one, you'll probably never need one again."

"I know. But I still prefer to have our *mafya* friends handle any real problems," Maksim said.

"Yes, yes," Vadim said impatiently. "They arrive tomorrow. But they will be handling things in Wyoming. Otto will be handling our problem in Washington. We want him ready for whatever he might have to deal with." Vadim turned to face Otto. "Since you screwed up the first time, I've taken steps to make sure you don't screw up again."

Otto sat silent as his uncle went on. "You know we have friends. Contacts in high places. In our business, it's vital. Our success isn't our own. It's also important to our clients and highly placed officials who like to share in our profits in exchange for information. I have an ace in the capital."

"Is the ace going to help me?" Otto asked in a cautious tone.

"Yes. Our people watch their people. Their people watch our people. Everybody knows that. But some are better than others."

"Ours are better?" Otto asked.

"Much better," Vadim said. "As soon as I knew our White House target had survived, I asked this contact to share his file on her. He's the military attaché at our embassy, so he knows where she lives and when she goes to work. I might get the file before you leave."

"A military type? Does he sell arms like you?" Otto asked.

"That's not important right now. The point is, he has access to their surveillance reports on White House officials. Now we'll have access too," Vadim said with confidence.

Maksim pulled into the parking lot of the range and killed the motor. The three of them trooped over to a low, concrete building with an Office sign on the door to get their weapons and ammunition, then they joined a dozen people standing outside.

"Folks, listen up," the manager called out to the group gathered at one end of the compound. "Range safety is pretty obvious, but anyone who doesn't follow it gets kicked out. Everyone understand that?" He heard mumblings, but they all eventually nodded. "Okay, always keep your finger off the trigger until you're ready to fire. Always keep your firearm unloaded until you're in the shooting booth and ready to fire. Always keep the action of your firearm open when you are not at the firing line. Got that?"

The group nodded again. "For you new folks here today," he glanced over at the trio of Russians. "No one who's had a drink or any kind of drug is permitted here at any time. Got that?" Vadim, Maksim, and Otto all glared at the man. "Got that?" he repeated.

"Yeah, we got that," Vadim said. "It's too early to drink anyway." A few others chuckled.

The manager went on. "Do you all have your goggles and ear protection? Anyone who doesn't have his own, we've got extras in the shop. Have to protect your eyes and ears whenever you're on the range. And no smoking. Now then, can't let anyone under the age of eighteen on the range." He looked over at Otto. "How old are you?"

"I'm twenty-two."

"I can vouch for that," Maksim said. "He's our nephew."

"Guess he looks old enough. One more thing, no fast firing is allowed. You have to wait at least two seconds between shots. Everyone got that?" Again, the group mumbled their agreement. "Any questions?"

Otto spoke up. "Do you take Bitcoins for payment here?"

"Sure we do," the manager replied. "Neat new system. Less paperwork. And we don't have to pay credit card fees. You got a Bitcoin wallet, come see me later."

Otto smiled.

The manager turned to leave and said over his shoulder, "Okay, you all have a booth assignment over there, so spread out. Just remember to follow the damn rules, and we'll all be fine."

Otto walked to a vending machine near their booth and fed it a few coins. He punched a few buttons until a candy bar dropped to the bottom. After he scooped it up, he said, "That guy's like you, Uncle Vadim. A man with a lot of rules."

"Pretty annoying if you ask me," Vadim said, ambling toward their booth. "I paid the guy to rent these guns. Bought the ammo. He's making a profit. He shouldn't worry so much. C'mon. There's our place over there," he said, pointing to a long row of covered, wooden-partitioned spaces with numbers hanging in front. Inside, each one had a ledge under an opening that looked out at a series of targets set many yards away. They took their guns and equipment to space number seven and scanned the area. Then Vadim turned to Otto who was adjusting his head gear.

"This Glock you rented for me…it's different from the one I used back home. Must be new," Otto said.

"Change is inevitable," Maksim said.

"Except from a vending machine," Otto said with a smile. "Anyway, this one isn't heavy at all. I've seen these in movies, but I didn't know they were so light. What are they made of?"

"It's a polymer frame," Maksim said. "This is a Glock 19. When you pull the slide back, there's a striker that moves back and locks. That means it's ready to fire."

Otto stared at the slide. "We use a 9-millimeter bullet, right?"

"That's what these are." Maksim held up a tiny, mixed-metal tube. "The bullet goes in, the trigger releases the striker, and a spring hits it into the bullet. When the gun goes off, that forces the slide back again. There's no on-off safety on this gun. They've got a different kind of safety system so that nothing happens unless a lever inside the trigger is pulled back."

"I get it," Otto said. "Let me try." He followed Maksim's lead and stood with his legs apart and one arm extended slightly longer than the other. He held the gun with two hands, stared at the target, took aim, and gently squeezed the trigger. "I hit something," he exclaimed, putting down the Glock and adjusting his head gear.

"Something," Vadim said. "Just nothing near the middle. Keep shooting." All three of them loaded their guns and took their shots, waiting the obligatory two seconds between firings.

Otto didn't want the manager to have any reason to remember them. So, he kept his hoodie over his ear protectors and didn't talk to anyone else at the range. The news reports he had seen about the Naples bombing always included a request for anyone who knew a waiter named Otto Kukk to notify law enforcement. Each request was accompanied by the FBI's sketch of him. At least Vadim and Maksim hadn't seen it. They didn't watch much news. They stuck to sports channels and occasionally checked the financial reports. But what about everybody else?

He fired another shot and glanced to his right. He noticed a man in a nearby booth who was high-fiving his friend. The man turned toward him, inclined his head, and then said something to the guy next to him. Both men looked at Otto for a moment before turning back to their target.

Otto started to perspire under his sweatshirt.

Did they recognize me?

Terrifying possibilities started racing through Otto's mind. Would they call the police? The FBI? He couldn't tell Vadim he had to leave without explaining the FBI sketch. Besides, his uncles were still shooting, taking turns every two seconds.

He stole another glance at the two men. They were firing their weapons. He let out a breath and decided to play it cool. Maybe they had noticed him because he was the youngest guy at the range. After all, he was just practicing, like everybody else.

He started to relax when he remembered that he'd be leaving for Washington tomorrow night. Vadim was making him take the red-eye since it was the cheapest flight. When he got to D.C., he needed to be prepared to monitor that White House woman and figure out how to get rid of her.

Otto adjusted his goggles, took aim, and hit the target.

TWELVE

"HEY, BRETT. COME IN HERE AND GET A LOAD of this," Dominick Turiano called out.

"Be right in," Brett said, hanging up his suit coat and rolling up the sleeves of his white shirt. He walked down to the other agent's office and stepped inside.

"Trevor wanted me to show you the latest," Dom said. "The team—well, *your new team*—might find good uses for some of these."

Brett strode over to a long table where several devices were displayed along with a stack of papers and a colored brochure. Dom handed him a tiny object.

"Looks like a screw to me," Brett said, rolling the small metal cylinder between his fingers. "What does it do?"

"Look close," Dom said, grabbing the screw and holding it up. "One end is a miniature drill. It can work its way into basically anything that's wood, plaster, or drywall. Only goes in a fraction of an inch. Then it pivots and inserts the other end, which contains a listening device. If it doesn't pick up any sound or conversation, it pivots around again and drills another hundredth of an inch. It repeats the process until you can pick up normal talking."

"These are much better than the ones we used in Chicago," Brett said, squinting at the little screw. "Any suggestions for placement?"

"I wouldn't recommend heating or air conditioning ducts. Too much rattling and hissing. Kitchens are also too noisy. I'd concentrate on rooms that would give us the most useful intel. Places where people might have meetings or talk on the phone a lot. Offices, living rooms, maybe dining rooms too."

"How long does it last?"

"That's the beauty of this thing. It's powered by a self-charging, internal battery."

"And you think we can use these in embassy properties?"

"Yep. We just got a shipment of these, so they're ready to go whenever we need them." He moved down the table and picked up a round device with lined edges that fit in the palm of his hand. "This isn't for embassies, but it's useful for big cities or stadiums. And for our troops too. That is, if the Pentagon gets its act together, tests, and orders them. It's a bomb preemptor."

"Looks like a hand-grenade," Brett said, opening his hand as Dom passed it to him.

"One of the smallest jammers ever made. Weighs about two and a half pounds. It activates when you pull a safety catch, just like a grenade. Then you throw it wherever you think there might be an IED or regular explosive. It uses electrons to disrupt communications channels."

"So, an IED or bomb can't be triggered by a cell phone, toy car, drone, or whatever the hell they try to use these days?" Brett asked, fingering the device.

"Exactly. Those jamming modules have been miniaturized. They even have antennas printed on internal circuit boards. And the whole thing is cushioned, so the circuitry doesn't get screwed up when it's thrown onto something hard."

"Amazing," Brett said. "How many have we got?"

"Only this one right now. It's a prototype. The manufacturer is showing it off to us, but it's still making its way through the development pipeline. Which is great. It already has a lot of impressive features. No one has seen it in action yet, but the manual says it can be reused because it has a heat-absorbing element that saves the internal battery compartment."

Brett said, "I'm sure they'd be great for our troops. Not just in Syria or Afghanistan, but wherever ISIS sets up shop next. Last numbers I saw about IEDs were incredible. There were something like seventeen thousand explosions where militants are currently operating. Africa, Malaysia, Somalia—tons of places. Sure hope the vetting process for these is accelerated at the Pentagon."

"So do I," Dom said, moving down the table. "Now this one's a lot bigger."

"Something else to stop an explosion?" Brett said, eyeing what looked like a briefcase.

Dom opened it. Inside was a square object that resembled a large flashlight with an antenna on one end, a small screen on the side, and a set of buttons along the edge. "This thing is better than a bomb-sniffing dog."

"What do you mean?" Brett asked, studying it.

"It's got a biologically based sensor. Picks up C-4 and a lot of other bad stuff."

"I feel like I'm in the middle of a James Bond movie and your name is Q," Brett said with a laugh.

"This is nothing compared to the secretary of defense's science and technology group. They've got bullets that go around corners."

"Well, the secretary of defense has a pretty big budget. Ours is miniscule compared to DOD's." He picked up the little screw again. "We're practically a pack of nails compared to the secretary's whole tool box."

"Yeah, but our stuff works. Usually," Dom said. "Now, back to the bomb sensor. You have to get fairly close for it to work. It sucks in a bit of air and then generates a digital readout once its sensor processes the sample. For example, .90 or .99 means there is a high probability of an explosive, but .50 to .60 is a zone of uncertainty.

"If we find the bomb, there is a jammer in the case that can stop a cell phone signal," Dom explained. "At least we hope it can. It hasn't been tested enough yet for us to be sure. But if it doesn't and there's no trip wire or set timer on the explosive, you can pull out the bomb's trigger so that nobody can set it off."

"Pretty dicey stuff," Brett said.

"Of course, but think of it this way: better to have sensors that give our people a fair chance, right?"

"Absolutely," Brett agreed. "So, when will all of this be tested?"

"Don't know. The contractors keep sending us prototypes to get our opinion. Our bomb guys are still going over everything and preparing to send them a report. I just thought you'd like to see them. By the way, have you seen that real estate lady the boss has been ranting about?"

"Yep," Brett said. "Met her a little while ago. Name's Eleanor Clay. Fairly new in town, so I'm pretty sure she doesn't know the routine about being, well, helpful to the FBI."

"What's she like?"

"Let's just say she comes off like a predator. Or a drone looking for a target."

"I'm sure you can handle her," Dom said. "You're single, right?" he added with a grin.

"Have been for a while. But I didn't know spending *private* time with informants was part of our job description. Not the kind she seems to want anyway," Brett said. "She's already sent me a follow-up text suggesting dinner tomorrow. Of course, she said it was so we could discuss some properties she thinks I might buy."

"You think you can turn her?" Dom asked. His grin widened as he added, "I said, 'turn her,' not turn her on."

"I better be able to. Trevor is already driving me up the wall. But you know how he is about getting the advance on any building that changes hands around here."

"I do. Well, I gotta get back to my own investigation."

"You're heading up the bank robbery team, right?

"Bitch of a problem," Dom said, nodding his head. "Trying to coordinate with the local police, marshall's office, and park service is like herding cats. There are just too damn many enforcement agencies in this town. Have you had the same problem dealing with the Naples blast?"

"Not really."

"Anything new on that front?"

"Nothing yet. We've had some calls from people who think they saw the waiter in our drawing, but none of those leads have panned out. And we haven't gotten any hits on any of our databases. Foreign or domestic," Brett said.

"Whoever he is, must be a clever little bastard," Dom said, turning to his desk. "Or maybe his handlers are the clever ones."

THIRTEEN

WEDNESDAY MORNING: SAN FRANCISCO, CALIFORNIA

"STAS. LUBOV. YOU MADE IT," VADIM SAID, giving each man a bear hug. "Come in and let me show you the view. You'll see right away why there's no better place to invest some of our profits. And we need more of those," he muttered.

The two guests hauled in their luggage. They looked around the room with its contemporary furnishings and well-stocked bar. Then they gazed out the windows where a bright sun illuminated an expanse of white buildings and blue waters.

"Very impressive," Stas said, tossing his black leather jacket over one of the side chairs.

Lubov slumped down on the couch and asked, "Got any good food around here? Stuff on the plane was awful. Vodka was about all I could take."

"I called for takeout. We'll have it in a little while. But first, will you join me in another vodka?" Vadim asked.

"Of course," Lubov said. "Now why are we here? Couldn't you have told us something over the phone? After all, how many times have we done deals together?"

Vadim sauntered over to the bar and took a bottle of his finest vodka out of the fridge along with four chilled glasses and began to pour. "I don't trust phones any more. Not here, what with all the surveillance the Americans are so famous for." He glanced around. "Misha will be out in a minute. He's just changing." Vadim poured the drinks and handed them to his guests. "He and I have been working out the details of this new plan. Ah, here he comes now."

Maksim walked in from a bedroom and hugged each man. "Great to see you! No worse for wear, I see. Your businesses must be treating you well," he said in a jovial tone. He sat in the side chair without Stas's coat on it.

"We do all right," Stas said, joining Lubov on the couch. "Recently had to get rid of some competition, though."

"Yah," Lubov said. "A few well-placed tips, and the guys heading most of the Trincher gangs were history. The jerks were moving in on our territories and running millions through some shell companies in Cyprus. And look at what happened to those accounts."

"Don't forget we also lost a lot in that Cyprus shakedown," Vadim said.

"We know," Lubov said. "But you never get raided by the FBI or anybody else. And neither do we. We're too careful to get caught, and no one has been stupid enough to rat us out to any feds."

"Which is exactly why I asked both of you to come," Vadim said, handing each man a large cocktail glass. "I see you obviously didn't have any trouble getting into the country."

"Of course not. We have enough passports and visas to get almost anywhere." Lubov took a swig of his drink.

Vadim pulled up a chair and focused on the two *mafya* leaders. Stas with his sloping forehead and Lubov with the long, beaked nose. "To start. As I said, we lost a lot of money in Cyprus. Then the sanctions kicked in. Our fortunes go up and down as yours do. But now, Misha and I have put together a plan that will change that. It's nothing like our other operations, which have relied on shipping arms where they are needed most."

"Go on," Stas said.

"That money is from militants in tough regions. We've switched our focus and started looking at the world's financial centers where the real money is made or lost. That prompted a question: if something were to happen to most of the major central bankers and financial leaders, what would happen to the markets?"

Lubov and Stas suddenly began to stumble over each other with rapid-fire questions.

"What do you mean *happen*?"

"What central bankers are you talking about?"

"How could something happen to most of them?"

"You're not talking about mass murder, are you?"

"Are you crazy?"

Vadim sat back and took another drink. He let them simmer down and then said, "You didn't answer my question. What would happen to the markets?"

Stas and Lubov both stared at their host.

"They would tank," Stas shouted.

"Stock market would take a huge hit," Lubov echoed.

"Market here cratered after 9/11, not to mention other corrections now and then. But after that attack, they said the American economy lost a ton in just days," Stas said.

Vadim set his glass down and folded his arms. "Exactly. And how did *certain* people protect their investments from that crash *before* 9/11?"

Lubov thought for a moment. "I heard they shorted the market."

"So, what would you do *before* an event that would wipe out a lot of top bankers and others like them if you knew it was going to happen?" Vadim asked, narrowing his eyes.

"I'd preserve our investments. I'd short the dollar. I'd…I'd do all sorts of things to protect our businesses," Stas answered.

"So, if you could help set up this event you knew would happen well in advance, what would that be worth to you?"

"Wait a minute," Lubov said, jumping to his feet and pacing in front of the window. "Are you saying you want us to do a massive hit that crashes the market and lets us all make money on the deal? How in hell would we do that?"

"Relax, Lubov, come on. Sit down, and let's discuss this idea like the good businessmen we all are," Vadim said.

"I don't know," Stas said. "Lubov's right. What kind of crazy scheme have you come up with?"

"Have you ever heard about the Federal Reserve Conference at Jackson Hole?"

"Jackson Hole?" Lubov asked, looking bewildered. "Are you talking about the ski place?"

"Precisely," Vadim said. "Every year the American Federal Reserve Governors get together for a conference in Wyoming at that ski resort. But it's also a summer resort."

"So? You think you're going to put a hit on a dozen of those guys in a meeting?" Stas asked, raising his voice. "That's nuts."

"Not a dozen of those guys," Vadim mimicked. "There will be over a hundred top bankers, finance ministers, and CEOs from all over the world. All in one place having meetings, lunches, dinners. All in the mountains with minimum security." He sat back and let that thought settle in.

Stas looked at Lubov and then over at Maksim. "And you think it's a good idea to attack one of those meetings?"

Maksim took a deep breath. "Vadim and I have been all over this plan. The more we look at the possibilities, the more we think it's absolutely brilliant. We would all work together to set up the hit, but we would arrange our finances ahead of time in separate small trades so that no one could possibly connect any of us to the attack. Then when it's over—and they're trying to figure out how to replace their top people and repair all the damage—we take our profits and lay low for a while."

There was silence in the room, except for some occasional sounds emanating from a bedroom where Otto was playing a video game.

"Who's in there?" Lubov asked pointing to a door.

"That's our nephew, Otto. He's learning the business," Maksim said. "Still a little green, but I think he's got the right instincts. At least for money. I'm not sure yet whether he really has an appetite for the more extensive problems that sometimes need to be handled."

Lubov shrugged. "That's the thing with the younger ones. They feel entitled to the profits but don't want any of the dirty work. If we're going to work together on any of this, we have to stick with experienced people. Not some *nephew* along for the ride."

"We know," Vadim said. "Don't worry about Otto. He won't be included in the Jackson op. In fact, we're sending him to Washington tonight so that he can take care of one particularly difficult individual. It'll give him a chance to prove that he actually *can* deal with an extensive problem."

Lubov got up and walked to the windows. He looked out toward the Golden Gate Bridge. "If we pull off that conference stunt," he paused and then continued, "I might like to buy a place here too. Not a bad view."

The corners of Vadim's mouth turned up slightly. "You are beginning to see the possibilities of my idea."

"The trouble is," Stas said, "We all sell weapons, but none of us actually has experience using them at this scale. You're talking about a lot of important people. I have to think about this."

"And how many people get killed by the arms we sell? I'm talking about taking out a few dozen. Hell, they murder more than that in a week in Chicago or Los Angeles. Yes, these people are some of the most important in the world when it comes to managing money. But many of them are the very people who put sanctions together, not just against North Korea and Iran, but against *us*." Vadim said as his knuckles turned white against his cocktail glass.

"I guess you have a point there," Lubov said.

"And just how do you propose to *take out* a few dozen of these important people?" Stas asked.

"We'll discuss the strategy and develop a plan we can all agree to. In fact, we already practiced taking out a whole room full of people. So, we have a lot of insight that will give us a head start."

"You took out a room full of people?" Lubov called out. "We never heard anything about that."

Vadim held up his hand in a calming gesture. "No. What I meant was that we staged an experiment to target an individual. We weren't concerned about collateral damage. It didn't come off as planned, but we did learn a lot about tactics, explosives, and timers. I'll explain all of that later. The important thing now is for all of us to agree to focus on this Wyoming event and figure out how to make it profitable."

"I don't know," Stas said, rubbing his forehead.

"To win big, you have to think big," Vadim said.

"But we've never been to Jackson," Lubov said. "All of our operations have been in familiar territory in Russia. We wouldn't know where to begin in Wyoming."

Vadim stood up and walked over to a large black desk by the window. He scooped up a fist full of papers and maps and handed them to Lubov and Stas. "Take a look at these. They'll give you a sense of the Jackson area, let you scope it out, and get some ideas about where to stay. You'll be heading out there right away." He turned and walked toward his bedroom. "Excuse us for a few minutes. Misha and I have some calls to make."

Maksim joined his brother as the *mafya* men held the papers and exchanged questioning looks.

FOURTEEN

"RIGHT THIS WAY, MISS REID. MISS MARCONI IS waiting for you," said the maître d' of one of the most exclusive eateries in the world. He stepped away from his mahogany rostrum in the basement of the West Wing and led Samantha down a short hall. They passed a replica of the USS *Constitution* encased in Plexiglas and then entered the White House Mess.

They walked past a large round table just inside the door. Everyone called it the Staff Table. If senior staff members didn't have a reservation or plans to sit with a particular colleague, they could take an open chair at this table. It was the best spot to pick up news and gossip from other directorates.

Samantha nodded to the head of legislative affairs who was evidently sharing a joke with the Associate Director of the Office of Management and Budget. She wondered how he was handling the new Congress's latest round of budget cuts. Later, she'd have to find out if they were going to reduce the Homeland Security budget. She hoped not. There were better places to cut money than

81

from departments protecting the country, like the White House Barber Shop. Or the fund for presidential cuff links and tie clips. Or the alphabet soup of commissions. Or, better yet, some of the examiners and staff specialists ensconced in the new executive office building. No one had any idea what those people did.

As she walked, she saw the press secretary sitting at a table with the communications director. They were probably trying to figure out how to explain the strategy the president and the British Prime Minister had been developing to counter some of Putin's potential moves on Latvia and Lithuania. She had heard about all of that in the morning NSC staff meeting.

She spied her friend, Angela Marconi, Deputy Director of the president's Scheduling Office, seated at a small wooden table by a wall where paintings of ships decorated the spaces between sections of carved paneling.

"Glad you could get away for once," Angela said with a grin as Samantha sat down and grabbed a blue menu with a piece of gold braid trailing down the center.

"I don't have much time," Samantha said. "It's been crazy as usual, but I always love to get down here. The one place I *know* I won't run into a member of the press."

"Yes, you must be dodging them left and right these days what with the bombing. Have you learned anything new about the Naples investigation?"

"Nothing really," Samantha said. "The FBI sent over an agent—really nice guy. He had a drawing of a server who disappeared after the blast. And I think I remember seeing that server in the ballroom, but nobody knows whether he actually had anything to do with it."

"You *saw* him?" Angela asked, raising an eyebrow. "If you saw him, he probably saw you. Do you think he was checking you out? Everyone around here thinks *you* were the target of that explosion, and I've been worried about you ever since. Maybe whoever it was will try to get you here."

"Relax," Samantha said. "It's not like we're under siege. Nothing like what happened in Naples is going to happen here."

"Well, I can't help but worry about my best friend," Angela said with a slight frown.

"I appreciate it, but I'm fine," Samantha said perusing the menu. "Although I have to admit that every time I relive the whole bombing scene, I feel a little off-kilter."

"You know, I always wondered. What's a kilter?" Angela asked with a slight grin.

Samantha smiled back, grateful her friend was trying not to worry her about the bombing.

A waiter clad in a dark blue blazer walked up to their table, tablet and pen in hand. "What may I get for you, Miss Reid?" he asked.

Samantha was always proud of the way all the waiters remembered the names of the staff in this room. "I'll have a tuna on whole wheat with a side of fruit please. Oh, and an iced tea too."

He jotted it down and turned. "And for you, Miss Marconi?"

"Just a bowl of vegetable soup today. And ice water."

"Very well," he said and quickly strode toward the kitchen.

"Just soup? On another diet or something?" Samantha asked.

"As usual. Thought I'd try the vegan thing for a while, although I have to kill it every time I go to my mom's for one of her big Italian dinners."

"Her cooking is fabulous," Samantha said. "I love her Sunday dinners. Sorry I haven't been in a while."

"You haven't missed much. She's still trying to introduce me to a cavalcade of losers."

Samantha started to laugh. "Like who?"

"Remember the dentist she fixed me up with last month?"

"The one who gave you the toothbrush sanitizer for your birthday?" Samantha said, shaking her head in dismay.

"That's the one. She finally gave up on him when I told her to stop inviting him over. But now she says she met a very nice man at a farmer's market."

"And?" Samantha asked.

"I'm supposed to meet him Sunday. She says he owns a macadamia nut farm in Costa Rica."

Samantha couldn't help laughing again. "Are you excited?"

"Are you kidding?" Angela said, "When she told me about him, all I could think was 'That Don't Impress Me Much.' How about you? Heard from Tripp?"

"Just a quick email saying I should come see his new apartment sometime," Samantha said. "Sometime? Like when?"

"Well, even if he had asked you on a concrete date, would you have time to go right now?"

"I guess not. But still." She thought for a moment and added, "I've been thinking that our relationship isn't completely over, but it's definitely fading." And so were her spirits. Samantha had been depressed ever since her meeting with Ken Cosgrove and the order to go to Jackson Hole next week.

"Here you are, ladies," the waiter said, walking up to their table. He placed a large bowl of soup in front of Angela and a plated sandwich with fruit in front of Samantha. "And here are your drinks. Anything else I can get you right now?"

"I think we're good," Angela said, eyeing the bowl. "Well, maybe a few crackers."

"Coming right up," he said, and returned to the kitchen.

Samantha took a bite of her sandwich as the Tetons loomed in her mind. "I meant to tell you about some travel next week. Ken is sending me to Jackson Hole to give a speech at the Federal Reserve conference."

"That's a pretty high level group. As my dad used to say, 'Above whom there are no whomers,'" Angela said.

Samantha leaned forward. "But you know that's the last place I'd want to go."

Angela reached over and touched Samantha's hand. "I know, kiddo. But look at it this way, it's been years since the last time you were there. And, it'll get you out of town. At least for a while. I don't like the idea of you possibly being a target in Washington. Or anywhere."

"Don't worry. If I ever feel like I'm in trouble, there are a lot of people I can call, like the Secret Service."

"What about the FBI agent who came to see you?" Angela asked.

"Well, yes," Samantha said. "He did give me his cell and said to call him any time."

"And what does this FBI agent look like, I wonder," Angela said, tasting her soup and cocking her head to one side with a smile.

"Not bad, I guess," Samantha said. "Tall, good build, well dressed."

Angela's face lit up. "What else?"

Samantha shifted in her seat and said, "Oh, all right. He's got short brown hair. He's probably thirty-five or thirty-six. And he had this way of looking right at me...Then again, no one else was around except Joan."

"Could be interesting, especially with Tripp more or less out of the picture."

"I didn't say he's out of the picture," Samantha said defensively. "I just don't think his focus is centered much on me these days. Besides, I'm not ready to think about other men."

"You don't have to *think* about them," Angela said. "Just keep that FBI phone number handy."

Samantha heard a low buzz. She pulled out her cell, read the newest message, and pushed her chair back. "Gotta go. Sorry to cut out on you. There's more talk about a threat at a Cubs game."

"A threat at the stadium?" Angela asked wide-eyed.

"Don't know too much about it yet," Samantha said as she stood up. "Maybe we could meet tomorrow night since we'll both probably be working late?"

"Good idea. I'll text you when I've wrapped things up in our shop. Good luck with the Cubs."

Samantha nodded and briskly walked toward the entrance.

FIFTEEN

"HOW ABOUT A ROCK MASSAGE?" STAS SAID,
with a big laugh.

"What the hell is a rock massage?" Lubov asked, getting up
from the couch and walking to the glass and chrome dining room
table in their hosts' vast penthouse.

Stas shifted in his chair in front of the table and showed
Lubov a picture of a gorgeous girl lounging next to a hot tub.
"You can get one in this spa for a hundred and ninety American
dollars. Vadim must have printed this out as an inducement."

Lubov grabbed the page and scanned the different treat-
ments. "I think the four-handed massage sounds better, especially if I can pick which four hands I want." He pulled up a chair
and started pouring over some of the maps and articles spread
out on the table.

"Check out this article," Stas said. "It has a very useful dia-
gram. Apparently, the finance people always stay in a lodge up

north near Jackson Lake. I wonder if they have all their meetings there or if they fan out over the valley."

"Even if they don't spread out, I'm sure they'll have security everywhere. Every one of those minister types probably has his own body guard."

"Yah. But we won't be targeting people individually."

"We still need to figure out all the places they might go as a group."

"What we really need is their schedule. Maybe Vadim can get a copy of it," Stas said.

Lubov picked up a map and studied it. A large lake some miles from Yellowstone caught his eye. "That big park there. Is that the one with all the geysers and hot springs?"

"Yes. Don't think we'll have time to check it out, though. Look over here," he said and pointed to a road. "You follow this down from the big lake, there are a couple of smaller lakes, and over a little east is the Snake River. It says here they have good fishing. Maybe we'll find time to catch some trout."

"Sure," Lubov said. "Wait. There's a section on fishing here, and, let's see—damn."

"What?" Stas asked.

"We can't eat 'em."

"Why not?"

"They have a catch and release policy."

Stas broke into a laugh. "I thought that was America's immigration policy."

Lubov ignored him and grabbed the map again. "So, farther down is the Teton Village. That's the big ski resort with all the mountains, gondolas, and everything. Says they've got the longest vertical drop in the country, and you can see the whole valley from the top. Could be fun."

"We'll be there to work," Stas said.

"Yah, but look at the other stuff on this list. Kayaking, rafting, paragliding."

"All things to keep in mind if our car breaks down," Stas muttered. "But this isn't going to be a vacation." He leafed through a few more pages on the table and added, "On the other hand, they do have some pretty decent restaurants in Teton Village and Jackson."

Lubov glanced over Stas's shoulder and said, "Everything from the Four Seasons to the Mangy Moose. Whatever the hell that is."

"Speaking of food," Maksim said, walking in with Vadim, "here's the delivery from the Red Tavern. It took a while, but it's worth the wait." He turned and shouted to his nephew. "Otto? Food's here."

A bedroom door opened, and the young man poked his head out, surveying the scene. "Hi," he said cautiously.

"Get in here. We have guests from Moscow." Vadim waved his hand toward Lubov and Stas. "Take these bags into the kitchen and get the food out. Bring the silverware too."

Otto nodded to the men, picked up the food, and disappeared.

Vadim pulled out a chair and joined the *mafya* bosses. He sat at the head of the table. "So, you've looked at all of this?" he said, pointing to the pile.

"More or less," Stas said. "How much time should we take out there?"

"You need to be careful not to get ID'd, so not too long," Vadim said.

"A conference schedule would be more helpful," Lubov said.

"Here you go," Otto said, setting down two large platters of food on the table. One was piled with shredded cabbage, tomatoes, and cucumber and dill salad. The other was crowded with *pelmeni* meat dumplings and zucchini pancakes with salmon tartar and sour cream. "I'll get the plates and forks." He turned and rushed back into the kitchen.

The men eyed the spread, and Maksim said, "Would you like me to pour more vodka? Or should we have water first?"

"Vodka. Always vodka," Lubov said.

Otto reemerged with individual plates, silverware, and paper napkins. He hesitated as he looked down at all the food.

"Why don't you take some and go back to your games," Maksim suggested. "We have business here."

Otto looked relieved. He took a plate, swiped a couple of dumplings, grabbed a spoonful of salad, and then quickly retreated to his room. As they all heaped multiple servings onto their own plates, Maksim handed out four glasses of vodka, and Vadim resumed the conversation.

"We should be able to help with the time tables. I told you about Alexander Tepanov being promoted to that director job at the central bank." They grunted their agreement as they ate. "With all the problems between the U.S. and Russia, Putin may decide to send more people to the conference. Tepanov could be one of them. He needs someone to put on a good show, maybe cut some trade deals on the side, and distract the press from what he's trying to do in Eastern Europe."

"He is clever," Lubov said between bites. "But do you think a guy like Tepanov would be invited?"

"Could be," Maksim said. "Since he was just appointed, it has to mean he's been accepted into the inner circle."

"And if Tepanov goes," Vadim said, "I can talk him into getting us a copy of the agenda. He owes us some favors. Besides, it wouldn't cost him anything."

"Wait," Stas said, leaning back and holding up the palms of his hands. "If Tepanov actually goes to this conference, how can we be sure he's not one of the victims?"

Vadim squinted and said, "Once we get what we need, if there is a bit of additional damage, there's not much we can do about that. Is there?"

"I guess not," Lubov said. "Will you need him in the future?"

"Moving our accounts will take some time, but it will be done before the conference. I just called him early this morning. He had already left for the day, but his assistant told me when to call him back."

"Sounds good," Stas said.

"Now for *pryamoi razgovr*," Vadim said, raising his glass. "Time for straight talk about our undertaking." They all raised a glass and took a gulp as Vadim continued. "I wanted you to study all the places these people may spend their time so you won't miss anything that will help us carry out this great opportunity. The opportunity for us to shape financial events, control world markets, and make a killing.

"Now, we will give you the parameters and assure your payments. Half down when you set a viable plan in Jackson. Half at completion. We will be anxious to hear your ideas. When you figure out how to execute all of this, send us a simple text. Then we'll know your preliminary work is finished and you'll be coming back here. To get started, let's make your airline reservations. You should leave for Jackson first thing tomorrow."

Vadim glanced over at Maksim and added, "Of course, my brother and I will also be in Jackson during the conference to make sure everything goes smoothly. We will all fly there together on a private jet a day or two before it starts. So, check out the best places to land while you're there."

"You'll be shadowing us?" Stas said, raising his eyebrow. "Don't you trust us?"

"Of course. But prudence is always worth more than trust when you sell guns for a living." Vadim looked around the table, stood up, raised his glass, and gestured for another toast. *"Doveryai, no proveryai."*

Maksim smiled, raised his glass, and echoed, "Trust but verify."

SIXTEEN

WEDNESDAY EVENING: WASHINGTON, D.C.

BRETT SHUT DOWN HIS COMPUTER, SHOVED his cell into a pocket, grabbed his suit coat, and turned out the light. A few agents were still hunkered over their desks as he walked down the hall.

He also had a ton of work to do, but he couldn't miss his eight o'clock reservation. He had checked out the restaurant online and, judging from the menu, realized it might not fly on his expense report. But Eleanor had picked the place, and he couldn't afford to miss an opportunity to build trust. She had suggested a relaxed meeting over dinner since she had appointments all day long.

He headed out of the building, grateful for the mild breeze. It had cooled down to the sixties, and traffic had eased up since most of the government types had already headed out 395, Rockwood Parkway, or Route 50. A lot of the agents complained about the traffic tie-ups and claimed that even if they wanted to take the metro, there was never enough parking at the stations.

Yet, there they were, with Maryland homes and mortgages in Silver Spring, Wheaton, or Shady Grove. Some of them had bought down in Springfield, Virginia, along with a ton of military families. There simply wasn't reasonable space in the city for families. Or even nearby. The usual lament in all the bureaus.

Brett was glad he had snagged a decent month-to-month furnished place by the Mount Vernon Triangle. Nothing fancy. He didn't need fancy. He had a simple one-bedroom efficiency. In fact, if anyone came over, they might think he was in a witness protection program. Nothing personal in the place. His own furniture, pictures, and books were all still in storage back in Chicago. One of these days, he'd make another move. Just not yet.

He hurried down F Street, passed the rust brick National Building Museum, and turned left onto Sixth Street. Brett saw several Chinese restaurants up ahead and wished she had picked one of those. Still, he was grateful for the chance to walk. He hadn't been able to hit the fitness center in his apartment building for the past two days.

Brett followed Sixth all the way down to Pennsylvania Avenue and then took two rights onto Indiana. And there it was. Fiola. When he opened the door, set back from the street, the first thing he saw was a long, shiny, wooden bar crowded with well-dressed men and women leaning toward each other, trying to converse. The room was noisy, but that seemed to recommend it. Most restaurants had a decibel level equal to the quality of their food.

He asked a young woman standing at the front if Eleanor Clay had arrived yet. "Yes, sir. Let me take you to her. Careful on the steps," she said, leading him past the bar which was separated from the tables by a low wall covered in dark brown leather. They took three steps down to the dining area.

Brett spotted the real estate agent, perched in a half-moon-shaped booth lined with heavy beige fabric. He slid in across from her. "Evening, Eleanor. Hope I didn't keep you waiting."

"Not at all," she purred. "I did go ahead and order my martini."

The waiters look like walking ads for their wine, Brett thought as one passed by. Another appeared wearing a long-sleeved cotton shirt the color of merlot.

"May I take your drink order, sir?" the server asked with a practiced smile.

"How about a beer," Brett said.

"Certainly, sir. We have the Avery White Rascal, the Ballast Point Sculpin, Founders Breakfast Stout, a Great Lakes Lager, a Pilsner, the Moretti or Peroni, both from Italy, of course, or perhaps you would prefer our Port City Pale Ale."

"The Peroni would be fine, thanks," Brett said.

"You'll love the food here," Eleanor said. "Rather nouveau, I suppose, but quite like some of my favorite haunts in New York. Check out this menu." She handed him a heavy sheet with a headline that read, Market Tasting Menu Creations, on one side.

Ignoring the specials listed under the headline, Brett flipped the sheet and scanned the regular entrees on the back. "The Salumeria Biellese Wagyu Beef Bresaola is dynamite," Eleanor said. "Or maybe the Ahi Tuna Carpaccio for a first course. Are you a fish or pasta person?" she asked, raising her heavily blackened eyelashes at him.

"I was thinking about a steak," Brett replied. Then he noticed that the striploin at the bottom was served with radicchio *tardivio*, rosemary *zabaglione*, and Tuscan *lardo*. He had no idea what all that was. The steak was priced at sixty-four bucks. He wondered if they had A-1 sauce. Probably not.

"Well, a big man like you needs a big steak. Go for it," she said. "And remember, you're my guest tonight. After all, I'm the one who suggested we meet here, and you're my client."

"Sorry. It's on me," Brett said emphatically, knowing he couldn't accept a high-priced dinner from a civilian. He'd just have to do his best on his expense account.

The waiter put down his ale and said, "Have you folks decided on your dinner yet? No hurry, of course."

"Give us a bit of time," Eleanor said. "I don't want to rush things."

Neither did Brett, but he wanted to start easing into things. He took a sip of ale and looked directly at her. "There's something important I want to talk to you about tonight."

"Yes, I know. I have several listings with me." She reached toward the large shoulder bag sitting next to her.

"No, wait," Brett said. "I really appreciate the time you've spent showing me that townhouse and looking for apartment listings. I've been reviewing my financial commitments, and I've decided to wait a while to see how my new assignment shakes out. So, can we put those new listings on hold for now?"

Eleanor shifted on the banquette. She sipped her martini and said in a low voice, "I'm sorry to hear that. I thought you were serious. And here I've spent a lot of time poring through the MLS for you."

"I was serious," he said. "I just want to wait a while."

"So, what is this new assignment of yours? You never really told me what you do. You just said you worked down in this area. You'd think you were with the CIA or something."

"Well, I'm not," Brett said.

"Then what is your job, if I may ask?" she said.

"I'm a special agent with the FBI."

"Well, why didn't you say so?" she said, brightening. "There's nothing wrong with working for the bureau. Or are you on some sort of secret assignment you can't talk about?" She raised her face with an expectant smile.

"I'm working on a number of projects, and, now that you bring it up, I could really use your help on one of them."

"Use *my* help?" she said.

"This is a new one for me. I've spent a lot of time in the field but not so much on the research side of things. But now I'm replacing another agent whose responsibility was learning—no not just learning, *knowing* all the important real estate moves of certain foreign interests in Washington."

"State Department coordinates all the embassy moves. I'm sure you know that," she said with a slight wave of her hand.

"Yes, of course, we know their role. But ours is different than theirs."

"Then what *is* your role, and what could it possibly have to do with me?"

The waiter reappeared, tablet in hand. "Pardon the interruption. I just wanted to see if you had any questions."

Eleanor picked up her menu, glanced over it again, and said, "I'll start with the farm greens with hearts of palm and toasted pine nuts. Then, let me see which fish would be good tonight. Yes, I'll have the Adriatic *brodetto* of wild cod, mussels, and octopus."

"Excellent choice," the waiter said. "And for you, sir?"

"I don't really need a first course. I'll just nurse the ale here. But I guess I'll go for the steak, medium rare. Okay?"

"Of course, sir. Thank you," he said, making a note and leaving them alone again.

"Look, State facilitates the property searches for diplomats from all over the world. But we need to find out *ahead of time* when properties are changing hands."

"Why? Sales end up in public records anyway," Eleanor said.

"I know. I realize you're new in Washington, but surely you can understand that certain countries have agents that keep an eye on us just as we keep an eye on them."

"And you want *me* to inform *you* whenever I line up a sale to a foreigner? I can't believe this," she said, draining her martini. "I'm not some sort of spy."

"Of course not," he said in a calming voice. "But you could be a kind of consultant to the FBI. We already work with several top real estate agents in town. They're known as Clandestine Human Sources, a CHS. Think of it as doing something for your country's security. After all, that *is* our mission: keeping the country safe. I'm not asking you to break any laws. Nothing like that. I'm just asking for some information from time to time. That doesn't sound too bad, does it?" he asked.

She sighed heavily and looked like she was trying to decide something. "I have to admit that real estate agents talk to each other all the time. We trade listings, trade gossip, and this sounds like widening the circle a bit. I hadn't heard about these CHS's, but I guess they don't sound too bad. You just caught me off guard, that's all," she said somewhat apologetically. "But you said only the top agents are CHS's?"

"Of course." Looks like he might be able to close this deal after all. If he could just maintain a professional level of discourse and not let her get too personal, maybe he could learn something valuable as soon as tonight.

"Here you are, ma'am. Your first course. Everything is edible, including the blossoms," the waiter said, setting down a bowl. "Greens, rhubarb, nuts, and goat cheese sprinkled with lavender petals. Enjoy." Brett looked over and was glad he was just drinking ale.

Eleanor sampled the salad. "You're missing out on a wonderful vinaigrette here," she said. "But back to your proposition."

Brett hoped to hell she would stop using that language.

"About letting you know before a contract is signed. Is that all you want to know?" she asked.

"It would be especially helpful to know the moving dates as well." He wasn't about to tell her that before anyone moved into a new property, his team would be there planting a whole host of listening devices.

"Well, now that I think about it, I've handled two international contracts in the last week. Burkina Faso is buying a house for their commercial attaché, and then there is another property on Belmont in Kalorama. Third house from the corner at Massachusetts. I just sold it to a Russian official. It's across the street from the Islamic center. Do you care about any of those sales?"

"I didn't know we had that much trade with Burkina Faso, but in general, yes. Information on several different countries could really help us out." Brett said. "Especially Russian, Chinese, Middle Eastern countries, South American, certain South Africans. You're smart; you can imagine where our interests would be. But if you're not certain, just contact me and let me know the state of play on various deals." He took a sip of ale. "About the Russian one on Belmont—do you know the buyer's title?"

"I believe he's their new military attaché," she said, taking another bite of her salad. "He's been living at their embassy. But he mentioned a promotion and bringing his family over from Moscow. So, he's getting the house."

"What about the move-in date?" Brett asked. "And is it occupied now?"

"No. This one is vacant. The man who owned it is a foreign service officer who's already gone overseas. He said FSOs often have to travel on short notice. I don't know if the new owner is doing any renovations. He seemed to like it the way it was. Kitchen and bathrooms are in good shape. He'll be closing right away and could move in a matter of days."

The waiter reappeared, removing Eleanor's salad and serving their main courses. "Will there be anything else? Perhaps wine to complement the meal?"

"I could use a glass of your Talley Vineyards Chardonnay," Eleanor said. "Do you want something, Brett?"

"I think I'm good, thanks," he replied, eyeing the steak. Suddenly, his tension evaporated and he was ravenous. "This looks terrific." He cut off a piece and tasted it. "Sure as hell beats Jack-in-the-Box."

Eleanor burst out laughing. "You know, word about this place has really gotten around. Members of Congress are in here all the time. McConnell, Pelosi—both sides of the aisle."

Must have bigger expense accounts than the FBI, Brett thought.

But he suspected tonight's tab would turn out to be worth every penny.

SEVENTEEN

"THIS NEW INFRA-RED LIGHT IS PRETTY
handy," Brett whispered, watching his locks team specialist fid-
dle with the bolt on the back door of the Kalorama house. She
grunted in reply and continued her work. The two-story red
brick house was uncomfortably close to its neighbors, but at least
there were tall fences separating the properties. Brett said a silent
prayer that no one next door would see or sense an intrusion.

While he waited, he surveyed the rest of the area. It was a
half block off the Massachusetts Avenue area known as Embassy
Row. Extending several streets, this section of Washington was
home to politicians, delegations, and interests from around the
world, including the Islamic mosque right across the street Eleanor had mentioned.

The side roads were usually packed with cars, especially
when the faithful obeyed the muezzin's call for Friday noon
prayers. They would fill the elaborate lime stone building with
its mosaic inscriptions of Qur'an verses written in blue Arabic

101

script just above the five entry arches. Only one car was parked there now: a black sedan with two FBI watch officers inside. It was three o'clock in the morning.

"Everything okay back there?" a watch officer spoke softly into his two-way radio.

"Just made the lock," Brett answered quietly. "Let us know if anyone shows up."

"Right," he replied. "Good luck."

Brett, Dom, and several staff specialists pushed inside. Wearing night-vision googles, black pants, and black shirts, they moved silently through the kitchen and entered the dining room. Two agents carried their equipment upstairs.

Rays of ambient light from a street lamp filtered through the windows that didn't have shutters or drapery. Brett and Dom crouched along the periphery, studied the chair rail and chandelier, then focused on the baseboards and crown molding.

"I'm glad Trevor let me join your little group. I want to make sure the new system's installation is as easy as it should be. I'll have one of the experts start in here," Dom whispered as he crouched to open a case filled with small tools and dozens of tiny screw-type listening devices. "The screws last up to three years, but I think we should connect a couple of them to the electrical system for backup."

"Good idea," Brett said in a low voice, motioning to the rest of his team to pick up their devices.

Dom extended a small ladder he had carried in and leaned it against the wall. "We should install the first ones up here and place others across the room," he said, pointing to a mitered corner of molding above crimson wallpaper. "They'll look for these, but our guys at the apartment across the road won't turn the system on until after their sweep team leaves," he added.

Brett stepped into a richly paneled study where he could easily imagine the Russian military attaché hosting meetings and, hopefully, conference calls. He surveyed the room and quietly discussed several locations for bugs with his crew. Thanks to Eleanor, this room could become a gold mine of information.

As he watched his surveillance staff install the tiny screws, his conversations with the realtor started replaying in his mind. She had been fairly pushy whenever they talked. Always asking him prying questions that made him uncomfortable. It had been a while since someone had tried to forge a personal connection with him.

Two years had passed since his wife had decided she wanted a more lavish lifestyle, asked for a divorce, and ran off with a bond salesman. She now lived in a mansion along Lake Michigan in Winnetka with a guy who probably came home for dinner. Brett envied her for knowing what she wanted, even as superficial as it was.

His thoughts were interrupted by static on his two-way.

"Got company out here. Stay low."

Brett quickly moved to the dining room and signaled Dom and the others to hit the floor. Then he crept up the stairway and motioned to the two agents in the bedrooms to get down as well. He continued to listen as the radio connection remained open.

"D.C. cops," he heard a watch agent say.

"Crap," another replied.

Brett heard the sound of approaching footsteps over the feed. Then he heard another voice. "License and registration please."

"We're not illegally parked," the driver said.

"No, but we got a call from a neighbor. Wants to know why you're sitting out here snooping, or whatever you think you're doing. What *are* you doing?"

"Not breaking any laws that I can see, officer," the driver said in a friendly tone.

"No, but I did ask to see your license and registration."

"We're FBI, keeping an eye on the mosque."

"At *this* hour?" the officer asked.

"Yes. We're part of a terrorism task force if you must know. And while this area is heavily patrolled by embassy security as well as your forces, we have a special reason to conduct our own routine surveillance of certain individuals. Here are my creds."

There was a long pause. Then Brett heard the officer say, "Just seems strange that you would be doing surveillance on an empty building."

"It's not always empty," the agent replied.

"Uh-huh."

Finally, Brett heard footsteps shuffling away and the sound of a car driving off.

"All clear," the driver said with a sigh.

EIGHTEEN

THURSDAY MORNING; GEORGETOWN, WASHINGTON, D.C.

OTTO WHEELED HIS RENTED ACURA INTO THE parking lot in front of the Georgetown Holiday Inn on Wisconsin Avenue. He gazed up at the five-story rectangle that resembled Stalin-era construction. It clashed wonderfully with the traditional architecture of a little white church across the street. He couldn't help but think the hotel looked like the box that church came in. Still, Vadim had told him it was in a good location and was reasonably priced. He failed to mention he could have booked Otto a room at the Four Seasons where he and Maksim always stayed, though.

Otto noticed his accommodations were a grade below the place Vadim had rented for him in Naples. He also realized they would continue to decline every time he screwed up. Maybe he would surprise his uncles and get upgraded to a four-star hotel after he completed this assignment. Though, the more he thought about Vadim sending him around the country to kill someone, the more nervous and upset he got.

He told himself again it was like gaining entry to the gangs in Russia. Otto didn't really want to be like Vadim, but he wanted to be established and well connected like his uncle. He had only set up that C-4 in Florida because Vadim had told him they'd all go broke if that woman and others like her kept trying to shut down operations like theirs.

At first it had seemed like a thrilling adventure ripped straight out of a movie script. And Vadim had assured him that an explosion at a big hotel would never be pinned on businessmen. Not with the number of terrorist attacks occurring throughout the world. Only potential or known terrorists would be implicated in the Naples bombing.

Now everything was getting complicated. At least Otto was away from Vadim's constant carping. Maybe he could just follow his target for a while and figure out how to keep Vadim off his back.

He shrugged as he opened the trunk, lifted his suitcase out, pulled up the handle, and dragged it into the reception area. Wearing his usual black jeans and hoodie, he rolled the luggage across the beige tile floor to a long, sleek registration desk. He rested his elbows on a faux marble countertop just as an attractive, young Asian girl turned toward him and asked, "Checking in?"

"Yes." He gave her a passport and a card. Two of many he carried while traveling. Different sets for different countries.

She studied the name and address on his passport. "Oleg Alimov," she read.

He had to think for a moment before responding to the alias he had chosen for this trip. Otto nodded and smiled.

"I see you are from Russia. We get a lot of tourists from Russia, India, and China. You might want to check out our gift shop," she gestured across the large lobby. "They have a nice assortment of maps and guidebooks that might be helpful."

She slid a form in front of him. "Sign here, please. And list your rental car if you have one so you'll have our special parking rate during your stay. Also, we have a fitness center, a swimming pool in the courtyard, and a nice restaurant down the hall that serves a full breakfast. I'm sure you'll like it. They have everything. Even grits," she said, giving him a wide smile.

"What's grits?"

"You'll see. Try it."

The more he looked at the girl, the more he wanted to try *her*. He wondered if she was allowed to spend time with hotel guests. He had a lot of time to kill. And being alone every evening would be boring. He'd have to think about that. He signed the registration sheet, added information about his car, and took the room key from her.

"Elevators are over there, Mr. Alimov," she said in a cheery voice. "Hope you enjoy your stay."

"Thanks," he said, reaching for the suitcase. "Oh, one more thing. I was told that there was a UPS store around here."

"Yes, sir. There's one just two blocks down on the other side the street. You can't miss it."

"Good. Guess I'm off to the gift shop," Otto said as he turned away and pulled his bag over to the shop's open door. He could access any guidebook or map he wanted on his iPhone. But he wanted to have an excuse to talk to her later, so he grabbed two candy bars, a map, and a D.C. guidebook from a small shelf. Otto signed his alias and room number for the items and then headed for the elevators.

He rode up to the fourth floor and found his room right away. It was next to the ice machine and across the hall from the elevators. Now he'd hear every guy who wanted a drink late at night, and he'd hear that little *ding* every time the elevator opened. He thought about asking for a different room but decided he didn't want to hassle the desk clerk. He'd rather try to impress her. Later.

He opened the door to his room and saw a stark group of furniture. A king bed with a straight wooden headboard, a simple desk, and a small navy couch that matched the carpet. At least there was a flat screen. He guessed it was about thirty-two inches. Not exactly up to the standard of Vadim's seventy inch that he loved. But in this small room, the thirty-two would probably work fine.

He flicked it on, glanced at a list of channels, and tuned to CNN. He had been checking the news each day and was relieved every time he saw a follow-up story on the Naples explosion that didn't include his sketch. It had only been shown on the national news channels a couple of times. He hadn't seen it again. The FBI still had it on their website, but he figured nobody paid attention to that.

There hadn't been any new developments. No news. No leads. No answers. Maybe Vadim was right. Maybe they were only investigating known terrorists. He listened to the announcer drone on about the British Prime Minister's visit and a reporter's update on some possible threat in Chicago. He relaxed. There was nothing to worry about. He just had to get settled, study the map, check in with Vadim, and do as he was told.

After unpacking and setting up his computer, he checked his email. Sure enough, there was a message from Vadim with an attachment. He scanned the note and then opened the attachment, which was a summary of her actions. Where she goes first thing in the morning and at what time. Occasional lunches and dinners at nearby restaurants. The time she leaves her office, where she parks, and where she jogs on Sundays. He was impressed by all the information the Russian Embassy had compiled on her.

It was their first report, and it said they would keep updating the information. So, Vadim had pulled off a deal with his military aide contact. He knew Russian government employees were good at surveillance and tracking people at home. It made sense that they'd be good at it here too. Plus, Otto was certain his uncle had made it worthwhile for the contact to slip him the target's file. After reading the entire message, Otto decided to start learning his way around town and begin shadowing the woman later that day.

Otto took the elevator back down to the lobby and headed out to Wisconsin Avenue. Once outside, he turned left, walked two blocks, and peered across the street. There it was. He waited for the traffic to move, spotted a break, and then ran across the street toward a sign that read, "P.O. Boxes, Etc. UPS." He opened the store's glass door and slipped inside. Behind a scuffed counter, an older man asked, "May I help you?"

"Yes. Is there a package for Oleg Alimov?" Otto said, walking up to the counter.

"Let me check," the clerk replied. Otto watched as the man combed through a stack of big envelopes in a large, cerulean, plastic bin behind the counter. He stooped down to push larger packages aside, checking each label.

"Ah, yes. This must be it. Addressed to Oleg Alimov. General delivery to this store. May I see some identification please?"

Otto fished in his pocket and produced a passport. The clerk held it close, compared the picture to Otto, and seemed to hesitate. Otto suddenly worried that the man might have seen his sketch on TV.

No. He's old. He wouldn't have remembered that.

Besides Otto wore a uniform in Naples. Now he was wearing a sweatshirt. No comparison there. Finally, the man handed him a package the size of a shoe box. "Sign here," he said in a gravelly voice.

Otto signed, grabbed the box, and quickly left the store just as a woman with red hair walked in. Looking across the street, he spotted a pizza shop next to a liquor store. He hadn't had much to eat on the overnight flight. So, he dashed back across the street for some pepperoni pizza.

It smelled wonderful inside the tiny family-owned shop. While he waited for his order to cook, he played with the idea of breaking one of Vadim's rules. It was small. Vadim said not to drink anything on this assignment. Said he needed to stay sharp. Well, he was sharp. And he could relax occasionally without losing his senses. Besides, a bit of vodka would pair perfectly with his jet lag.

After he paid for his food, he walked next door and picked up a small bottle of liquor and a couple of Cokes. He was glad the clerk didn't ask for an ID. He didn't want too many people to remember him or his alias.

Taking his box and bags back to his room, he set everything down on the desk and began to unwrap Vadim's package. It was covered with heavy tape. He tugged at it, cursing the airline for not letting him bring a pair of scissors on board his flight from San Francisco. Finally, he ripped the tape off and gingerly lifted the lid. The contents were surrounded in a heavy foil, probably to avoid screening devices. He undid the inner wrap and admired his beautiful brand new Glock 19.

NINETEEN

SAMANTHA HANDED HER DEPUTY A COPY OF
the Jackson conference program. "I got this from Treasury," she
said, poring through a stack of papers on her desk. "What do
you make of the line-up? And can you really see me fitting in
with that crowd?" she asked skeptically.

Jim pulled his chair closer to the desk and perused the list.
"Let's see. The Chairman of the Federal Reserve gives the opening speech. Couple of European finance ministers talk about
lowering their debt. South American central bankers get all
hyped about taming inflation. Pretty dry stuff."

Samantha shook her head. "When I first read it, I wanted to
be Reba McEntire and sing 'Consider Me Gone.'"

He laughed out loud. "Looks like all you have to do is say
something that keeps them awake."

"At least I'll be speaking at lunch," she said with a sigh. "But
look at the location."

111

He started to read the program. "'In a departure from previous itineraries, conference participants will leave the lodge in chartered vans and proceed to Teton Village. There, they will board the new aerial tram and travel 4,200 vertical feet to the restaurant at the summit of Rendezvous Mountain, take in views of the entire Jackson Hole Valley, and enjoy a luncheon speech given by the White House Director of Homeland Security.' That's you, babe," he said, looking up at her with a grin. "At least the view will be spectacular."

"But I can't stand spectacular views," she said. "Been there, seen that, fell down. Well, my husband did. You remember that," she said in a small voice. Suddenly she could see the entire disastrous trip unfolding. A decade had passed since she had met him in college and married him the day after graduation. They honeymooned in Jackson because he loved to hike and she was open to learning.

Images from their first hike came flooding back. The trail, the sudden storm, the lightning, then the wind gusts that cost them their footing along a narrow ledge. He was propelled sideways and fell down a jagged wall, landing on a pile of rocks. She fell too, but his body broke her fall.

When she caught her breath and rolled off him, she noticed he was lying at a strange angle. And he wasn't responding. She shook him, called his name, felt for a pulse. It was there but seemed weak. She frantically alerted the rangers on her cell and waited in agony for someone to come. In her panic, she screamed for help. But no other hikers were nearby.

Samantha tried to use CPR, but her arms were stiff and bruised. Nothing was working. It seemed like ages before the paramedics reached them. The rescue team checked her out and told her she'd had a close call, but her husband hadn't been so lucky. They loaded him onto a stretcher and transported him to a hospital. They tried to save him, but it was no use in the end.

Ever since that day, she had worked relentlessly to put her life back together, eventually accepting a few dinner invitations from friends and finally having the affair with Tripp. But she'd never been able to forget Jackson's vivid mountain scenes or overcome the fear of heights she'd developed after the incident.

She took a deep breath and refocused on the papers in front of her.

"Oh yeah, sorry," her deputy was saying. "But that was a long time ago. And this is a different gig. You won't be hiking. You'll be speaking."

"It isn't the speaking part that bothers me. It's the getting-there part. I can't even go on Ferris wheels. I don't like glass elevators, and the last time I went to an event on the top floor of the Hay Adams, I couldn't even go out on the balcony for cocktails."

"You'll be fine," Jim said in a reassuring tone. "Just focus on looking *up* at bankers, not *down* at boulders."

She grabbed another sheet and called to her assistant. "Joan, could you come in here?"

"Sure," Joan said, walking in with a folder. "Since you're already talking about that conference, I've got some updates too. Travel arrangements, hotel, all of that."

"What do we have so far?" Samantha asked.

Joan pulled up the other spare chair in the small office and opened her file. "Got you scheduled on a flight along with Secretary Pickering and some of his staff. That includes Homer Belford. He'll be working with you on talking points for the secretary's remarks after the fed chairman, and he said he has a few more ideas for your speech. So I've arranged for the two of you to sit together on the plane."

"Sounds good," Samantha said. "What about the hotel?"

"Everyone stays at the Jackson Lake Lodge. It has rooms in the main building and a bunch of cabins. Their website says it was all built in the '50s. Not sure what that means today, though," Joan said.

"So, I guess it all depends on what the meaning of '*was*' is," Jim said with a wry smile.

Joan threw him a glance. "From the looks of it, I don't think much has changed. As for décor, they have an Indian motif. A brochure I found says that tourists can stay in a yurt, but that's farther away," she said.

"A yurt?" Jim said with a laugh. "You're going to Wyoming not Mongolia for god's sake."

The administrative assistant ignored him. "I put you in the lodge rather than one of the cabins. I figured it would be nicer to be close in and not have to traipse through the woods at night."

"Good idea," Samantha said. At least the Treasury will have security on site. She wouldn't have to worry too much.

Joan continued to read her notes. "Under the list of amenities, they have a pool, but no TVs or radios. I have no idea about cell phone coverage."

"That's okay. There are always carrier pigeons," Jim said.

The assistant carried on. "At other places like the town of Jackson and Teton Village, your cell should work fine." She rifled through some more pages and started to laugh. "As for the formal sessions, they're casual. Since the sessions are in the morning, they leave the afternoons open for whatever you want to do. I researched a lot of options. Besides the usual hiking and raft trips, they've got art fairs, a bungee trampoline, a marching band at the Pink Garter Theatre, Art in the Park, a Hootenanny, not sure what that is, and a fair that includes pig wrestling and Arapahoe dancers. You can also look at elk, wolves, red-tailed hawks, pika, and marmots."

"What the hell are pika and marmots?" Jim asked, trying to suppress a laugh.

"I don't know, but I think you have to watch out for the bears," Joan said. "I pulled a video from the—" She glanced at her sheaf of notes. "Yes, here it is. The Grand Teton National Park Foundation. They produced a video about how to tell the difference between a black bear and a grizzly bear."

"You're really supposed to stand there and analyze the difference?" Jim asked.

"I guess," Joan said. "They also have five top tips for hikers. Number one is to remove your bear spray from your backpack and keep it handy. It should spray up to twenty-five feet. If you've got a grizzly in front of you, you're supposed to spray it for six seconds."

"Wouldn't it better to use those six seconds to run away?" Jim asked.

"You would think," Joan said.

"Are you two finished?" Samantha said.

"Not quite," Joan said with a smile. "I also read that there are mosquitos in certain places in Jackson. But don't worry. They provide food for birds and bats."

"Hey, you'll feel right at home," Jim said. "Congress just voted to make this National Invasive Species Awareness Week." He got up. "On that note, I'd better get back to work."

"Me too," Joan said, handing Samantha her file and heading out the door.

Samantha sat back and perused the notes. If she had an evening free, she could go to the Elks Lodge and see a play called, *Murder Rides Again—in Jackson Hole*. She stared at the listing and wondered if it was an entertainment prospect or an omen.

TWENTY

THURSDAY EVENING;
GEORGETOWN, WASHINGTON, D.C.

SAMANTHA LOCKED HER CONDO AND WALKED
down K Street toward one of her favorite restaurants. After cutting yesterday's lunch short, she was looking forward to a long dinner with Angela. They agreed to meet just a few blocks from Samantha's place at Chadwick's.

As she pushed open the restaurant's door, she was assaulted by shouts from the bar and the smell of beer and popcorn. Samantha glanced over and saw that the TV was tuned, as usual, to ESPN.

Chadwick's had been a popular bar since the '70s, and, judging from the photos along the wall, not much about it had changed. Groups of twenty- and thirty-somethings were gathered three-deep at the bar, all jostling for a better view of a game while a few outliers tried to engage in conversation.

"Hey, Samantha," Angela called from a table along the side wall. It was covered in a blue and white checked cloth and dotted with a votive candle and a couple of menus. "Glad you could make it. I always worry that some last-minute crisis is going to ruin another evening. But here you are. Finally. I already ordered my wine. Wasn't sure what you wanted tonight."

Samantha pulled out a wooden chair, hung her purse on it, sat down, and grabbed a menu. "I feel like a pinot noir. Although after a day like today, maybe something stronger."

"What's up?"

"It isn't just *what*, it's a whole lot of *whats*. We have a new situation in Atlanta. Not sure if it's a crank threat or something really serious. Some hacker got into the Center for Disease Control. That's bad enough, but he also sent a threatening message to what we thought was a secure server. So, either he's just playing with us and trying to look important, or there really *is* a threat. Can you imagine dealing with a bio-hazard?"

"Jeez," Angela said. "They can't find him?"

"Not yet."

"Hi. I'm Mark. I'll be your server tonight," an eager young man said, standing next to their table. "What would you like?"

"I'm fine with my sauvignon blanc for now," Angela said.

"I'll start with the house pinot noir please," Samantha said. "We'll wait a bit to order dinner. Thanks."

"Before you decide, just wanted to let you know our special tonight is chicken pot pie."

"Comfort food," Angela said as the waiter moved to another table.

"Sounds perfect," Samantha said.

Angela scrutinized her best friend. "There's something else, isn't there?"

"I have to leave for that conference next week. I don't want to think about it, but I need to prepare."

"Just follow your Rule of the Six P's," Angela said as an impish grin spread across her lips.

"Oh, proper preparation precludes piss-poor performance?" Samantha said with a small smile.

"And focus on the positives. That trip gets you away from threat scenarios. Let your staff handle all that for a few days. Plus, I bet the old financial types will appreciate having someone younger on the conference roster."

"I don't want to *be* on the program. The more I think about it, the more depressed I get."

"Have you tried Cymbalta?"

Samantha's smile grew a little as she looked at her friend.

Angela continued. "It won't be so bad. You give great speeches. You're a natural. And think of the great contacts you'll make. Besides, it's a pretty place. I've seen pictures. All those mountains and rivers and log houses with big stone fireplaces. One was featured in *Architectural Digest*."

"I don't know. I've never really been into antler chandeliers," Samantha said.

Angela grinned and cocked her head. "All the financial guys will probably have some sharp, younger staffers with them. You might meet someone."

"Can't say I'd be in the mood to meet someone in the same place I lost someone."

Angela softened her gaze. "I hear you. Let's try and think about other things tonight."

"Here's your pinot noir," Mark said, sidling up to the table with a wine glass he placed in front of Samantha. "Have you had a chance to check out our menu?"

"We've been here a bunch of times," Angela said. "I'll have your Niçoise salad."

"Got it. And you, miss?"

"The turkey sliders would be great. Thanks," Samantha said.

He nodded and walked away.

"By the way," Angela said, taking a sip of her wine. "Have you gotten any updates on the Naples case?"

"Looks like they've hit a dead end. Every time I check the news, I see the guy with the best hair saying, 'Good Evening.' Then he goes on to tell me why it isn't."

"Right," Angela said. "At least some of them are nice to look at."

"As for the case, the FBI is still analyzing everything, talking to all the hotel staff again, and hoping for a tip from someone. They said it doesn't look like terrorism, not in a town like Naples. No group has taken responsibility, and they haven't found a disgruntled employee with a motive. So, they've got no suspects."

"What about that one guy who disappeared?"

"He disappeared. There are no leads on his location. Anyway, let's talk about something else. I don't really want to think about that night. It was the last time I was with Tripp, and I still have nightmares about the explosion."

"No word from him in a while, huh?" Angela asked with a concerned look.

"I get an occasional email about his business trips. That's about it," Samantha said.

"Okay, we'll forget about him. For now."

"Any new talent in your playbook?"

"I did see a cute guy at the fitness center," Angela said, her eyes lighting up.

"He must be new. You go there all the time."

"Actually, he's in my class."

"What class?

"I decided to sign up for spinning classes. I figured they'd be much better than yoga, which is so, well, slow."

"Ladies, your entrees," the waiter said, setting their plates down. "Kitchen's not too busy tonight. Seems everyone is just hanging at the bar watching the Cubs game, so the chef got these out super fast." He smiled and hurried toward another group of diners.

"By the way, that threat at Wrigley Field turned out to be a hoax. Probably just some irate fan," Samantha said. "Oh, wait. I forgot to ask for water," she said, turning around and searching for Mark. Suddenly, she stopped and stared. What was that? At the window? She quickly turned back to Angela.

"What is it? You look like you've seen a ghost."

"Maybe I have," Samantha said in a low, shaky voice. "Don't look there now, but I think I saw a guy outside the front window who was staring right at us. He was kind of tall, skinny, and he was wearing a black sweatshirt or jacket. I couldn't see his whole face. He had a hood on."

Angela leaned across the table. "And?"

"And—no, I must be imagining things. There are a ton of students around here. Could be anyone."

"Who do you think you saw?" Angela asked. Her voice was sharp.

Samantha took a deep breath. "It looked like that waiter in Naples."

"You can't be serious. You have to look again," Angela said. "Why don't you go ask for water at the bar? You could just sort of glance toward the front again."

Samantha nodded and slowly stood up. She walked over to the bar and wedged between two couples. While she was waiting to catch the bartender's eye, she glanced at the window. Whoever he was, he was gone now. She got two tall glasses of ice water and returned to the table.

"He left," Samantha said, setting the glasses down and sliding back into her chair.

"But what if it really was him? What if he knows who you are, and he's stalking you?" Angela whispered.

"I don't know. You think he'd follow me all the way to Washington? That's just too weird," Samantha said, frowning.

"Strange or not, you should call it in."

"I can't call the Secret Service because I *thought* I saw a waiter who may or may not have been involved in an attack."

"Why not?"

"Wait a minute." Samantha reached into her purse, pulled out her cell phone, and dialed a number.

"Who are you calling?" her friend asked.

"This may be crazy, but I have an idea." Samantha sat back and listened.

"Agent Keating here," the baritone voice answered.

"This is Samantha Reid. From the White House, remember?"

"Of course. What can I do for you?"

"I'm sorry to bother you so late."

"It's not late for me. Are you still at your office?"

"No, I'm actually in Georgetown having dinner with a friend. But I just saw something, and I wanted to tell you."

"Saw something? What?" Brett asked.

"I looked out the window and thought I saw that waiter from Naples. The one whose drawing you had."

"Are you sure?"

"No. Not really. But he seemed to be about the same height and build. He looked like he was wearing a black sweatshirt with the hood up, so I couldn't get a good look. It's just..."

"Where are you?" Brett asked.

"Chadwick's. It's in the 3100 block of lower K Street."

"Stay right there."

"I didn't mean—"

"Stay put. Don't go outside. I'm on my way," he said.

Samantha clicked off. Now she was shaking. If that really *was* the missing waiter, what could she do? She had a horrible thought that he might be setting another explosive nearby. She glanced nervously out the window again. No one was there. She turned to Angela. "I'm going to speak to the manager."

She got up, walked to the kitchen, and asked a server to get the manager. She was standing in front of the swinging doors, shifting from foot to foot, when he walked up.

"Hello, I'm Armand, the night manager. May I help you?"

She took a deep breath. "Yes. I'm Samantha Reid, White House, Homeland Security."

"Yes, Ms. Reid. I've seen you here before. Is there a problem?"

"I hope not. But I need you to check the back of the building where the electrical boxes, air conditioning units, and any other equipment is stored."

"Check for what?" he asked, raising his eyebrows.

"I realize this sounds far-fetched, but I need to go with you and make sure there isn't some sort of explosive there."

"Explosive?" the man said. "What the hell?"

"Just take me back," she said, pointing through the kitchen.

"Should we be calling the police or something?" he said, staring at her.

"The FBI is on its way."

"God!" He quickly guided her through the swinging doors. "Do you have information about an attack or something? We need to get our customers out." He was almost shouting. Two cooks and a few waiters stopped to listen.

"No. It's a precaution. I'll explain later. Let's go," Samantha said.

They rushed past stoves, serving counters, doors to a large refrigerator, and finally arrived at a dimly lit walkway. The manager stomped outside and ripped open the circuit breaker box. "Nothing here," he called out and then sprinted to a large storage closet. He turned on its overhead lights as Samantha charged in and began examining the equipment. They scoured the entire area.

Finally, she turned and said, "Thank you for the quick work. I'm sorry for the alarm. I was afraid a suspect known for setting explosives might be in the area. As I said, the FBI is on its way."

The manager rubbed his forehead. "Well, thank you for the warning. This is unbelievable. At least we're okay for now. Right?"

"I think so. I'm going back inside to wait for the special agent."

"You do that," the manager said, leading her back to the main room with his hand on his chest. "Please keep me informed. I'll stay right by the bar."

TWENTY-ONE

BRETT HAD ONLY BEEN HOME FOR FIFTEEN minutes when he got Samantha's call. He put a lasagna TV dinner back into the freezer then grabbed his wallet and keys. Rushing into his bedroom, he shoved a gun into his shoulder holster and slung on a light jacket. Then he rushed to where he had left his briefcase lying near the front door. He rummaged through it, stuck a piece of paper into his pocket, and bolted to the parking garage.

He was still fleshing out his mental picture of the city's layout, but he had a vague idea of where the restaurant was. Brett jumped in his car and drove as fast as he could, grateful the commuter traffic had died down for the day. Georgetown was more crowded. Students from nearby universities clustered outside trendy bistros and leaned against old fashioned street lamps decorated with colorful flower boxes.

He hung a left on Thirty-First Street, drove to the bottom, and turned right. A block away, he saw an elderly couple slowly backing out of a spot. He turned on his blinker. While he waited, he scanned the area under the Whitehurst Freeway. People flooded out of a movie theater. Others gathered in groups in front of the Washington Harbour entrance. No one in a black sweatshirt. No one with a hood on. He pulled into the slot, locked the car, and hurried to Chadwick's.

He quickly spotted Samantha and another woman at a small table and walked over. "Hello, Miss Reid," he said.

"Oh, Agent Keating," Samantha said, looking up at him.

"It's Brett, remember?"

"Sure. This is my friend, Angela Marconi. She works at the White House too. She's with presidential scheduling."

He nodded to Angela then dragged a chair over from a nearby table. Sitting down, he said, "Now, tell me again. What *exactly* did you see?"

Samantha took a sip of her wine and glanced at her watch. "I will. But wait. Have you had any dinner? I appreciate you coming so quickly, but I don't want you to starve because of us."

"I haven't—"

"Food's great," Angela said, waving at a passing waitress. "You should get something."

"May I help you?" a young woman said.

"Mark's been our waiter. Is he still around?" Samantha asked.

"He's in the kitchen, but I can take your order."

"Anything that's quick and easy," Brett said.

"Hamburgers are good," the waitress suggested.

"That would be fine. Medium rare, and whatever comes with it. Thanks." He turned and focused on Samantha. "Now. Again. Tell me what you saw."

"I was looking out that window, the one right by the front door, and there was this guy, all dressed in black with a hood like I said. And he seemed to be staring in. Right at me. Immediately, I thought he looked familiar. Then it hit me. He might be the guy I saw in Naples working the banquet.

"I got so nervous that I had the manager show me all the places in back where someone might be able to hide an explosive. Well, maybe not all. But I was thinking that if it was the same guy, he had experience putting C-4 in an electrical box. We talked about evacuating the place, but we didn't find anything. He's anxious to talk to you if you think he should take any action. That's him standing near the bar," she said, pointing.

"That was good thinking," Brett said. "But how would the guy have known you would be here tonight? He wouldn't have had time to set up an attack."

Samantha thought for a moment. "Guess you're right. I have to admit I was frightened...I am frightened. I just wanted to check it all out."

"I get that," Brett said. "Back in a minute." Pushing away from the table, he walked over to the bar and spoke with the manager. When he returned, he said, "I believe the restaurant is safe for now. But don't come back here for a while in case the man you saw really is trailing you." He pulled the paper out of his pocket, unfolded it, and smoothed it out on the table. "This the guy?"

Samantha and Angela both examined the mock-up of a young man with a mess of black hair and a narrow but good-looking face. "Yes, that's the guy I *think* I saw tonight. I can't be sure, but you said to call if I thought of anything," Samantha said.

"You were absolutely right to call. Glad you did. Now, how long was he out there?"

"I have no idea when he arrived. I only saw him when I turned around. Then when I looked again, he was gone."

"He saw you looking at him and ran," Brett said.

"Evidently. But do you really think someone went to Naples to find me and then came here to find me again?" she asked.

"Best lead we've had so far," Brett said. He pulled out his cell and punched in a number. After a moment he said, "Dom, Brett here. We've got a situation that might tie into the Naples attack. I'm at Chadwick's in Georgetown. I've got Samantha Reid here, and she may have seen the Naples suspect. Can you get over here?" He listened and then said, "Great. See you in a few." He turned back to Samantha. "Any more thoughts, recollections, anything?"

"Guy looks kind of innocent in a way," Angela said. "But you never know. Lots of people look harmless. Until they're not."

"Exactly," Brett said. "Our Florida field office has been working this case from every angle, but as of now, we're going to take the lead."

"This is like hide and go seek," Angela said. "I don't mean to make light of it, but if this guy *is* stalking Samantha, can you find him? And more importantly, can you protect *her*?"

"Here you are, sir. Burger and fries. Ketchup is on the table. Anything else I can get you?" the young waitress asked, setting his food in front of him.

"A Coke would be great. Thanks," Brett said and then looked at Angela. "You can be sure that we are going to do our best to find this guy. And we *will* protect Miss Reid." He took a bite of his burger.

"Please just call me Samantha," she said. "What are you proposing? A bodyguard?"

"Yes," Brett said. "We need to make sure you're safe outside the White House."

"Here's your Coke, sir," the waitress said.

"Oh, thanks." Brett took the glass from her and faced Samantha. "We'll have an agent drive you to and from work, and we'll coordinate with the Secret Service during your normal working hours. I'm sure you use White House drivers when you have appointments or meetings outside the compound, right?"

"Yes. Assistants to the president and certain directors get drivers during working hours. The Chief of Staff and NSC advisor get one for commuting, but not me," Samantha replied.

"Whoever this guy is, there's no way he'd be stupid enough to hang around the White House, not with security around the periphery and cameras and microphones along the fences," Angela said.

"Unless this is his first time in Washington," Brett said. "Could be foreign. The name he used, Otto Kukk, is an Estonian name. It was obviously an alias, but it still indicates a foreign source. To us anyway."

"Well, at least he'd never get inside the White House grounds," Samantha said.

"No, but if he's following you, he might get inside your home," Brett said. "Where is that, by the way?"

"Just down the street," Samantha said. "That's why I come here a lot. It's a short walk."

"Did you walk here alone tonight?" Brett asked.

"Sure. But Angela met me here."

Brett lowered his eyes and finished his hamburger. He took a final swig of Coke and then motioned to the waitress for a check. When she returned to pick it up, he said, "Please keep the change."

"Hey, Brett. Got here as fast as I could," Dom said, hurrying over and pulling another chair up to their small table.

"Samantha, Angela, this is Special Agent Dom Turiano. He'll be working with me on this case," Brett said.

"Pleased to meet you," Dom said, extending his hand. "So, you saw the Naples waiter?" he asked Samantha.

"Right outside that window. But I'm not positive."

"That means stepped-up action for our D.C. task force," Brett said. "We have to strategize about focusing the search on the city and the surrounding area."

Brett and Dom chatted while Samantha and Angela paid their checks. When everyone stood up to leave, Brett asked, "Angela, where is your car?"

"Just down the street. I got lucky and found a spot," she said.

"Same here," Brett said. "Dom, why don't you walk Angela to her car? Samantha, I'll take you home. I don't want you out alone from now on."

"Got it," Samantha said. She pulled out her cell phone again. "I'm going to give my boss a heads-up on this."

"Good idea. We would have done that for you, but please go ahead. Who's your direct report?" Brett asked.

"Ken Cosgrove, NSC Advisor."

"Of course. He needs to know what's going on here." He turned to Dom. "Work on your plans. I'll do mine and call you later. Right now, I need to check out Samantha's place."

Dom nodded. The agents and Angela chatted while Samantha dialed Ken's cell and explained the state-of-play. After a few minutes, she said, "I would have called you first, but I wanted to check in with Agent Keating. He's the one I met with at the office. I told you about that earlier. He's here with me now."

"Yes, that's fine," the advisor said. "He'll be good for you on the ground. Secret Service has their hands full right now. It seems unlucky that this man suddenly showed up in D.C. Then again, it could be the break we've been looking for. Still, we don't want *you* out there as some kind of bait."

"I won't be," she said. "Brett, I mean, Agent Keating is very professional. Sounds like he really will stay on top of it. He said his office will take the lead on the investigation and search for the guy up here. He's also going to walk me home. I'll see you first thing tomorrow in the staff meeting."

"Yes, thank you, Samantha. Have a good night."

As she clicked off, she heard a groan from the stragglers at the bar. She glanced at the TV. The Cubs had lost. Apparently, no one was having a good night.

"Ready to go, Samantha?" Brett asked as Angela waved goodbye and headed toward the door with Dom.

"Absolutely," she said, grabbing her purse. As they walked toward the door, she eyed Brett out of the corner of her eye. Would he really protect her? He couldn't be with her all the time, but whenever he was, she knew she would feel quite secure.

When they reached the door, Brett poked his head out and scanned the area. He turned, nodded to her, and then took the lead down the street. She followed and watched him as he walked.

There was something about him. Strength, confidence, or was it competence? He certainly seemed to always know what he was doing. Were all FBI agents like that? The NSC had an undercover agent on staff, but she had never really seen him in action. From what she had learned of Brett, he certainly seemed like the take-charge type. She liked that. In fact, she liked that a lot.

"You and Dom are great to take care of Angela and me," Samantha said as they approached her apartment.

"Our pleasure," Brett said and waved over his shoulder. He never stopped scanning the street. When they reached the entrance to her low-rise, tan brick apartment complex, she pulled out her key and unlocked the front door. "How's the security in this building?" he asked, following her inside.

"Decent, I guess. There's a desk over there with an attendant during the day."

"What about at night?" Brett asked, surveying the lobby.

"They're on call if we need a manager or repairman."

"Not good enough," Brett muttered. "What about access to that front door?"

"Residents all have keys, and guests press our buzzers."

"Way too easy," he said. "First thing we need to do is get the name 'Reid' off the door list."

She nodded. "I'll tell the manager in the morning."

"Would you mind showing me your apartment?" he asked.

"Not at all. It's up this elevator on the second floor. I didn't want to be any higher. I kind of have this thing about heights," she confessed.

"Lots of people do," he said as they stepped into the elevator. Outside her door, she reached into her purse and produced another key. "Let me go in first," Brett said when she opened the door. One lamp illuminated the foyer. He spotted a switch and turned on some overhead lights. "Come in, but wait here," he said, moving cautiously through the living room. She stepped forward and put her purse on the hall table as he advanced to the kitchen. Finally, he moved through the bedroom, closets, and small bathroom. "All clear," Brett said, stepping back into the foyer with her.

"It's not very big," she said somewhat apologetically. "But it's nice being so close to work."

"I get that," he said, glancing around again at the tasteful furnishings, beige couch, dark green chairs, ficus trees in the corners, and wide picture window overlooking the park and Key Bridge. "Nice view. Just don't spend too much time looking out this window. Do you have a security system? I don't see a key pad."

"We don't have them in the apartments. At least I haven't seen any. I suppose I could get one."

"I'll take care of that first thing tomorrow. Do you have an extra key? I'll get a crew to install a system."

She went to the small table at the end of the living room. There was a drawer in its center filled with pens, tablets, stamps, envelopes, and her extra key. She walked back to the foyer and handed it to him. "I really appreciate this."

"And I appreciate that you called me right away. If this *is* the guy and he's here to track *you*, we're going to find him."

Samantha checked her watch. "I know it's getting late, but would you like a cup of coffee or anything?"

"No thanks. I'm good for now. By the way, when do you leave for the White House?"

"Around 6:30 every morning."

"So, you have a pretty regular schedule then?"

"In the morning. Hard to say when I get out at night. It's usually not until seven or seven-thirty. Sometimes later," Samantha said.

Brett glanced around the apartment once more, gazed out the window, and then looked back at her. "I said earlier that we're going to assign agents to be with you 24/7. Not when you're at work, but all the rest of the time. They'll be stationed right outside, and they'll drive you to and from work. And wherever else you want to go at night or on the weekends." He pulled out his cell and added, "I'll get that ball rolling along with the set-up for your security system. But right now, I don't want you alone in here."

"Oh, I'm sure everything is fine," Samantha said. "It's late, and I doubt anybody could get in the front door. They'd have to get someone to buzz them in. Plus, I've got a dead bolt."

"Sorry. If that guy really was at the restaurant, that means he's been following you. He could know where you live, what time you go to work, even what kind of car you drive. So, since you don't have an alarm system yet, I hope you don't mind me intruding on your privacy tonight. I'll take the couch."

"If you're sure. I hate to put you out."

"I'm sure," he replied, walking over and closing the drapes.

"Well, thank you. I'll get you a nice pillow and blanket. I have extras down the hall."

"That's okay. I won't be sleeping."

"Well, I'll bring out a few in case you change your mind," she said. "The bathroom is back there. Oh, you saw it already. I have extra razors and toothbrushes if you'd like either," she said over her shoulder and headed to her little linen closet.

"Thanks. That all sounds great. You said your apartment is small, but you should see some of the places I've had stake-outs. Makes this place look like the Marriott. Or the Mark Hopkins with that view."

Samantha returned with everything she had promised. "Okay," she said. "All set. Again, I really appreciate this. I'm sure we'll work out a schedule and routine sometime tomorrow." She handed him the pile and gave him a big smile. Then she turned and retrieved her cell from her purse. Samantha walked back down the hall to her bedroom. Before she closed the door, she heard Brett talking on his cell, giving Dom an update on his plans to secure her apartment and assign agents to her case.

As she got ready for bed, Brett's comments about the waiter knowing where she lived and what car she drove made her shiver.

Yes, there was a savvy special agent right outside her door. But even the entire Secret Service couldn't always protect the president. How could a couple of FBI agents always protect her?

TWENTY-TWO

"I HATE GETTING UP THIS EARLY," VADIM bellowed to Maksim, who was making coffee in the penthouse kitchen. Outside their picture window, the first rays of sunlight reflected off Coit Tower and warmed the gray Pacific Ocean lapping at the Golden Gate Bridge.

"Don't blame me for the time difference. When it's 6:30 in the morning here, it's 4:30 in the afternoon in Moscow. I can't change that," his brother said calmly, never pausing in his work.

"I'll place the call. You get me an espresso. And make it fast. Only a Putin insider could have been promoted to his position in the central bank. I need to be sharp when I talk to him," Vadim said. He grabbed his cell and punched in a set of numbers. When the call was answered at the bank, he asked for Alexander Tepanov and waited. After a full minute, a voice came on the line.

"Vadim, old fellow. Where are you?"

"On the road, as usual," Vadim said. He tried to keep things vague when he conducted business. "But first, your wife and your mother. How are they?"

"We spent a wonderful weekend at my *dacha*. Now that summer is here, we may take a month near the Black Sea."

"Sounds good. Congratulations on your new position at the central bank. It's a very prestigious posting," Vadim said in a jovial tone.

"Yes, thank you," the banker said. "Lots of new responsibility and more travel, I'm afraid."

Maksim handed Vadim a small cup of the strong espresso. His brother took a sip, nodded his approval, and continued speaking. "Will you be traveling to that financial conference in the states I read about? I imagine there'll be a lot of high-level officials and central bankers there," Vadim said in an offhand manner.

"Yes, I have an invitation to go to the American Federal Reserve Conference in Wyoming," Tepanov said. "Never been to Jackson Hole. Sounds pretty rustic. Why in the world would the top finance ministers want to go to a place where they stay in log cabins? They don't even have television there."

"I have no idea," Vadim said. "Maybe they're trying to create a good image for the public."

"I suppose some of the city dwellers think it's fun to get out of town and look at elk and moose. Not sure I understand why."

Vadim desperately wanted Tepanov to register for the conference and get that schedule. "It's probably just an excuse to network," Vadim said. "Think of all the power brokers who will be there. Not just from America, but Europe, Africa, East Asia. And I'll bet they strike all sorts of deals while they're at dinner or on fishing trips. You could make a lot of valuable contacts there, don't you think?"

Tepanov paused. "I suppose you have a point. My calendar does happen to be free next week. Maybe I should get to know the Americans in my new position. It wouldn't hurt to meet more Germans, Indonesians, or Chinese in the field either. Go where the money is, and make sure they all know I am more or less independent, not someone who should ever be sanctioned."

"Brilliant," Vadim said. "I read that the food is good too."

"I'll keep that in mind. Now then, I'm sure you didn't call to ask about my vacation plans."

"Not entirely. Did they include a schedule of events in that conference invitation?"

"Yes. Why?"

"Maksim and I were thinking of spending a day or two in Wyoming ourselves. So, I just wondered if you were going and when you'd be available. We thought the conference would be a good place for the three of us to meet and for Maksim and me to express our gratitude for your efforts on our behalf," Vadim said.

"We might be able to work that out."

"Great. If you wouldn't mind emailing me the schedule, we'll see if we can coordinate our calendars."

"All right," the banker said.

"Perfect. That will help us make our plans." Vadim smiled, picturing his list of assets that would skyrocket in value once Lubov and Stas finished everything. "Will you be available tomorrow morning?"

"Yes, I should be here."

"I may need your help to execute some trades. You've assisted us with stocks and bonds in the past, and I was hoping you could arrange to place some buys for us again through your contacts. With the usual commissions, of course. I have to work on my numbers, but I may have them by tonight."

"I have plenty of contacts who could do that. I'll wait for your next call. Please use my personal number." Tepanov read off the digits.

"Sounds good. I'll try you later then." Vadim hung up and called out to Maksim, "Tepanov is sending us the schedule. I'll forward it to Lubov and Stas so they can fine-tune their options. After breakfast, I'll figure out our own options. I'm looking forward to these trades."

TWENTY-THREE

OTTO SWIPED THROUGH LISTINGS FOR nearby restaurants on his iPhone, hoping to find one she would like. After stopping by her reception desk several times to ask stupid questions about the guidebook he had bought, Otto finally struck gold. The pretty Asian girl had asked if they could continue their discussion over dinner when her shift ended.

He couldn't stop thinking about her. With her short, jet black hair and dark, almond-shaped eyes, he thought she might be from Indonesia or Thailand. He hadn't asked her. All he wanted was to take her out. Vadim would never approve of his trying to get close to a girl when he was supposed to be following orders. But Vadim wasn't here. She was. And he wanted her.

Obviously, she hadn't seen that FBI sketch of him on the news. If she had, the police would have arrested him by now. But so far, no one had paid any special attention to him, except that weird look the Reid woman had given him when she saw him at

141

Chadwick's. He had run away pretty quickly, though. Otto no longer felt in danger on that front.

He started scrolling through reviews for places that were close to the hotel. From that list, he narrowed his search to two restaurants, the ones that were farthest away from areas where the White House woman hung out. As he swiped through photos of Martin's Tavern, it started to win out against its competition. The food looked great, it had private booths, and the prices were decent.

She got off at 8:00 p.m., so he made a reservation online for 8:15 p.m. and requested a booth. Then he opened his inbox and looked for new emails from San Francisco. There was one from Vadim asking him for an update on his activities. What could he say? That he had just shadowed Reid but was afraid to try again because she had some official driving her everywhere? He hadn't figured out how to deal with that situation yet.

He looked at his watch and realized it was almost 8:00 p.m. Vadim would have to wait. He ran into the bathroom, splashed some water on his face, ran a comb through his hair, and rushed downstairs. "Hi, Jolene," Otto said with a smile as he walked up to her desk. "About finished for the night?"

"Oh. Hi, Oleg." She turned to another young woman at the end of the counter. "I'm heading out. See you tomorrow." She logged off her computer, retrieved her purse from a drawer under the counter, and came around to join him.

She is a knockout, he thought.

"I'm sure you're the expert on restaurants around here, but I thought Martin's Tavern looked good. Would that be okay?" he asked in a hopeful voice.

"Sure," she said. "I haven't been there in ages. I usually go back to the dorm for dinner."

He escorted her through the lobby and out the hotel's front door. "Oh right. Georgetown University. You told me that. When do you graduate?"

"Next week. After finals," she said as they turned left and strolled down Wisconsin Avenue. The balmy night air made the walk rather pleasant as they passed the pizza shop and liquor store down the street. "It'll be so good to be finished with my degree and get a real job. Working at the hotel helps with tuition, but trying to fit in study time and all my classes has been tough."

"What's your major?"

"I'm getting a degree in business and economics. I added a couple of electives in history, art, and music when I could fit them in. I want to start my own business someday," she said.

"What kind of business?" Otto asked.

"I'm not sure yet. But everywhere I look, I see people, especially people my age, starting little companies. Some make it, some don't. But this is the one place in the world where I've decided I really can make it," she said with conviction.

"What about your family? Where are they?"

"Back in Thailand."

"So, what made you choose Georgetown? It's a little far from home."

"My father made me study hard. And I had heard so much about America that I really wanted to come here. After high school, I searched everywhere for a good place to go to college. We had been saving for my tuition, but it wasn't enough. So, I got the hotel job and then accepted Georgetown's admissions letter. Now, I don't want to go back home."

"So, can you just stay here?" Otto asked, raising his eyebrows.

"It's kind of complicated. I have a student visa. If I can get a good job, I can ask my employer if they'll help me with the paperwork to stay on. They'll have to say that they couldn't fill the job with anybody else. As part of the business program, we have computer classes. So, I am hoping that will make my resume more competitive and bump me up the applicant list."

"I'm sure it will. Everybody is advertising for computer programmers these days," he said.

"Oh, I don't think I'm good enough to do that. Maybe something a little less technical," she said with a smile.

"It's not that hard to pick up. I've learned a lot just by watching free tutorials online," he said.

They reached N Street, waited for the light, and then crossed over to the restaurant. He noticed there were a few small tables outside. Maybe those would be better than a booth inside. They'd be more out of the way. He would just have to hope that nobody recognized him. He could hardly wear a hoodie when he was trying to impress a woman like her.

Then again, it probably didn't matter where they sat. Who would notice him if Jolene was sitting there? He pointed to the restaurant's patio area. "Would you rather sit outside or inside?"

"Outside would be nice if we can get one of those tables. It's a lovely night."

The maître d' showed them to a small, wrought iron table for two under an awning and handed them menus. Otto took a seat facing the wall. "Your server will be along shortly," the man said and scurried back inside.

Before opening her menu, Jolene looked at Otto. "I've told you about my future. What about yours? Are you here looking for a job?"

"Oh no. This is just a trip," he said, trying to sound casual.

"You mean a vacation?"

"Sort of."

"We have a lot of foreign students at Georgetown. Did you finish college in Russia? You said earlier you're from Moscow," Jolene said.

"Yeah. I studied English. And I took a bunch of computer courses."

"So, do you work in computer programming back there?"

"Not really. I'm kind of working for my uncles right now," he said.

"Oh, a family business. That's nice. My father runs a laundry in Bangkok. It's hard work, doesn't pay much, and I wanted to do better. I'm hoping I can make enough to send some home to them. What is your uncles' business?"

He wasn't sure how to respond. But mentioning one of their ventures probably wouldn't be too risky. "They're into all kinds of things. Like car dealerships."

A young waiter hurried through the door and approached their table. "Something to drink?"

Jolene opened the menu and glanced at the wine list. "May I have a glass of the pinot grigio please?" she said pleasantly.

"Sure thing. And for you?" the waiter asked.

Otto was going to break Vadim's no-drinking rule again. Being out with a major beauty like her required reinforcements. "How about a Heineken?"

"No problem," the waiter said. "Back in a minute."

Jolene kept looking at the menu. "I think I'll try the crab cakes. What about you?"

"How are the lamb chops?"

"I've never had them, but I'm sure they're good. This is a pretty popular place." She looked up from the menu and smiled. "So, are you going to go back to Moscow and sell cars for your uncles or something?"

He wouldn't be selling cars. Those dealerships were probably just fronts, and he wasn't sure he wanted to work for his uncles forever. Maksim was okay but Vadim was obnoxious. Always complaining and criticizing every little thing he did.

Otto knew Vadim only took him on as a kind of intern because his mother wanted him to learn how to be a good businessman. But she had no idea what Vadim actually did. She couldn't. Having Otto shadow Vadim was her way of ensuring he stayed away from gangs. If she knew some of the things Vadim had asked him to do, she'd probably say prayers for his soul or something.

But he wasn't an assassin. In fact, he was incredibly relieved when that fire alarm went off in Naples and everyone escaped the bombing. The whole incident helped solidify a plan that had been quietly taking shape in the back of his mind: no matter what, he was going to find a way to get out from under Vadim's thumb.

"Oleg?" Jolene said. "You've got a strange look. Did I say something wrong?"

"No. Sorry, I was just thinking about your question."

"Here's your wine. And the beer," the waiter said, setting the glasses down. "Have you decided on dinner?" he asked.

"I'd like to start with the spinach salad and then the crab cakes," Jolene said.

"Clam chowder and lamb chops please," Otto said.

"Sounds good," the waiter said and walked back through the door.

Jolene took a sip of her wine. "If you don't want to sell cars, why don't you stay here and get a job? As I said, companies all seem to want people who are good with computers. You could probably get something pretty quickly."

Stay? The thought had never entered his mind. But as he stared at Jolene, he wondered about it.

He was here on a mission, one he was being paid to carry out. In fact, when he left San Francisco, Maksim had hinted Otto might get a bonus when he finished this assignment. The trouble was he wanted the bonus, but he didn't want to finish the assignment. And after the screw-up in Naples, he wondered if he could ever escape the FBI. They were still circulating his portrait. Someone somewhere was bound to recognize him eventually.

He took a deep breath. "I doubt I could stay here," he said, taking a swig of beer. Then he added, "Until I figure it out though, it would be really nice to see you again." He sat back. Now he had a lot more figuring out to do.

TWENTY-FOUR

FRIDAY EVENING: THE WHITE HOUSE

SAMANTHA SLIPPED ON STRAPPY, VINTAGE, juniper green heels and smoothed her slim, silk, black dress one last time. She brushed her hair, twisted it behind her ears, and held it in place with two pearl clips. Pearl stud earrings completed the look.

Turning away from the mirror, she left the ladies room and retrieved her evening bag from the desk in her office. Samantha walked down a flight of stairs and hurried through the West Wing. She stepped out the door to the colonnade next to the rose garden and hurried along to the entrance of the Mansion, as everyone called it. There, she climbed back up a flight of stairs that lead to the Cross Hall where guests were gathering to honor the new Prime Minister of Great Britain.

Even though she was running on very little sleep, Samantha was determined to stay awake and attempt to be charming tonight. After all, Brett had stayed up all night so that she would be safe to live and work as normally as possible.

At 6:00 a.m., he had introduced her to two of her new FBI bodyguards. They drove her to the southwest gate of the White House at 6:45 a.m. and only left when they saw her walk safely inside. She had thought that would be the end of the day's excitement. But Homer surprised her with another meeting to analyze a new suspicious set of accounts in Siberia.

Homer explained there were concerns that the money in the accounts was payment for more illicit arms sales. They had already tied the accounts to some phony end-user certificates. Samantha suggested the weapons were purchased on the cheap from former Soviet stockpiles and sent out by freelance merchants. She knew that whenever arms were shipped to another country, an official had to sign an end-user certificate, or EUC, to confirm the weapons would *only* be used by a government, not resold to militant groups. Homer backed her theory, and the Treasury was already trying to match the approximate value of the sales to the new Russian accounts.

After that meeting, Samantha had rushed to the bathroom to get ready for the reception. With the hours she worked, going home to get ready would have been impossible. But she was not the only member of the White House senior staff who had dragged a hanger bag and formal shoes to the office that morning. A cardinal rule for these dinners was never to arrive late. In fact, you had to arrive long before the honored guests.

Senior staff members were constantly reminded that there were only four possible reasons to refuse a president's invitation to a state dinner: a death in the family, a serious illness, a wedding, or an official mission that required working overseas. She had heard about senators who had literally checked out of hospitals to attend these evening affairs.

Stepping into the Cross Hall, Samantha noticed the usual people were already there, including the White House Chief of

Staff and National Security Advisor as well as the Secretaries of the Treasury, State, and Defense. Seeing them made her feel rather special for being included tonight. Though, she was pretty sure she had only been invited because the security issues she was dealing with dovetailed with the ones England was facing, and a friendly exchange was in order.

She meandered into the Red Room where Gilbert Stuarts's famous portrait of Dolley Madison had been prominently displayed for generations. She wondered if the Prime Minister would remember that Dolley was the one who saved a picture of George Washington when British troops looted the White House in 1812. Maybe he wouldn't notice.

She took a glass of wine from a passing server and moved into the oval Blue Room. She had always liked its eighteen-foot ceilings and the official White House Christmas tree it showcased every year. When the president and first lady weren't posing in it with Christmas party guests, the room was used for special occasions. The most important one had been the wedding of Grover Cleveland, the only sitting president to get married in the White House.

As she stood against the wall, she nodded to the chairman of the House Intelligence Committee who was deep in conversation with the majority whip. She hoped they were talking about a controversial bill that would increase instead of cut the CIA's budget. Suddenly, she saw the Treasury Secretary walking toward her.

"Good evening, Samantha. Glad you'll be joining us in Jackson next week," he said.

A smile automatically spread across her face. "Thank you, Mr. Secretary. I just hope I can help encourage a bit more allied support for your. . . and our. . . initiatives."

"Yes. We're all in this together. If you'll excuse me, I'd better go talk to the British Chancellor of the Exchequer."

With a pleasant nod, he moved away. Could she help with anything in Jackson if she was still afraid to show up? She tried to push that thought aside as she moved past a senator and entered the Green Room.

With Duncan Phyfe furniture dating back to 1810 and parlor walls covered in green silk, she glanced down and saw that her shoes would blend right in. She was constantly amazed that these antiques had held up for so many years and through so many official functions. Of course, hardly anyone ever sat down on those pieces. It was too tempting to work the rooms, see and be seen, and occasionally cut a deal with an opposing member of Congress, even though only top leadership ever seemed to make the guest list.

She heard a murmur and realized it was time to return to the Cross Hall and watch the President, First Lady, and their guests of honor come down the stairs from the residence. Once there, Samantha stepped aside to let others get a better view. The press pool snapped the obligatory photos, and then the Press Secretary ushered the media back to the Press Room to file their stories. When they finished, the President led the way to the State Dining Room.

Samantha followed the crowd and noticed the Social Secretary standing at the door, directing people to their tables. Samantha saw her name written in perfect calligraphy on a place card and was pleased that she had been seated next to her British counterpart. He was one of the Prime Minister's chief terrorism specialists. Samantha had been on a conference call with him a week ago, but this was her first chance to meet him in person.

"Good evening, Ms. Reid."

She turned around and met a large set of light brown eyes. The man they belonged to had dark auburn hair and a sharp smile.

"I'm delighted to finally put a face to your voice," he continued. "It's very nice to talk to you on such a pleasant occasion rather than on those frantic calls where we share information about another suspected threat." He pulled out her chair. She smiled and sat down.

"Yes, last time we talked, it was another suicide bomber at Heathrow targeting that plane to New York. I was amazed by how quickly your people neutralized the situation," Samantha said.

"We got lucky. And with the new protocols, we hope to maintain our record."

"New protocols?" she asked.

"We just concluded a meeting with your National Security Advisor and Director of National Intelligence. We all agreed on a faster and more thorough exchange of information between our MI5 and Interpol and your CIA and FBI. Now that there is *so* much information flooding into our agencies, it can be difficult to analyze and know what to pass along."

"Agreed," Samantha said. She took a sip of wine. "Thank you so much for your cooperation not only on the immediate threats but also on tracking bank accounts we think are tied to bad transactions."

"Yes, I know that's one of your key areas," he said. "I saw a dispatch that said you will be one of the speakers at the Federal Reserve Conference in Jackson Hole. Our Finance Minister will be there. I hope you will have an opportunity to meet him."

"I look forward to it." Samantha immediately felt guilty about lying to her dinner partner. She snatched up her menu card and tried to switch the subject. "I heard they were going to repeat the dinner they served in the '70s during our bicentennial when Queen Elizabeth was here."

The menu included New England *langouste en bellevue*, a saddle of veal with rice croquettes, a garden salad with trappist cheese, peach ice cream bombe, and finally petits fours. She couldn't eat all that, but she'd definitely taste it. Samantha exchanged her reception wine for a glass of Sterling Chenin Blanc that her waiter had just poured and settled in for a long evening. After the meal and all the toasts, they would be herded into the East Room for entertainment, music, and dancing.

What was it she had read about that dinner for Queen Elizabeth so long ago? Something about dancing? Suddenly it came back to her. President Ford had leaned over and respectfully asked the Queen for her presence on the dance floor. So, she got up, he took her hand, and just as she stepped onto the floor, the Marine Band started playing "The Lady Is a Tramp." Samantha smiled to herself, remembering the musical gaffe. She hoped she would have a few more opportunities to enjoy the evening. Though, with her recent luck, she doubted she would.

TWENTY-FIVE

VADIM WENT OVER THE NUMBERS AGAIN.

He had about fifty million dollars left after the Cyprus confiscations and sanctions enforcement. It included payments he had received for the shipments to FARC and the Lashkar group. With the help of Alexander Tepanov, he had spread his wealth around until no one was the wiser. Ten million disappeared into a series of accounts in Malta, and the other forty million trickled through a network of accounts in the Siberian branch of a Moscow bank. Now he wanted to arrange contracts for the money so that he could cash in after the conference.

He needed the Malta balance to pay Stas and Lubov their five million as soon as they returned. Vadim had sent the conference agenda to them that morning and was expecting an overview of their plans to arrive any minute. He didn't mind waiting a little longer for it now that it would include Samantha Reid.

It was a stroke of pure luck that her name was listed as one of the conference speakers on the agenda. The conference was

155

next week, and no one believed Otto would handle her before then. So, without telling Otto, Vadim decided their strategy for the conference would include her.

A chime sounded, and Vadim saw a text from Lubov light up his cell. "Figured it out. Details on return," it said.

That was fast, Vadim thought.

He narrowed his eyes and skimmed through his calculations one final time. Then he picked up his cell and called Tepanov's personal number. When the call was answered, Vadim said, "Good morning. I trust you had a pleasant evening last night."

"Very pleasant, especially after I accepted the Federal Reserve's conference invitation. I am already looking forward to seeing you and Maksim next week in Wyoming. My secretary is coordinating my trip with our embassy in Washington since one of our ministers is attending as well. Now, what can I do for you?"

"Well, I have been analyzing the markets, and I suspect that the American economy will take a dive soon. We should get in front of that," Vadim said.

There was a long pause on the line. "There have certainly been ups and downs recently, but I've seen no indication that another major move will occur," Tepanov said.

Vadim ploughed ahead. "In any event, here's what I want you and your associates to do. Take the money I have in your Siberian branch and buy a series of puts on the major stock indices. Spread them around so they will attract the least attention."

"Wait a minute, Vadim. Are you trying to short the market?"

"Relax," Vadim said. "I've checked the calculations. So, to begin, buy about thirty million worth of puts on the Dow. Then another thirty million puts on the S&P 500, less appropriate commissions, of course."

"Wait. Wait," Tepanov said, sounding exasperated. "Last I checked you had about forty million in those accounts. How can I buy sixty million?"

"I want to go on margin. I know I can margin up to fifty percent of the cash value of my total account. So, let's do that."

Tepanov sighed. "Vadim, you say you have made all the calculations. I do a lot of calculations too, and I hope you realize that if the market is higher before these contracts expire, you would lose everything. And I mean *all of it*. There would be margin calls, and you'd be in debt. Your options would expire worthless."

Vadim gave a reassuring laugh. "Don't worry. I've figured it all out. We just need these orders executed carefully."

The banker was silent for several minutes. "And if I can do this without anyone noticing, we will meet in Jackson to *finalize* our relationship?"

"Precisely," Vadim said.

"All right. I still don't understand your reasoning, but you sound very determined about this. And, after all, it is your money. I'll get the trades executed for you."

"Thank you. Don't email the confirmations. Send them by DHL to my address in the states, like you did with the paperwork for those new accounts. I always prefer old fashioned paper and the delivery systems for financial transactions. You never know who's monitoring what these days."

"It's true," the banker said. "Well, that's enough business for one day. I look forward to carrying out the trades and seeing you in Jackson."

"Thanks again." Vadim said. "Keep in touch."

He clicked off the call, leaned back, and turned in his chair to face Maksim. "I'm shorting the market just like I said I would.

When Lubov and Stas get back, I have a feeling they'll do the same thing."

Maksim handed Vadim a glass of vodka, raised his own glass in a toast, and then leaned against a wall. "I thought you said we should always keep twenty percent of any asset for schmuck insurance in case things don't pan out. Shouldn't we keep that reserve?"

"No need," Vadim said, clinking his glass to his brother's. "You heard me. I've checked the math. All we have to do now is fly to Jackson Hole and watch the fireworks. It should be a pretty good show."

TWENTY-SIX

"ARE YOU SURE YOU WANT TO DO THIS?"
Samantha asked, getting out of Brett's car, parked across the
street from Montrose Park.

Summer in Georgetown was glorious until the humidity hit.
Right now, dogwoods still flowered in front of brick row houses.
But it wouldn't be long before the white blossoms were replaced
by a heavy canopy of dark green leaves and stifling tempera-
tures. She wanted to get out and enjoy the mild weather while
she could.

"Yes," Brett said, locking his car and pocketing the keys. "I
know you usually work on Saturday mornings, but I am more
than happy to be your security detail if you want to run today.
Besides, I need the exercise, and the scenery here is much better
than my apartment building's fitness center." He scanned the
area and only saw two couples strolling along R Street. "Okay,
which way?"

Samantha started walking across the street. "Over there. Sometimes I run along the river, but I discovered this trail a while ago that will be perfect for a day like this. C'mon."

They entered the park and started jogging along her familiar route. When they reached a set of monkey bars, they stopped for a quick drink from their water bottles and continued.

Sidestepping a fallen branch, Samantha glanced over at Brett who was wearing a gray T-shirt and navy shorts. He looked good in a suit but even better in running clothes. She could see the muscles in his arms and calves and the outline of a gun in the waistband of his shorts. Samantha was used to seeing him carry it. He had taken many turns with other agents to drive her around town since that first night.

Tripp had been too focused on finalizing his next contract and securing his next promotion to call or email lately. She hadn't heard from him since he left for his latest foreign assignment, negotiating an oil deal somewhere in Mexico. But she was starting to learn that absence doesn't always make the heart grow fonder. Maybe it gives it license to wander sometimes.

She thought about that as she leapt over a hole in the path. Clearing the gap reminded her of when she used to play hopscotch with her grade-school friends in Houston. They would draw squares on her driveway with colored chalk and see how many they could hop over without losing their balance. She wished she could still hurtle over problems that way.

Brett suddenly jogged behind her and matched her pace on the other side of the trail. She smiled at him and realized how calm she was whenever he was nearby. As long as he was the one coordinating her security, maybe she could keep her balance after all.

They kept running at a good pace for thirty minutes and then circled back to the park entrance. "That was good," Brett said, sitting down at one of the picnic benches. "This where you want to cool off?" he asked, taking a swig of water.

"I usually go next door. There's a pretty little cemetery and chapel over there." She pointed to the left. "Want to see it?"

"Sure," Brett said. "Just stay close."

They walked slowly past a pair of open iron gates. Looking down the path, Samantha noticed an old man sitting on a wrought iron bench with a golden retriever lying quietly by his side. "I've seen him here a few times. His name is Wilkinson," she said, motioning toward the bench. "He's become a bit of a friend. His family's buried over there. He worked at the State Department eons ago. Come say hello."

"Okay," Brett said.

When they reached the bench, Samantha said, "Hi, Will. Good to see you today. I want you to meet someone. This is Brett Keating."

The old man was hunched over. He slowly looked up at them and smiled. "A new young man for you?"

"Well, no. He's kind of a colleague," she said, somewhat embarrassed.

"Good to meet you," Will said, extending a shaky hand to Brett who walked up and shook it. Brett noticed a wooden cane lying in the grass next to the bench.

"Samantha tells me you're here a lot," Brett said, gazing around at the freshly cut lawn and scattered flower beds. He also spotted a nearby fountain with a small bird statue in its center. "I can see why."

"Yes, it's usually very quiet. It's been pleasant seeing Samantha sometimes on the weekends. I don't think I mentioned it before, but she reminds me of my granddaughter, Brittany. Same long hair. Same nice smile."

"Really?" Samantha said. "You haven't told me about your family, just your wife."

"They don't live around here. My son is an ambassador now. To Switzerland."

"That's impressive," Brett said. "And what about your granddaughter?"

"Oh, she's in college now. Dickenson University," he said proudly. "Please sit if you need to stretch your legs. You both look like you've been running."

They gratefully joined him on the bench and stretched their sore muscles. "It's such a nice day. I hope we have more like it before the humidity comes," Samantha said.

"Me too. The heat and humidity will be moving in soon, but we may get lucky," Will said. They chatted for several minutes. Finally, Wilkinson sighed and scooped up his dog's leash. "I'd better get back. Time to feed Roosevelt," Will said, lifting the dog's leash with a wink. "It's been nice seeing you two." He grabbed his cane and struggled to push himself up.

"Wait," Brett said, helping the man stand up. "Let us go with you. We're done here anyway. Right, Samantha?"

"Absolutely," she said. "We'll walk you to your car. Is it parked nearby?"

"Just down the block," he said. "Not too many cars on R Street on a Saturday. Of course, that's never the case during the rest of the week."

They walked out of the gate and started to cross the street. Roosevelt broke free and raced across the crosswalk with his leash trailing behind him, leaving Samantha to lead the trio's slow charge. Brett took Will's arm and followed her. She paused in the middle of the street and tilted her head, listening to something.

A black Acura suddenly screeched around the corner and barreled straight for Samantha. Her eyes widened as Brett dropped Wilkinson's arm and dove for her. He shoved her toward the curb just as the car careened past, hitting Will and knocking him to the ground before speeding off.

The dog barked furiously as he ran into the street. Roosevelt put his nose on Wilkinson's face and began to whine.

"Oh my god," Samantha screamed as she scrambled up and ran to the old man.

Brett jumped up and squinted to read the license plate of the car, but it was already turning down a side street. He watched it disappear and then raced to where Samantha was kneeling next to Will.

"He's unconscious," she sobbed.

Brett fumbled in his pocket and ripped out his cell phone. "Calling 911." He punched in the number, explained what had happened, and then described their location. "We have to get him out of the street," Brett said, hanging up the phone. "Though I hate to move him. Can't see if anything's broken."

Roosevelt started to howl and paw the pavement next to Wilkinson.

"I don't believe this," Samantha said in a shaky voice as tears streamed down her face. "That car was heading for *me*. I know it. And the bastard hit Will instead. We've got to help him."

"EMTs should be here pretty quickly," Brett said. He took the man's pulse. "Kind of weak, but he's hanging in there. I don't see any blood. Let's try to lift him."

Just then, several other people ran out of the park. Roosevelt barked at the gathering crowd as it started firing off questions.

"What happened?"

"Heart attack?"

"Is he badly hurt?"

"Should I call 911?"

"Did that," Brett shouted. "We just need to get him off the road," he called out as two teenage boys reached down to lift the old man's legs. Brett put his arms under Wilkinson's chest and turned his head toward Samantha. "Support his head and neck."

She immediately cradled Will's head and neck with her hands. The group gingerly lifted his limp body and carried it to the sidewalk. They gently laid him on the ground and waited several anxious minutes before they heard a siren wailing in the distance. When the ambulance appeared around the corner, the crowd had grown and Roosevelt was trying to lick his master's face.

"Let me talk to them," Brett said in a low voice to Samantha. "I don't want the local police involved in your case or getting in our way over this. Hit and run. That's what it looked like, okay?"

Samantha was trying to swipe away tears with the back of her hand. This was no accident. This was attempted murder. She was sure of it. She began to shake. "Brett, this isn't—"

"I know. I know. This is terrible. I should have saved him, but—"

"You saved *me* instead," Samantha said with a hard look.

Brett looked at her and touched her chin. "Let's stay together on this. We'll find that guy."

She nodded and hung her head. "I want to go to the hospital with Will. I want to see if he'll be all right."

"Of course," Brett said. "We'll both go." Brett grabbed Roosevelt's leash. "C'mon, boy. Stay with me. We'll take care of you at headquarters for now."

Samantha watched the ambulance pull up. A team of EMTs quickly poured out of the vehicle and onto the sidewalk. As they conducted their initial exam of the body, Brett explained what had happened. Then the EMTs retrieved Wilkinson's identification from his wallet and started strapping him into a stretcher. As soon as he was safely loaded into the ambulance, the driver turned to Brett and said, "We're headed to Georgetown Hospital. Entrance Three on Reservoir Road is Emergency. If you can follow us, they'll want a statement and any help you can give."

"We'll be right behind you. Got my car over there," Brett said.

The ambulance pulled away and drove off with its siren blaring. Brett, Samantha, and Roosevelt walked to Brett's car in silence. As Brett led the dog into the back seat, Samantha buckled herself into the passenger seat and thought a long, wordless prayer for her friend. Then she wondered when she would be targeted next.

TWENTY-SEVEN

SATURDAY LATE AFTERNOON: SAN FRANCISCO, CALIFORNIA

"WHAT DO YOU MEAN THERE'S BEEN NO action?" Vadim screamed into the phone.

"Um. . . what I meant was I've been waiting for the best opportunity to take care of this project. It just hasn't happened yet. She's never alone," Otto said apologetically. He didn't want to say too much on a cell phone. You never knew who might be listening in or trying to track your calls.

Otto also didn't want to tell his uncle that he had tried to hit Samantha Reid with his car. He wasn't trying to kill her, just put her out of commission for a while. That way, she wouldn't be a threat to Vadim's businesses, and he would have some time to figure out his next move. At least, that had been his plan.

"I send you there, pay your expenses, give you one simple job, and you come up with nothing. How much longer before you get this done?" Vadim said.

Otto paused, wondering what he should say next. He had no idea when he would be able to get close to his target again. And he didn't want to leave Jolene any time soon. She was the first girl who had paid him any attention, and he was getting hooked. He cleared his throat and tried to come up with a logical answer to Vadim's question.

"Do you have a certain date in mind when you want everything finished?" Otto asked.

"As soon as possible. I keep seeing articles about how certain people are working with other governments to shut down a lot of accounts. We don't want those accounts to be on anyone's radar. Not in this business."

"Sure. I get that," Otto said, stalling for time while he thought up a new excuse. "Tell you what. I have the equipment you mailed me, and I'm getting to know the city pretty well. If you give me more time, I should be all set in another couple of weeks."

"Another couple of weeks?" Vadim exploded. Then he paused for a long moment.

By next week, he would be in Jackson taking care of his own assignment, and the Reid woman would be there too. What would he do with Otto? He had no plans to fly him to Wyoming. He'd probably screw up something else if he were there. But he didn't want the kid hanging around the San Francisco apartment while it was empty.

The more he considered the situation, the more it made sense to leave the boy back East. What were another couple of weeks at a Holiday Inn? As long as Otto kept out of sight and didn't get tied to the Naples bombing, it would be nice not to have to think about his useless nephew for a while. He wouldn't say anything about Reid attending the conference. After all, if Otto nailed her first, they could just concentrate on the financial leaders.

"All right, but you listen to me," Vadim said. "Don't do anything stupid. I'm letting you stay there for now. Maksim and I have our own projects to attend to. Out of town."

"Oh? Where are you going?"

"We have some business in Wyoming. It doesn't concern you. I'll contact you when we get back. Meanwhile, just do your job and keep a low profile. Got that?"

"Yes, Yes. I get it. And I will."

Vadim switched off the call and walked to his bar to pour himself a drink. By the time he returned to his desk, he saw that Stas had sent him another text.

"Returning to SFO tomorrow night to explain grand plan," it said.

Vadim took a sip and smiled.

TWENTY-EIGHT

SUNDAY AFTERNOON; GEORGETOWN, WASHINGTON, D.C.

SAMANTHA AND BRETT STOOD IN FRONT OF the Georgetown Hospital reception desk, waiting to hear if Wilkinson had been moved out of intensive care and into a private room. The volunteer manning the desk confirmed that he had and gave them his room number.

"Thank God," Samantha said. "You have no idea how many prayers I've been saying."

"I understand," Brett said. "When the car first hit him, I was afraid he was dead. But he must be tougher than he looks."

Brett and Samantha walked to the elevators and rode up two floors. The smell of alcohol and antiseptics greeted them as they stepped into the hall and started looking for the right room. It was an unwelcome reminder to Samantha of the time she had spent in her husband's hospital room just before he died. "Here it is," Brett said, making a beeline for a door in the middle of the hall. "Looks like somebody's in there with him."

171

They knocked on the open door and heard a young woman's voice. "Come in."

A lovely girl who looked nineteen or twenty sat next to Wilkinson's bed. Her long, auburn hair was held back with a colorful blue headband. As they stepped into the room, she jumped up and held out her hand. "Hi. I'm Brittany. You must be Samantha and Brett, right?"

Samantha quickly closed the gap between her and Brittany. Instead of shaking hands, she gave the girl a quick hug. "Thank you so much for coming. When I got your number from your college, I didn't know if you could get away, but I figured you would want to know," Samantha said.

"Of course I wanted to know. Thank you so much for calling," Brittany said. "Please feel free to pull up those chairs. I can't thank you enough for getting Grandad here and checking in on him until I could borrow a car and drive down last night."

Brett got the chairs while Samantha leaned over the bed to touch Wilkinson's arm. "How are you doing?" she asked. "Are the nurses taking good care of you?"

Will was sitting up in bed with a tube trailing from his right hand to an IV machine that stood next to him. His other arm was in a sling, and a few bandages covered his head in patches. "Considering what you told Brittany about that driver, I feel pretty lucky. Just a small break below the elbow and a mild concussion. Could have been a whole lot worse."

Brittany scooted her chair closer and took his hand. "Grandad, you're strong. I knew you'd be okay. I'm just glad the accident gave me an excuse to get out of some classes and head down here."

"When do you have to go back?" Samantha asked her.

"I'll stay until he's ready to go home. You mentioned the FBI is taking care of Roosevelt. I hope he hasn't been too much trouble. He's usually wonderful."

"Not at all," Brett said. "After we leave here, I'll bring him to Wilkinson's house. Can you take care of him until your grandfather is released?"

"Oh sure. No problem."

"Here's my cell," Brett said, handing her a card. "Just call me when you leave here, and I'll drive him over."

"Sounds like a plan. I only have one more final, so I'll just study here. The doctors said Grandad will probably be discharged in another day or two. When I get him home, I'll make sure he has someone who can be there 24/7 to cook for him and all of that. He has a housekeeper who can be there some of the time, and we've got friends in the neighborhood. I'm working on it."

"Good for you," Samantha said. "With your folks overseas, I'm sure they're proud of you coming to the rescue like this."

Brittany grinned. "I texted my dad. He's in Geneva. He said he was grateful I could be here. They can't get away right now, but he knows I'll take care of everything. So, we're good."

Samantha turned to Wilkinson. "Getting any sleep?"

The old man shook his head and gave her a thin smile. "In a hospital? Not a chance."

"Tell them about last night, Grandad," Brittany said. "You won't believe it."

"It *was* strange. I was trying to relax when an alarm went off. They announced something called code red. Then it sounded two more times over their loud-speaker system. Turns out there was a suspected fire in a room on the fourth floor. Then a nurse came into my room twice during the night to take my blood pressure. Then I heard an announcement for a code blue, so every available doctor on the floor raced down the hall. When that was over, it was the middle of the night, and I was trying to fall asleep. But this little machine here," he said, pointing to the IV dispenser, "makes that beeping sound. Hard to get used to that."

"Tell them the rest," Brittany said.

"Oh yes," Will said. "When I wanted to go to the bathroom, I had to call a nurse to help me with this machine and all. That happened twice. Then at about 5:45, another nurse covered me with a blanket. I was too hot, so that was a useless exercise. Then they brought my breakfast at 6:45, and just as I thought I might be able to doze off, in comes this fellow with a dog."

Samantha burst out laughing. "A dog?"

"They called it the hospital therapy dog. Evidently, some patients like to pet it. Calms them down." He sat up a little straighter and continued. "I really don't need someone else's dog calming me down." He glanced over at Brittany. "I'd much rather have my granddaughter here to talk to. I don't know what I would have done without her."

"We would have looked after you. And Roosevelt too," Brett said. "For as long as it took."

Will looked at Brett and nodded his head with a smile. "I thought you looked responsible. Hope you're taking good care of Samantha here."

"I'm trying my best," Brett said.

Samantha leaned over and gave Will's right wrist a gentle squeeze. "Let's stay in touch, okay?"

"I'd like that, young lady," he replied.

Samantha fished in her purse, pulled out her business card, and handed it to Brittany. "Here's my contact info. Please keep me posted on how he's doing."

The young girl glanced at the card and raised her eyebrows. "The White House? Wow. Grandad, did you know that she's the Director of Homeland Security there?"

Wilkinson smiled at Samantha. "I always knew you were a bright woman. If anyone can keep things safe around here, I'll bet you can."

Samantha gave her old friend a serious look. "We all try," she said. As she and Brett turned to leave, she shook her head slightly.

If we can't even protect a sweet old man like Wilkinson, how can we protect the country?

TWENTY-NINE

"THERE THEY ARE," MAKSIM SAID, POINTING
to the exit of the San Francisco Airport. He shifted the driver's
seat into an upright position and then pulled the door's handle.

"Right on time," Vadim said, opening the passenger door.

Maksim pushed the door open and then walked around
the Lexus sedan to pop the trunk. Vadim stepped out and
slammed his door. "Easy with that," Maksim said. "This may
not be the Bentley we have back home, but it's still a decent
piece of hardware."

"If you can't slam a door when you feel like it, must be lousy
engineering," Vadim said. He turned and greeted the two men
who approached the car. "Welcome back. Glad to see you. At
first I thought you might decide to stay in Jackson until the conference started."

"We thought about that," Stas said, tossing his bag into the
trunk. "But we didn't want to be seen around town too much.
Someone might remember us."

"Yah," Lubov agreed. "And since we're taking a private plane out there, we thought it would be a good idea to have commercial airline records of us leaving Jackson. That way no one can connect us to the attack. I assume we'll all be using different names for the trip next week."

"Right," Vadim said. "Let's get in. There's a special place we're going to see today. After spending time in the mountains, I thought you might enjoy some time on the water."

"A boat trip?" Lubov asked.

"Yes, a little diversion," Vadim said. "But one with a purpose. Besides enjoying the view, that is."

"Sounds fun," Stas said. "We're happy to have you show us around."

"Yah," Lubov said. "The water will be a good place to discuss our plans for Jackson."

"Can't wait to hear," Maksim said, putting the car in gear and driving north out of the airport.

"I've already set our financial plans in motion," Vadim said. "I'll explain it all later."

They drove up Highway 101, turned off into the city, and continued on to Fisherman's Wharf, finally finding a parking spot near Pier 33. From there, they walked to the dock and boarded a Hornblower Hybrid yacht along with a crowd of tourists. The four men climbed to the upper-level, aft deck and found seats under a canopy close to an outdoor bar.

"I want to impress upon you the seriousness of our undertaking," Vadim said as Maksim, Lubov, and Stas settled into their chairs.

"We know you're serious," Stas said.

"Yes, but we have to be careful," Vadim said. "Everything must be in place. And none of us can be tied to the operation in any way. Look over there," Vadim said, pointing. "That's where we're going. Alcatraz. It was the most famous prison in America. Maximum security. Minimum privilege as they say."

"Couldn't have been worse than Lubyanka when the KGB ran it," Stas said.

"Probably not," Maksim said. "From what I've heard they didn't torture the prisoners here, but it was still a pretty tough place. When I checked the website and made the reservations for a tour, I read that a bunch of people tried to escape, but no one knows if any of them actually made it. I mean, it's a rock, the water's cold, and you either got shot or you drowned."

"What's that?" Lubov asked, pointing to a piece of land jutting into the bay. It was studded with large houses.

"Oh, that's Belvedere Island," Maksim said. "Pretty, high-end real estate with views of the San Francisco skyline. It's spectacular, but it takes a long time to drive over the Golden Gate Bridge. That's why we opted for Russian Hill."

The conversation died down as the yacht drew closer to Alcatraz Island. They looked up in silence at the desolate island and the concrete penitentiary it still housed. Stas was the first to disturb the quiet. "Look, they're tying up," he said.

"Great. Let's go see this rock," Lubov said, standing up.

"We can fill you in on everything on the way back," Stas said, pushing back his chair. "We can sit near the engines. With all the motor noise, nobody will hear a damn thing we say."

They followed dozens of other passengers down a short gangplank and stepped onto the dock. A tour guide escorted them inside a receiving area where several people picked up equipment for an audio tour.

"Do we need those things?" Lubov asked.

Vadim shook his head, grabbed a couple of brochures, and handed them around. "Nah, let's just do our own tour. Here's some stuff about what happened here."

As they read through the booklets, Stas suddenly pointed to a page. "Is that Al Capone? I've heard of him. Into a whole lot of stuff that sounds familiar, right?" He gave the others a wry grin.

"Guess you could say that," Lubov said. "Says here that what they really got him for was tax evasion. Jeez, he only served seven years. But wait, poor bastard really went downhill. Had syphilis, pneumonia, and a stroke. Died at forty-eight. Not a good way to go."

"I guess the lesson there is be careful and don't get caught. But if you do, keep a good doctor on retainer," Maksim said.

Vadim laughed, slapped him on the shoulder, and said, "C'mon, let's check this place out."

They stayed several steps behind the others in the tour as they moved through the deserted prison. It was just as drab and dank on the inside as the outside. The tour swept them past "the hole" where inmates were stashed in solitary confinement and the place where prisoners staged food riots and protests. When they finally stepped back outside, wild flowers and birds' nests offered a stark contrast to the penitentiary's morbid interior.

Staring at the San Francisco skyline shimmering in the late afternoon sun, Vadim found it hard to imagine that anyone, even a hardened criminal, could stand being held prisoner in a tiny cell while looking out his window at all that beauty just three miles away.

The tour group boarded the yacht for the return trip, and the four men went to the upper bar to order vodka on the rocks. After they found seats near the engines, Lubov glanced around and saw that the other passengers were seated some distance away. "Now we can talk a bit. I'm glad things have changed since those mobsters were stuck in there. We don't operate like they did. We've got more secure systems to run our businesses, we move money around whenever we want, and we've got our own gangs that nobody touches."

"That's because we've developed a good network of people to pay off," Stas said. He also surveyed the deck. Other passengers were either drinking, standing along the rail taking pictures, or engaging in their own conversations. Nobody was paying much attention to the Russians.

"Speaking of our networks, we've figured out how to pull off the conference with their help. We stayed in a hotel in Teton Village," Lubov said, keeping his voice low. "But we drove over to the Jackson Lake Lodge where all the conference attendees will be staying. Can't do anything there. Too remote. Only one road out. And we have no idea where everybody will go after the speeches. Some might go hiking or fishing. Others could go anywhere. But when you sent us the official agenda, we noticed that they are going to have a lunch meeting at the ski place in that village."

"You think you can pull it off there?" Vadim asked.

"Yes." Stas said. "We took out a PO box, just like most of the residents in that town, and arranged to have our contacts ship in some of the supplies we'll need. The lunch meeting is going to take place in a restaurant at the top of Rendezvous Mountain. We've already scouted the area and found places to install a system before anyone gets there for the meeting."

"Wait a minute," Maksim said. "You're going to plant something at the top of the mountain? What kind of triggers will you use? They don't always work," he added with a frown.

"We know that," Lubov said. "We'll have multiple items installed all around the restaurant and in a few other places. You don't have to know all the details. That's what you've got us for," he added with a conspiratorial grin.

"So far so good," Vadim said. "Where should we stay?"

"We'll stay in Teton Village but in a different hotel," Lubov said. "I think you should stay in the village too in that really nice place. Remember the picture you printed out of that girl by the pool?" When Vadim nodded, Lubov continued. "That's from the Snake River Lodge and Spa. Lots of foreigners stay there. And it has great massages."

"Sounds like a good idea," Vadim said. "Now what about the plane? You said you'd also scope out the best place for us to land."

"We did," Lubov said. "We'll land at Idaho Falls. Has a decent runway. We'll also rent two cars. Stas and I in one; you and Maksim in the other. It will take us about an hour to reach Jackson from the runway. There's no security in Idaho we'll have to worry about. And, when everything's over, the Teton Pass will be our escape route. It'll only take us about ten minutes to get to the pass from Teton Village. Then it's back over the mountain and on to the airport.

"Nobody would be able to put up a road block in that period of time. Besides, everybody flies out of the Jackson airport, not Idaho Falls. So, once we're in Idaho, we fly back here, stay quiet for a while, check the markets, and count our money," Lubov said with a note of triumph in his voice. He took a drink of vodka and asked, "Speaking of money, now that you know the plan, what about our down payment?"

"It's waiting for you at the penthouse. A promise is a promise. That's the way we do business," Vadim said.

"And *stay* in business," Maksim added.

Stas smiled. "So, where should we go out to celebrate tonight?"

Vadim swirled the ice around in his glass, took a big gulp, sat back, and thought for a long moment. "I was thinking of taking you to the best strip joint in town."

Lubov's eyes lit up. "You have a good one here?"

"What's it got?" Stas asked, leaning in.

"The place is called the Mitchell Brothers O'Farrell Theatre," Vadim said. "Poles on the stage. The women dance. They even do some shows in private rooms. It's down in an area of the city called the Tenderloin District."

"I'm game," Lubov said. "I could use some entertainment after that depressing prison and after driving all over that crazy town filled with cowboys and tourists. More booze wouldn't hurt either." He held up his glass. "Hope they have better stuff than this."

"That could be a problem," Maksim said "They don't serve liquor there. Oh, and there's a hefty cover charge."

"A cover charge for nude women?" Lubov laughed.

"Maybe we should skip it and get ourselves some first-class takeout instead," Stas said.

"Sure," Maksim said. "There's plenty of takeout places in San Francisco. The city has about four thousand restaurants."

"Four thousand? That's about half the population of Jackson," Stas said with a smirk. "I like a city with a lot of choices. Eating in sounds like a good idea. Besides, you guys have a first-class bar in that penthouse."

"One of my priorities. Goes along with our preference for a life of luxury," Vadim said. He raised his glass in a toast they all drank to. Then he tossed back the last of his vodka, leaned back, and grinned.

THIRTY

BRETT STOOD IN FRONT OF AN OLD APARTMENT building half a block from the new Russian military attaché. He knew there was a camera in the apartment's window air-conditioning unit that filmed everyone entering or exiting that house. And the house's listening devices were recording conversations 24/7.

Nori Hotta was doing a great job translating the recordings. She meticulously searched for keywords that might tip them off to things like breaking trade embargoes, infiltrating agencies, conducting cyber-crimes, or anything else that threatened national security.

Recently, Trevor had been pestering Brett for updates on multiple monitoring projects, especially the Russian military attaché one. So Brett decided to check in with Elise Vaughn, the agent stationed here. He walked into the apartment building and recited the apartment number to a man at the desk. The desk clerk called upstairs then nodded his okay and pointed to the elevators. He rode up to the third floor and knocked on the door.

185

A young woman with short blonde hair and a face full of freckles opened it. She smiled at Brett and allowed him to step inside the sparsely furnished room.

He quickly closed the door and then turned to her. "How's it going? Anything new to report?" he asked, walking over to the window and peering across the street. "Any important visitors lately?"

"We spotted their sweep team checking out the place before that military aide moved in," Elise said.

"Thanks for that," Brett said. "We were able to shut down the audio probes just in time."

She sat down at a desk covered in stacks of paper. "Right now it looks like the new owner spends most of the day at the embassy. Sometimes he has meetings at the house or makes calls at odd hours, though. That's when it gets interesting. He calls Moscow a lot. And with the time difference, he's either up early or talking late at night. I know you get the translations from Nori, and NSA is undoubtedly picking up a lot of conversations. But they've got so much to analyze. Our being here is much more effective. At least for now."

"I agree," Brett said.

"I know a smattering of Russian, which I know is why you gave me this plum assignment," she said with a rueful grin. "I've picked up a couple of things. Not sure what they mean though."

"Like what?" Brett asked, pulling up a metal chair placed near the desk.

"Well, I hear the words 'White House' now and then. And last night I heard the word 'conference' or 'meeting' a bunch of times. Of course, there are a lot of conferences at the White House, but I haven't heard about any recent ones involving Russians. Have you?"

"No. But maybe they're referring to other meetings. The British were just in town. Does it sound like they were trying to get inside information on what happened with the Prime Minister?"

"I don't think so. I'm sure Nori can make better sense of it, though," Elise said. "In another conversation, they mentioned a central banker from Moscow, Alexander Tepanov, and a minister who works for their ambassador here. The minister makes sense, but maybe you should run that Tepanov name. Could be that he's going to some conference with the embassy guy. Might be nothing. But they spent a long time talking about it, so it must be important to involve a military attaché too. What do you think?"

"If a Russian minister is scheduled to go somewhere, he'll want protection. He'll have to get permission to travel outside their permitted radius too. If it is a conference, I wonder where it would be. Anything else?" Brett asked.

"Oh, the other word I heard a lot was '*finansists.*' That means 'financiers.' Some of their words sound a lot like ours," Elise said.

"Well, if it's something involving a Russian banker, it would make sense that other financial people are involved. Doesn't sound too sinister to me." Brett checked his watch and got up. "I just wanted to stop by and see how you're doing. Take a decent dinner break tonight. The cameras and bugs will do the work just fine for a while, but keep me posted."

Brett left the building and walked back to his car parked a block away. Before he started the engine, he pulled out his cell. A new email from a friend in Chicago popped up in his personal account, and he opened it. It included a photo of his ex-wife at a charity dinner with the bond salesman she had married.

Staring at the grainy picture of her wearing an extremely low-cut dress and a stern look, he couldn't help but compare it to the memory of Samantha wearing her more conservative outfits while always looking gorgeous with that wide smile of hers. The more he thought about it, the more he realized that his ex-wife was the best bullet he had dodged in Chicago.

As he slipped his key into the ignition, a text from Eleanor Clay flashed across his phone's screen. This time, she invited him to an evening of "entertainment" accompanied by the details of a new embassy purchase. She had tickets to the revival of an old show, *Shear Madness*, at the Kennedy Center. He always needed any intel she could give him about foreign sales, but he was busy and didn't want to encourage her in any personal way. Maybe he could pawn her off on Dom.

As he considered how to answer her message, he reflected that the name of the show mirrored the state of his most important assignment: the Naples investigation. Everything about Samantha's situation—the explosion, the stalker, the hit and run driver—was complete madness. For her sake, he wanted to solve the case as soon as possible.

He shoved the cell back in his pocket and started the car. He needed to stop by a few other clandestine locations on Embassy Row before picking up Samantha at the southwest gate of the White House. Protecting her was turning out to be the best part of that assignment, even if some nutcase was still out there trying to track her down.

THIRTY-ONE

EARLY MONDAY EVENING;
WASHINGTON, D.C.

OTTO STUDIED THE EMAIL FROM VADIM again. It was a follow-up to the testy conversation they had had about him staying in D.C. a little longer. While he hated reading the imperialistic tone of Vadim's writing, he was glad he had finally won a round with the man. Staying in D.C. meant spending more time with Jolene. The flip side was Vadim's demand that Otto finish the job he had been sent to do.

He pushed his laptop off his lap and then swung his legs over the side of his hotel bed. Otto walked to the bureau, rummaged through a stack of jeans and T-shirts, and fingered his brand new Glock 19. It had never been fired. He put it on the desk next to his latest batch of notes on the Reid woman's whereabouts. Recently, she had started getting rides with different people to and from work. Had to be some kind of bodyguards.

He wondered if she remembered him from the Naples dinner. It didn't seem very likely, but it would explain the sudden driver routine that kicked in right after she spotted him at that

189

restaurant on lower K Street. Then when he screwed up the hit-and-run and knocked down that old man, she had gotten even more protection. He hoped that man was okay.

Figuring out how to get his bonus without killing the woman was turning out to be a lot more difficult than he thought. Maybe he could scare her into leaving town for a while. That would remove her from her government action and allow Vadim to operate more freely. Perhaps that would satisfy him.

While he figured out his scare tactics, there were still things he could do to fill his reports to Vadim. He would continue to trail her from a distance and keep the gun in his car from now on. Just in case. It wouldn't be a bad idea to do some surveillance near her apartment later in the evening. Right now, he had better plans.

He was going to see Jolene and help her move out of her dorm. She had just graduated and had already found an apartment near DuPont Circle. After he helped set up her new place, he planned to surprise her with a nice bottle of cabernet he had bought from his now-favorite liquor store.

Otto glanced at his phone and realized he needed to start getting ready. He quickly undressed and stepped into the shower. While the warm water ran through his hair, his thoughts wandered back to Jolene. She had been on his mind a lot. He had never met a woman who was so unlike the girls in their gang back home.

Jolene always talked about her parents with respect, and she was never angry or belligerent. She had ambition. As far as he could tell, she never used any kind of drugs. She didn't even have tattoos or piercings, at least none that he had seen. It would probably take a few more dates before he got that close. But a guy could dream.

He finished showering, shaved, and picked out a pair of fairly clean blue jeans and a polo shirt. Then he went through his usual routine of grabbing his keys, wallet, and credit cards. This time, he also grabbed the bottle of wine and wrapped his Glock in a T-shirt before heading down to the parking lot. Otto stashed the concealed Glock in his car's glove box and locked it.

It took him less than ten minutes to drive to the campus. He pulled the Acura to the side of the road leading to the guard gate and texted Jolene. Then he sat back and waited. After a few minutes, he saw her waving and running toward the car.

"You're right on time," she said, opening the passenger door and leaping in. "I'll show my pass to the guard. You can park right next to my dorm. You are so nice to come help me tonight. It's kind of chaotic with everyone moving out, but those are the rules."

"No problem," he said, pulling through the gate. "Glad to be of service."

I'd like to service her sometime.

"We just have a short drive. Go up the hill and turn right."

As he followed her directions, he appraised the girl of his recent dreams out of the corner of his eye. Her short black hair was swept away from her flushed face. Her dark eyes looked mysterious and inviting at the same time. How did she do that? And why wasn't she always surrounded by other guys? Why was she so willing to only go out with him? She had told him that she recently broke up with a student from China. Maybe he simply came along at the right time. Now, he wanted to spend all his time with her, or at least as much as he could manage.

He flicked on the radio as they drove. As soon as he switched it on, he heard George Strait singing "Give It All We Got Tonight." Jolene had also told him she liked American country music, so he had gone through great pains to program the right stations. As George sang, "My god, you're somethin', like nothing. If I'm asleep girl, let me dream," Otto looked at her and couldn't believe his good fortune to be awake with this gorgeous creature sitting next to him.

"I like that one," she said. "Don't you?"

"Mmm-hmm," he muttered, glancing around at all the SUVs and trucks along the side of the road.

"Over there," Jolene said.

"I see it." Otto pulled into a spot, and they trooped into the dormitory.

Jolene had already packed her clothes into several suitcases, all sitting in a line on her dorm room's floor. She also had three boxes of books, her computer, a printer, a lamp, two posters, and a shopping bag filled with shoes sitting on top of a small fridge. It didn't take long to load everything into Otto's trunk and back seat, drive to her new building, and haul it all inside. When they were finally finished, Otto retrieved the bottle of cabernet from the car. He walked back to her new apartment and handed it to Jolene.

"Wow! This looks great. Thank you. And thank you for all your help. You sit down. I'll open this, and we'll chat for a while."

"These are pretty nice digs," Otto said, plopping down on a tweed couch and stretching his legs. He was relieved to be inside where no one could see him and possibly tie him to the ongoing news reports about Naples. Tonight, he could really relax. He just hoped that one night he could relax with her. He thought about that as he glanced toward the bedroom.

"I really lucked out," she said. "The landlord offered it to me partially furnished. Nothing elegant, but at least I've got the basics." She grabbed two glasses and came to sit next to him.

"You know, Oleg," she said as she poured the wine, "when we've been together, we've talked about my family, my classes, my finals, my job plans. But you haven't really told me much about yourself. Don't get me wrong, it's nice of you to show so much interest in me. I mean, a lot of guys I meet do nothing but talk about themselves, their sports, their trophies, how they nailed an exam, how they're going to make a million dollars with a start-up, whatever. But you're different. You're almost…secretive," she said. "It's like you don't want to tell me about your family or your life. So, tonight I just decided I'd come right out and ask you about it. Do you mind?"

Otto shifted in his seat. How much could he tell her without scaring her or chasing her away? He didn't have much to be proud of. No sports, no trophies, no money. His only hope for a million dollars was to stay tied to a man he couldn't stand. Was that his plan? His only plan?

He hesitated, sat back, and then took a deep breath. "I don't know what I should say. I told you I went to school in Moscow. My mother lives on a small farm. My dad died in a tractor accident. I don't have any trophies or an idea for a start-up. Guess that's not very impressive, right?" he said with a slight frown.

"Hey, wait a minute. Being impressive has nothing to do with it. I'm just curious about what you'd *like* to do."

"I don't know yet," he said. "But look at you. You've got all sorts of ideas about jobs you can get, things you can do, money you can make. It's terrific. You've got it all sorted out."

"Not quite," she said. "Sure, I've got ideas, and I have been *looking* for a job. In fact, I've got a few leads I was going to tell you about. But I don't have everything figured out yet." She leaned forward and took his hand. "And I think you're a lot more impressive than you realize. You're nice, you're tall, you're cute—"

"Cute?" he said with a half laugh.

"Well, I think you're cute. And you've got good hair," she said with a grin. "You're also smart and great with computers. You know more than most of the students did in my senior computer class. I've told you before that you could probably get a good job around here. One of the things I wanted to do tonight was try to talk you into giving it a shot."

"You mean look for a job and stay in Washington?"

"Why not? The place is booming. I saw an article in the *Post* that said thousands of graduates come to D.C. from all over the country. There are government contractors everywhere you look and lobbyists all over town. And every company needs computer help, especially for security."

"What's a lobbyist?" he asked.

"Oh those," she said. "They work on legislation. Big companies or associations of smaller ones or nonprofits send them to Washington to get things passed that they want. They talk to members of Congress and try to get them to vote for bills that would be good for their businesses. Anyone has a right to lobby for a cause."

"'Lobby' is a strange word," he said.

"It comes from way back. People would stand in the rooms just outside Congress, out in the lobby or hallways, and try to talk to the members to influence them. So, they're called lobbyists. See?"

"I get it, but I don't know anything about legislation or politics. We don't get involved in that stuff back home. I don't think they'd pay any attention to us even if we wanted to. I mean, we have elections, but I think they're pretty well fixed. Come to think of it, a lot of stuff back there is fixed. If you know the right people."

"Knowing the right people here helps too, but I don't think the elections are fixed. Oh, they've definitely got some problems, but we don't have to talk about that. What I wanted to focus on was the *possibility* of you staying, not the reality of it. So, what do you think?"

"I think I'd like to spend more time with you. For starters anyway. Oh, and I just got word that I *am* going to stay here a little longer."

"That's great," she said with a big smile. "That means I have more time to get you to make a decision."

Could he possibly make such a big decision after being in the country for such a short time? He had spent some time in San Francisco, but that was different. Out there he was just an errand boy. An intern. An acolyte. That was a word his mother used a lot, and he didn't think he wanted to spend the next several years in some sort of servitude. No, maybe Jolene had it right. Maybe he could start checking the job boards and see what was out there. The sooner he was no longer dependent on his uncles the better.

Perhaps his bonus could speed things up. Maksim never mentioned an exact number, but it might be enough for him to live in D.C. for a while and create a start-up or even go into business with Jolene. In fact, maybe he could get it all over with and start living a new life later tonight.

THIRTY-TWO

LATE MONDAY EVENING:
THE WHITE HOUSE

"HAVE A GOOD NIGHT," SAMANTHA SAID AS SHE nodded to the Secret Service agent who was seated at a desk by the basement door of the West Wing.

"You too, Miss Reid," the man replied. "FBI picking you up as usual?"

She stopped. "Yes. I guess you know that."

"We all know," he said. "Stay safe out there."

"Sure thing," she said and pushed open the door. She hurried down the walkway along the parking area known as West Exec and approached the southwest gate. She waved to the agent inside the guard shack, went out the door, and looked around. Brett's car was double-parked down the street with the headlights flashing. He stepped out of the car, ran over, and walked next to her until she scrambled inside. He got in on the driver's side. "Where to tonight?"

198 Karna Small Bodman

Samantha looked over at him. "You know, it's been a really long day. Most of my meetings ran late. As usual. I think I need to go straight home."

"Got it." He started to drive down E Street, heading for Virginia Avenue. "So, how was the day that wore you out so much? Anything you can talk about?"

Samantha leaned back and sighed. "Let's see. I went to a Cabinet meeting. Whenever I go to one of those, I sit against the back wall with other staff where they don't even pass the M&Ms."

He chuckled. "Probably classified info."

"Yes. I also had to sort out plans for a trip I have to make."

"Where?" A note of concern touched his voice.

"They're sending me out to Jackson, Wyoming, to give a talk on one of my favorite subjects right now: the money-laundering and illicit arms sales we're trying to track. It's a conference put on by the Fed. The Treasury Secretary has the lead. But with a lot of finance ministers and central bankers coming, my boss thinks I can convince them to help us close bad accounts. Anyway, we'll have Treasury security with us, so you'll get a break. I'm sure I'll be perfectly safe."

As Brett turned onto K Street, he remembered the listening devices picking up the words "conference," "financiers," and "Tepanov."

Is this the conference they were talking about?

"Have you ever heard the name Alexander Tepanov? He's a Russian banker," Brett said.

"Tepanov? Let me think. Homer over at Treasury has been working with his staff to trace a bunch of new Russian accounts. I don't think he's mentioned that particular name. Why?" she asked.

"He might be connected to that conference out west. By the way, I have some questions about that, especially your role, the schedule, and the security setup."

"Well, we're here," she said as Brett pulled up to her building. She rummaged in her purse. "I brought my door opener, so why don't you pull into the underground garage. I have an extra spot for a guest. Then you can come up for a few minutes, and I'll tell you what I know."

"Good idea. I always want you off the streets as fast as possible," Brett said.

He drove into the garage and waited until the garage door came down behind them before parking. They rode the elevator up to her condo and walked down the hall to her door. Samantha opened it, entered her new security code on a keypad, and they stepped inside.

"I'm glad your security system is working. Be sure to put it on STAY whenever you come home," Brett advised.

"Yes, I do that," she said. "Before we talk about the conference, would you like something to drink? Coffee? Juice?"

"Just water, thanks." He followed her into the kitchen and accepted a glass of ice water while Samantha poured some juice for herself.

"Anything new on that waiter from Naples?" she asked.

"We've been looking all over town. Our agents are using the sketch, hitting hotels and motels, car rental agencies. The works."

"An all points when we're not even sure of his name?" Her eyes widened.

"Yes, but it takes time. Do you know how many hotels are in D.C.?"

"Not a clue," she admitted.

"One hundred and ninety-six. And that doesn't include all the suburbs. He could be staying at someone's house," Brett said.

"It's been tough trying to focus on my job while always wondering where that maniac might be. Wherever he is, though, I feel so much better when you and the other agents are around." She said, leaning against the kitchen counter. "I was reading something last night, and I came across an old poem by Mearns. It struck a chord. 'As I was walking up the stair, I met a man who wasn't there. He wasn't there again today. I wish, I wish he'd stay away.'"

"I can see how you'd feel that way. I promise, we're trying our best to keep you safe."

She eyed him, paused, and said, "How did you become a special agent?"

"Well, if you really want to know. I grew up outside of Indianapolis. Got a scholarship to Purdue and a degree in engineering. But I decided I didn't want to be an engineer after all. My dad was in the military; Mom was a teacher. She taught civics and used to drum things like citizenship, voting, and the Constitution into me all the time."

"Sounds like you were lucky. I don't think they teach enough civics in schools these days. Have you ever seen those man-on-the-street interviews on *Watters' World* on Fox?"

"Yeah," Brett said, taking a drink. "I saw one where a group of college kids were asked about who should be on the Supreme Court. One girl mentioned the Kardashians."

Samantha burst out laughing. "We should get some sort of initiative going at the state level. Not a federal edict, but something local school boards could do. They could require high school students to pass the same naturalization test immigrants have to pass in order to become American citizens. The questions are all online."

"I think that's a great idea," Brett said. "Everyone who wants a driver's license has to study to pass a driver's test. Why shouldn't everyone who wants an American high school diploma have to study to pass a civics test? I think I'll pitch your idea to my mom. Maybe she can get the ball rolling on it back home."

"You have to start somewhere. Was your mom the one who made you want to work for the government and join the FBI?"

"In a way. But to be honest, I used to read a lot of mysteries and crime novels when I was a kid. Guess I sort of inhaled the idea of becoming an agent who would bring down bad guys," he gave her a slight grin. "Kids get notions in all sorts of strange ways."

"Do you have any?" she asked cautiously.

"Nope. Might be nice someday. I was married for a while, but she never got used to my hours or what I was doing. Ran off with a bond dealer. Haven't bought a bond since. Just a few stocks," Brett said with a shrug.

"Oh, I'm so sorry. Is your dad still alive?" she asked, changing the subject.

"He died three years ago. He's buried at Arlington. It's an honor to be there. Before I moved, I hadn't visited D.C. since his ceremony. I visited the site as soon as I got here. What about your family?"

"My parents are gone. Mom had cancer when I was in college. My dad had a heart attack when he was overseas. He was in the oil and gas business. He taught me a lot. I have a photo of them on my coffee table I can show you." She walked out of the kitchen and headed toward the couch in front of the picture window.

Brett followed her and noticed that the window's curtains were open. "Better let me close those curtains. Sorry, I should have done that earlier."

"No problem. I'll take care of it."

As she pulled the cord, a bullet tore through the window. Shards of glass shot into the back of the couch, and Brett cried out, "God, no!" He leaped, threw Samantha to the floor, and covered her body with his.

THIRTY-THREE

BRETT ROLLED TO THE SIDE AND STARED AT Samantha. "Were you hit? Open your eyes. Tell me," he demanded.

Samantha blinked, looked at him, reached up, and rubbed her forehead. "A shot. There was a shot. Next thing I'm on the floor."

He heaved a sigh of relief. She was alive, but had she been wounded? "I tackled you," he said, reaching over to touch her face. "Are you okay?" he asked anxiously.

She moved her shoulders from side to side and said, "I think so. Nothing hurts. Well, except my head a little bit. Maybe when I hit the floor."

"Sorry. Had to get you away from that window." He glanced up and saw where the bullet had smashed through the glass. "I can't believe someone was able to take a shot at you in that one minute you were exposed. My god, Samantha! He could have killed you." He kneeled beneath the window, scanned the street below, and shook his head. "I've got to get out there. The shooter must be gone by now, but someone may have seen something or

got a license." He reached for her hand. "Here, let me help you."
He stood up with her and then closed the drapes. "Stay away from
the window. Lock the door after me, use the bolt. Got that?"

She nodded as Brett grabbed his jacket and gun. He raced
out the door and tore down the stairs. On the street, he didn't
see any cars racing away or people walking in front of the building. He ran past Chadwick's and headed toward Wisconsin
Avenue. When he got to the corner, he saw several cars driving
slowly by the entrance to the Georgetown Park garage. Others
were stopped at the light on M street. As he ran, he pulled out
his cell and called for backup.

Holding his phone to his ear, he hurried up the street, peering
into every car on his way. He saw two couples in a Buick, then
an Explorer with a family inside. No lone driver. No black Acura.

*Damn. How could I let someone get a clear shot at Saman-
tha? How could I be so stupid? How in god's name could I—*

He continued to mentally tear himself apart. She hadn't been
hit, but what would the incident do to her mental state? She was
usually cool and calm. But after this? Who the hell knew? He just
knew he and the other agents had to step up their game and put
an end to this nightmare.

When he finally got through to headquarters, he reported the
attack. There was no evidence that proved Samantha's stalker
and the shooter were the same person, but he knew in his gut
they were. He explained his suspicions in his report, listed the
address of the attack, and said he was heading back to the apartment but needed help ASAP.

Samantha buzzed him in when he returned to the apartment
building. He hit the stairs and saw a teenage girl looking down
the hall from behind her door. She called to him. "What's happening? I thought I heard a gunshot or something."

"Someone shot a window from the street. Did you see any-thing?"

"Uh, no. I wasn't looking outside. I just thought I heard something. Is everyone okay?" she asked.

"Yes. Everyone's fine," Brett said. He flashed his badge and took out a card. "I'm Brett Keating. FBI. If you think of anything or talk to anyone who may have seen something—a person, a car, anything at all—please contact me right away, okay?"

She stared at the card, nodded, and said nervously, "Uh, sure. What were they shooting at anyway?"

"That's not important," Brett said. "We just want to find whoever went out for target practice tonight." He turned, walked over to Samantha's door, knocked, and hurried inside.

"Find out anything?" she asked expectantly.

"Afraid not," Brett said, sloughing off his jacket. "I can't believe I left those curtains open. Where the hell was my head?" He stared at her, raked his fingers through his hair, and mut-tered, "You could have been hit."

"For heaven's sake, don't blame yourself. I should have thought of it myself. I only leave the drapes open during the day so the plants get some sunlight, and I usually close them right away when I get home. I just forgot about it today. Besides, it was so late, we went straight into the kitchen."

"Are you sure you're all right?" Brett said, looking her over.

"No worse for wear. Pretty scary stuff though," she said, a flicker of fear in her eyes.

"Damn right it is. I called it in. Agents will be here in a few minutes. Why don't you have some wine or something to eat? Might help you to relax. I want to see if I can find the damn bullet."

He walked over to the wall across from the window and looked up. "The guy was obviously firing from the sidewalk or from inside a car. If he was in a car, he would have parked in front with the driver side window open and headed toward Wisconsin or straight ahead toward the parkway. I checked Wisconsin, but now that I think about it, the fastest way out of here would have been straight down K Street."

"You're right about that," she said. "I just may have that drink." She went into the kitchen and grabbed a bottle of wine, but when she tried to open it, her hands were shaking. She went back to the living room, bottle in hand.

"Here, let me help you with that," Brett said, pulling out the cork and handing it back. He turned to the wall again. "So, if he was firing from his car, which makes the most sense, the trajectory to the second floor was at a pretty steep angle. That means the bullet could be…" He scanned the area above a painting of what looked like a field of daisies. The painting was fine. No damage there. He looked higher.

"Can I grab one of those?" he said, coming over to the dining table. She nodded as he took one of her wooden dining chairs, carried it to the painting, stepped up, and said, "Here it is." He reached into the pocket of his pants for the small folding knife he always carried. He opened it and carefully started to dig the bullet out of the wall, just below the crown molding.

He got down from the chair and examined the bullet. "Nine millimeter. Could be from a Glock. Just a guess, though." He didn't want to tell her what a bullet like that could have done if the shooter's aim had been better.

In a matter of minutes, three agents were examining the apartment. Dom was one of them. "Don't imagine you saw anything? Anyone?" he said.

"No. When I ran out and checked the street, there wasn't anybody on the sidewalk," Brett said. "Get everyone to fan out through the building and the other apartments facing the street. I already talked to a neighbor next door. She didn't see anything, but she did hear the shot. Maybe somebody else saw something. And check down the street at Chadwick's. See if someone there heard the shot or saw a black Acura." Brett opened his hand. "Here's the bullet." He pointed to the wall. "From up there. Need to bag it and have it analyzed. Might be a Glock."

"Will do," Dom said, turning to give instructions to two other agents.

Brett joined Samantha at the table. He looked into her troubled eyes, took in her nervous demeanor, and tried to concentrate. "Tell me again how you feel. How's your head?"

Samantha touched her forehead. "I'm sure I'm okay. I know your people are here, but I have to call this into the White House too," she said. "They'll be glad to know you're on it. I'm not sure what we should do next, though."

"I do," Brett said. "We're going to increase your protection so there'll be one agent outside and one inside at all times. We're also going to recirculate that drawing we have of the Naples waiter. Along with the hotels, we'll get it into the airports and train stations. We'll double-check all the rental car places for anyone who's got a black Acura. Actually, we've already been working on that, but there were so many of them. We're still trying to find some of the renters, but we'll double our efforts. There's a lot of work to do. But we *will* find the guy."

Will we? And how the hell can we keep this woman safe? Can't keep her locked up here or inside the White House every second.

The more he thought about it, the more he cared about protecting her. He cared more about her safety than the safety of any others he'd had to protect in Chicago. Other informants, other potential witnesses. No, this time it was different. He realized that when it came to taking care of Samantha Reid, it wasn't just professional. It was getting personal.

THIRTY-FOUR

LATE MONDAY EVENING: GEORGETOWN, WASHINGTON, D.C.

DID I HIT HER? I TRIED TO AIM HIGH. JUST TO scare *the shit out of her. But she went down.*

Otto tried to gulp fresh air from the open window, but the smell of gun powder still hung in the air. He coughed and roughly massaged his ears.

Shaking off the shock of the blast, he shoved the gun into the glove box and slammed the Acura into gear. Otto drove at a moderate speed down K Street, picked up Route 66 near the Kennedy Center, and headed out to Dulles Airport. It was time to switch gears. Immediately.

When his target was inside the White House for work, he toured Washington, learning the complicated parkways, the quickest routes to the airports, and the places he'd hole up in if he had to. He also made lists of hotels and car rental companies.

Vadim had given him three sets of passports and credit cards for his trip. He had used the first set for his airline ticket from San Francisco to Washington and the Acura rental from Hertz.

He used the second set with the name Oleg Alimov when he checked into the Holiday Inn. He was saving the third set for his next car and escape out of town. If it came to that. Right now, he had to ditch the Acura.

As he drove, he tuned the radio to WTOP, which he knew broadcasted news all day long. He wanted to check for reports about a shooting in Georgetown. Nothing yet. It was early. He'd keep checking. He drove just under the speed limit as he navigated the Dulles Access Road and finally took a turn-off to the right at a sign for Rental Car Return.

He swerved into the Hertz lot and parked the car. He reached over and grabbed a baseball cap and a T-shirt. Otto put the cap on, wrapped the shirt around the gun, and tucked the bundle under his arm. Next he removed the reservation form from the glove box, noted the date and mileage, snatched the keys, and popped the trunk. He took out his roller bag filled with a change of clothes, put the gun and shirt in it, and walked into the rental office. He was glad to see several people standing in line. At this time of night, the lone clerk looked harried as she tried to process the travelers as fast as she could.

When he reached the counter, he laid the form and keys on the desk and said, "You need anything else?"

The clerk quickly glanced at the form, took the keys, and shook her head. "Charges will be on your credit card. Hope you enjoyed your stay."

"Yeah. Heading up to New York now. Got a lot to see."

"Have a good trip," she said, turning to the next customer.

He reached for his suitcase, paused by the door, and when the Hertz van drove up, he dashed out and hopped on board. The van wound around the terminal and finally stopped at the entrance to the United Airlines ticketing area. He gave the driver a small tip, heard him mumble, "Thanks," got out, and headed inside.

Making his way down the escalator to the baggage area, he turned and walked out the door again to join the taxi line. He finally got in one marked Washington Flyer, put his bag on the seat next to him, and said, "Reagan National Airport please."

During the taxi ride, he replayed the rental car return in his mind to make sure he hadn't made any mistakes. If the FBI tried to track him down at the airport, he doubted that the Hertz woman would remember him. Even if she did, he had told her he was going to the biggest city he could think of. That should keep them busy for a while. He figured those agents were also checking hotels and knew he would have to check out of the Holiday Inn soon. But he hadn't figured out how to explain the move to Jolene yet.

He sat back in the seat as the taxi driver navigated the parkway going south and finally took the airport turnoff. "Which airline?"

"Drop me off at Delta. Thanks." Otto paid the fare, took the suitcase, and calmly walked inside. This time he went into the men's room, changed into dark jeans and a hoodie, packed his polo shirt and ball cap, shifted the wrapped-up Glock to the bottom of his bag, and then once again walked down to the baggage area.

Back outside, he flagged down a van with Enterprise Rent-A-Car on the side. That afternoon, he had reserved one of their cars online knowing he could always cancel it if the shooting had gone awry. He had even thought to find a nearby hotel to list as his local address. He didn't intend to stay there. It was in Crystal City. Too far from Jolene.

Once inside the Enterprise office, he saw another tired agent dealing with a rather unruly and equally tired family of five. The children kept grumbling that they were hungry while their father argued about getting a van. The clerk kept saying they were all sold out and that he might have better luck at another company. Finally, the father settled for a large sedan, filled out his paperwork, and it was Otto's turn.

He pulled out his new passport and credit card, gave the clerk his reservation number, listed the Crystal City Marriott as his destination, thanked the clerk for the keys, and then walked outside to locate the car. This time it was a tan Nissan Versa. He had seen a lot of them in D.C. and figured it wouldn't attract attention. Plus, it was pretty cheap.

Before he left the parking lot, he programmed the radio to WTOP, another station that played country, and a third that featured hard rock. He needed to keep up with the news, keep Jolene happy, and have a little musical escape for himself from time to time.

Otto already planned to tell Jolene that he had had some engine trouble with the Acura and decided to switch. He drove onto the parkway and headed to Key Bridge, Georgetown, and then the Holiday Inn. He had found a back door to the inn he would use tonight. Otto didn't want Jolene to see him with a suitcase and start asking questions. He needed to get to his room, keep checking the news, and plan what to do next.

THIRTY-FIVE

"THIS IS UNBELIEVABLE," ANGELA SAID, barging into Samantha's office. "I got your text. Somebody is trying to *kill* you, and you're sitting here looking calm. Or are you just *trying* to look calm?"

"I guess I'm just trying to do my job," Samantha said in a weary voice as she stared up at her friend from her desk. "Look, I've got the FBI with me and the Secret Service is all over it too. What else can I do but try to concentrate on other things?"

Angela leaned over the desk and gently put her hand on Samantha's arm. "I know, kiddo. I just worry about how you're going to get through this. I'd be a basket case."

"I'm not so sure about that. I think when something like this happens, we instinctively try to find ways to cope."

"Maybe I can get Dr. Phil on speed dial for you," Angela said with a half-hearted smile, pulling up a chair and sitting on the edge of it.

213

"Thanks for trying to cheer me up. But seriously, when it comes to coping, look at Brett."

"Your FBI guy?"

"Yes. He's amazing. I know he's had a lot of training, but he always manages crises so well."

"But we haven't had his training," Angela said. "We get manuals about White House operations, classified documents, best practices and ethics. And they tell us where to go if there's a terrorist attack. But I haven't seen any memos about what to do if some nutcase is trying to gun us down at home!"

"I know, I know," Samantha said. "Here I am dealing with national security, and I've never seriously thought about my own security. But Brett sure does."

"I thought he and those other agents were *supposed* to be handling your security last night."

"Yes, well. . . it all happened so fast. I went over to the window and next thing I know, the window smashes, and I'm on the floor with Brett on top of me."

"Why wasn't there an agent outside watching the place?"

"Shadowing me was Brett's job. I only have one agent with me at a time. In a way, it's my fault for inviting him in to talk about my Jackson trip. We got to talking about our families, and I was going to show him a picture of my folks. That's when I walked over to the window. You should have seen him right after it happened. He was really undone. He was blaming himself for not closing the drapes."

"Does he usually unravel like that? I thought you said he was good at crisis management," Angela said.

"He is. As soon as the initial shock wore off, he immediately took over the crime scene sweep and gave the other agents their marching orders to find the shooter. He's usually very balanced.

He gets intense, but he also has a pretty good sense of humor. Sometimes, he looks at me for a long time like he's trying to memorize my face or something. But I think all FBI agents are trained to memorize faces."

"Are you kidding? That's not training. That's attraction. Is this guy single?"

"Yes. He was married for a while but his wife left him for some bond salesman."

"Sounds like he's better off," Angela said. She looked at the floor and smiled slightly before looking back at Samantha. "I assume you haven't heard from Tripp in Dallas or wherever he is."

"Nope. I have no idea what he's up to, and I haven't told him about any of this. But I don't really want to talk about him. I only have a few minutes before my next meeting. Can we change the subject and talk about the guy you met at your fitness club?" Samantha asked.

"Oh, we went out for dinner, and he keeps calling. I guess he's okay. He comes from a really small town in Texas. He said their phone book has three pages."

"I'm having a hard time picturing you with a small-town type."

"Me too."

"Well, how about work? Anything new?"

"Let's see," Angela said. "There's a group that's been demanding a meeting with the president ever since their protest at HHS fizzled out."

"Why did it fizzle out?"

"They swarmed through the building, staging a sit-in, and the Secretary didn't want to confront them. So, she just told her security people to lock the bathrooms. They were all gone in about two hours."

"Clever," Samantha said. "I like her style."

"Oh, and we got the weirdest request for a meeting. I kid you not, it's from the South Central Cotton Boll Weevil Eradication Committee," Angela said.

Samantha shook her head. "Still sounds better than my next meeting."

"What's it about?" Angela asked.

"My trip to Jackson. I leave tomorrow, so we're coordinating with Treasury and finalizing the speeches and logistics."

"At least that'll get you out of town and away from that maniac," her friend said.

Samantha sat back in her chair, sighed, and replied, "That's true. But I can't say I'm looking forward to it. In fact, to quote my dad, 'I can't think of anything I'd less rather do'."

Angela chuckled. "I hear you. But look on the bright side. You'll get to network with finance ministers and relax a little bit between meetings."

"I guess," Samantha said. "At least I'll feel safe out there. Treasury's got several security people coming along, so worrying about another attack is the one thing I can put out of my mind for now."

THIRTY-SIX

"RIGHT THIS WAY, GENTLEMEN," THE PILOT
said, leading the four men out of Signature Aviation, the fixed-
base operation for private aircraft at San Francisco Airport. They
walked through the glass doors of the waiting room to the tarmac where a sleek Citation X was waiting, fueled and ready to
go. "Weather looks good. We should make it to Idaho Falls in
about an hour and a half. We'll keep you posted."

The group watched the other pilot supervise the loading of
their luggage into the baggage compartment at the back of the
plane. Then they scrambled up the few steps to the cabin to
inspect the long, narrow passenger area with gleaming wood
cabinets, beige carpeting, and seating for eight.

"Here are today's newspapers—*Wall Street Journal, New
York Times, USA Today*," the pilot said, pointing to a stack on
top of a bar. "Coffee is in here, liquor and wine in this section,
ice in the compartment below, snacks are in there, and your
catering is in the right-hand drawer. If you need anything, please

let us know. We'll get underway in a few minutes. Make yourselves comfortable."

There were four plush leather seats facing each other in front
and two more on each side of the aisle behind them. A long bench
with seating for two stretched into the back where the restroom
was. Vadim took the seat on the right, which faced forward and
contained the main controls for heating and push buttons for the
lights, music volume, and window screen adjustments. Maksim
sat in the left-hand seat facing forward.

"Where do want us?" Stas asked.

"Why don't you sit back there for takeoff? When we have
lunch, you can move up, and we'll continue our conversation,"
Vadim said. He glanced toward the pilots who were running
through their checklists with the door open. "*Maybe* we'll continue our conversation."

They stowed their briefcases and jackets behind the seats,
grabbed newspapers, and sat down to fasten their seat belts. The
pilot came back and briefed them on the escape routes. They
feigned attention, and he finally returned to the cockpit. They got
their clearance from the tower and took off, heading northeast.

"Sure as hell beats flying commercial," Lubov said, reaching
for the sports section of *USA Today*. "When we flew out to
Jackson last week, we had to wait in all those stupid lines. Then
we had to change planes. But now we have a nonstop, and there's
no security check at all."

"That's why we chartered this one," Vadim said over his
shoulder. "Besides, if there's a storm, we just tell the pilots to go
around it. I always say, I'd rather be late than absent," he laughed.
"We're in charge on these flights." He turned back and said to
Maksim, "Have you read that last email from Otto?"

Maksim rubbed his chin and thought for a moment. "Yes, but it wasn't clear to me. He says he *believes* he has completed his assignment. *Believes*? What the hell does that mean?"

"Exactly," Vadim said. "I haven't seen anything in the news, though they might be trying to keep it quiet for a while. Governments do that a lot."

"At least the ones we're most familiar with," Maksim said. "Let's just hope he's finished it."

"Yeah. And if that's the case, I can only assume he's smart enough to move around. He mentioned switching cars, so that shows the kid is thinking."

"I'm sure he learned a lot in Naples," Maksim said. "But we'll see how well he stays out of sight. Did he say when he's coming back?"

"No, that's the strange thing," Vadim said, narrowing his eyes. "When he asked to stay longer, I got the impression that Washington was starting to grow on him."

"That does seem odd. He doesn't know anybody there. Of course, there are several colleges in D.C. Maybe he's met some students or graduates his age."

"He better not," Vadim said, slightly raising his voice. "He's there to do a job. And if anyone finds out—"

"Relax. Nobody is going to find out. One thing that kid is good at is disappearing."

The plane climbed through the clouds and leveled off. After perusing the papers for a while, Vadim turned to Lubov and Stas. "Come up here. We'll have lunch."

"Where is it?" Stas asked.

"It's up front in a drawer on the right. You can get it," Vadim said.

Stas frowned at Vadim. He didn't like being ordered around, but he walked up and retrieved four boxed lunches. Vadim and Maksim pulled up the tables from a casing under the window and unfolded them between the seats. Stas distributed the food, complete with silverware and napkins sporting the airline logo. There were rare roast beef sandwiches on sourdough bread along with pasta salads, fruit, condiments, and cookies.

"Damn, better than what you'd get on a commercial flight," Lubov said, uncovering his box and digging in.

"We could have ordered shrimp cocktails or Caesar salads or many other things," Maksim said. "But since this is a short flight, we thought we'd keep it simple. When we get to Jackson and settle in, we'll look for a good dinner restaurant."

"We found a bunch of those," Stas said. "The Four Seasons is right up the road in Teton Village, but maybe we don't want to be seen there too much."

"Probably not. Their staff might remember us," Maksim said. "What else?"

"There's a nice place just outside the downtown part of Jackson called Rendezvous Bistro," Stas said.

"Then going into town," Lubov said, "you've got the Gun Barrel Steak House. And on the town square there's the Snake River Grill and the Million Dollar Cowboy Bar where they've got pool tables, a great bar upstairs, and a restaurant downstairs."

"Since we'll be there a couple of days, we should check out more than one," Maksim said. "We need to be careful, though, and not be seen together too much. Might even order room service once in a while."

"Sounds reasonable," Lubov said.

Turning to Stas, Vadim said, "The pilot showed us where the liquor cabinet is. Get us some vodka to go with this."

Once again, Stas gave Vadim a mean look, but he decided that a shot of vodka was a pretty good idea. He squeezed out from behind the table and brought back four small bottles and a handful of glasses filled with ice.

Vadim glanced at the cockpit and noticed that the pilots had kept the door open. He said in a low voice, "There's engine noise, but I think we better wait until we get to town to talk more about this trip."

"Good idea," Maksim said.

"One thing I thought I would mention, though," Lubov said. "We talked to our mutual friend, that banker, Alexander Tepanov. I told him to short our accounts. Remember I said we might do that too?" Vadim nodded as he chewed his sandwich. Lubov continued, "Since he's got all the right contacts, he told us he would buy leveraged exchange traded funds for three times the down side. He gave us the ticker symbol SDS so we can track them and watch our fortunes skyrocket when the markets tank."

"What about that twenty percent for insurance we always talk about?" Maksim asked.

"Nah," Lubov said. "We only kept about ten percent this time because we *know* this is going to work."

The Fasten Seat Belts sign came on. Stas gathered up the boxes, used napkins, and other detritus from their lunch and put everything back in the drawer. The he returned to his seat to buckle up. The plane descended, made a smooth landing, and taxied to Aero Mark, the Idaho Falls FBO. Before they filed out, Vadim went to the cabinet, grabbed several small bottles of vodka, and shoved them in his pockets.

Maksim thanked the pilots. He and Vadim retrieved their luggage and piled into one of the waiting rental cars. Lubov leaned into the driver's window and said, "You guys follow us.

We figured out the route over the pass when we were here before. It'll take about an hour or so." Then he hurried to his own car and led the way out to the main road.

They drove past a couple of small towns, empty fields stretching for miles, and several ranches where herds of cattle meandered through the grass or slept under sparse trees. When they reached the pass, they saw towering mountains where ski runs on the Idaho side cut swaths through groves of pine trees stretching up to the summits.

"Incredible scenery," Maksim said as Vadim followed Stas's car.

"Yeah. San Francisco has hills, but nothing like this. They say it's even better on the Wyoming side."

"Almost makes me want to learn how to ski," Maksim said.

"You can think about going to the Alps or someplace like that next winter. Right now, we've got to concentrate," Vadim said. "Once we're done here and get back over this pass—" he paused and looked out the window at the sheer drop-offs—"*if* we get over this damn pass again, we'll fly back to San Francisco, wait for the news to filter around the world, and start raking in our profits."

"When do you think we should go back to Moscow?" Maksim asked.

"Not for a while. The FBI will be watching all the airports. They won't be able to tie us to anything, of course, but they might decide to watch everyone with a foreign passport. So, we'll hole up in the penthouse where we know we're safe and then think about how we're going to get out later."

"Sounds good to me," Maksim said.

Once over the summit, the winding road descended at a ten-degree angle into the town of Wilson, Wyoming. They drove past a gas station, what looked like a rustic café, a post office, and a general store and saw a big sign advertising the upcoming Annual Firemen's Fried Chicken Picnic.

"Now *that* could be useful," Vadim said, pointing to the sign. "If all the law enforcement guys are at some stupid picnic, it means less people will be watching what Lubov and Stas are doing."

"That would be good," Maksim said. They kept following Lubov's car and turned left onto Teton Village Road. "Jeez, we're surrounded by mountains," he said, gazing out the passenger window. "Big buttes over there, and look at those peaks to the left. There's snow at the top even though it's summer. Reminds me of Russia. I wonder how cold it gets here."

"I don't know, and I don't care," Vadim said. "I just want to get to our hotel, check in, and look around a bit. I want to make sure Stas and Lubov know what they're doing."

"They said they did. Remember, they've got a PO box. Maybe it's at that little place we passed on the way in."

"Probably. They assured us they were having the C-4 and triggers shipped over. In several different boxes, of course."

"Exactly. So, why worry? Their organization knows how to handle shipments. That's what we're paying them for," Maksim said.

When they approached the village, they saw a golf course on the left and a series of two- and three-story dark wood houses built close together. "Guess a lot of people have ski chalets here," Maksim said. "What's that?" He pointed toward the mountain where a huge red and black tram car the size of a small bus was inching up the side on a series of wires.

"Lubov told us they had a new cable car that holds a hundred people," Vadim said. "It's not just for skiers. In the summer, people take it up to the restaurant and look at the view. That must be the target."

"Over there, I see the entrance to the village. I'll call his cell." Maksim punched in Lubov's number. "Do we both go in the same way?"

"Yes, but you'll go off to the right," Lubov replied. "We'll drive around to the left. Our hotel is in the back. You'll see yours as you go in. Look for a building with a steep roof."

"Okay, I think I see it. We'll get organized and check in later about dinner."

Vadim drove into the village where they saw hotels, restaurants, and a gaggle of tourists. Hikers with backpacks and teenagers in T-shirts, shorts, and sandals milled around while what looked like a tribe of Indians sold jewelry and pottery in the valley area. Gangs of little children were playing tag in front of the display tables.

"Hope they don't have noisy kids staying at our hotel," Vadim said.

"At those prices, probably not," Maksim said. He pointed to the right "There it is. Next door to something called Alpenhof Lodge. I like the sound of ours better: Snake River Lodge and Spa."

They gave the rental car to the valet, grabbed their luggage, and checked in, each one using a fake passport with a credit card to match. "Your rooms will be ready in a few minutes," the clerk said with a smile. "If you'd like to leave your luggage over there, you can visit our lovely pool and spa area. It's just down the hall."

"Let's go," Maksim said. Vadim shrugged and nodded. They strolled along the corridor and were surprised to discover a free-form pool, half inside and half outside, with a large rock formation rising out of its center. A stone terrace was filled with lounge chairs where several young women were sunning themselves in the eighty degree weather. "I thought this place was at a high elevation. I had no idea it would get this warm," Maksim said.

"Doesn't bother me when it includes things like this," Vadim said. "See that brunette over there?" He pointed to an attractive, young woman in a bikini, sipping a drink.

"What about her?"

"Looks like that Reid woman," Vadim said, narrowing his gaze. "We need to get up to the room and call Otto. I want to know the whole story."

"Right," Maksim said as they walked back to the reception area. "But remember, if for some reason Otto didn't complete his job, her name *is* on the conference schedule. All we need to do is make sure Lubov and Stas know precisely where she'll be. And when."

THIRTY-SEVEN

"SO, WHERE ARE WE?" TREVOR MASON shouted toward Brett's office cubicle. He poked his head around the corner, looked at Brett, and said, "If the Naples bomber and the Georgetown shooter really *are* one and the same, what kind of progress are you and your team making on this?" he demanded, his face grim. "I'm getting pressure from headquarters, the White House, everywhere. And unless you've got some rabbit in a hat I don't know about, looks like you're still nowhere."

Brett looked up from his computer and motioned to the stacks of papers and files on his desk. "I told you in the last staff meeting that we're coordinating with every jurisdiction in town, checking airports, rental agencies, hotels, databases. You name it, we're into it."

"I can't believe that some twenty-something has evaded the notice of an entire FBI investigative team," Trevor said, shaking his head.

"If we ever find him, maybe we should ask him to work for us," Brett muttered.

"Get serious. This isn't some rerun of *White Collar* for god's sake. There's an insane bomber-assassin who's possibly still in town, and you talk about recruiting him. What are you smoking these days?"

"Just venting, Trevor," Brett said with a sigh. "Look, I'm as frustrated as you are. If it's the same guy, he's been moving around. But we've got Samantha Reid under constant surveillance."

"And how much is that costing us in agent overtime?" Trevor demanded.

"Actually, she's heading out west later today to speak at some conference. She'll be with the Treasury Secretary and his security, so we've cut the protective team for a few days and redeployed them to the search efforts at hotels."

"Thank god for small favors," Trevor said. "What's the latest from your real estate contacts? Any new properties changing hands?"

"That new agent, Eleanor, who tipped us to the Russian deal, has been pretty helpful," Brett said. "Almost too helpful," he said under his breath.

"What about other things *you're* supposed to be handling?" Trevor said.

"My team is on several of them. The Israelis are exercised about a possible ISIS cell inside the United States that could target synagogues. And we've all reviewed the additional warnings about home-grown terrorists who might target Disney or other vacation venues. But you know about that," Brett said.

"We elevated both of those," Trevor said. "Anything else hot right now?"

"The team picked up some chatter from the Nigerian Embassy about chemical weapons," Brett said.

"Nigeria? I thought they were focused on oil wells and stealing credit cards, just like the East European crowd."

"Yes, but we've alerted the CIA and others. I'll make sure you get the details by close of business," Brett said, anxious to end this interrogation and get back to his computer.

The boss nodded and finally turned to leave. "Keep on the bomber. We've *got* to nail that bastard."

Brett swung his chair around and read another classified report with no new leads. He pushed back from his desk and headed to the coffee room. He saw Dom pouring what was probably his third cup of the morning. "Is that stuff fresh or the usual rot gut variety?" Brett said.

"Just made this, so it'll be okay for a little while," Dom said. "How's it going?"

"The usual BIAT."

Dom laughed. "You mean Boss In A Twit?"

"Yep," Brett said, reaching for the fresh pot. "He's bitching about the bomber investigation which, as you know, is *our* investigation. Florida's got nothing. And even after that hit-and-run and the shooting, *we've* got nothing."

"I know. I've seen all the reports, the cross-checking, matching the drawing, the bullet, the databases. It's endless," Dom said.

Brett nodded. "The more technology we get, the more complicated and time-consuming it gets. And Congress isn't helping."

"When was the last time they did?"

"I know. They look schizophrenic to me. Right after 9/11, they were all over us, the CIA, everybody for not connecting the goddamn dots and not *sharing* enough information when it was that Attorney General who put out the ruling separating our intel from the CIA. Remember she said CIA had to operate just overseas, and we have to work here. Well, you know about that box they put us in. So, then they create incredible bureaucracies and layers that do what? Force us to file more reports so that we *share* our info.

"Then they make everybody upgrade all the computer systems," Brett continued, "so that it takes a shitload of contractors to deal with them. Then all the hackers—the Chinese, the Iranians, Saudis, Russians, Israelis, French, and lord knows who else—try to steal technology, disrupt systems, plant viruses. So, we have to build bigger and better firewalls, which means hiring even more contractors. Then the whole Snowden thing hits, and we have to cut back again while foreigners gear up. You probably saw that report about how cyber spying against us is up 700 percent in the last couple of years?"

"Yep. And that's not gonna stop," Dom said, staring at Brett with a slight smile.

"Well, Congress is demanding more court orders for the surveillance while the intelligence committees demand more briefings, the president demands more action to find terrorists, and the ACLU files lawsuits over just how much data we can collect while we're trying to find them."

Dom leaned against the counter with a bemused look. "Are you ranting or raving?"

"Definitely not raving," Brett said, blowing on his coffee to cool it. "Just letting off some steam."

"Hey, I hear you. If we had a name or an actual photo of that bomber, we could do a lot more."

"Like get an Interpol Red Notice so he would be stopped if he tried to fly out of this or any other country," Brett said.

"So, is that *all* the boss was yelling about today? The kid we can't find?" Dom asked.

"No," Brett said. "He wants constant updates on our embassy listening programs. I know that's a routine exercise around here, but ever since he added it to my, well, *our* team's basket of tricks, he asks about what we're hearing almost every day."

"What are we hearing? Anything we should be *sharing*?" Dom asked with a grin. "And what about that realtor? Seems like you've turned her into a pretty good CHS."

"She's given us some good intel lately, but she keeps asking me to dinner. Even to the Kennedy Center. Can you believe that?"

"Sure," Dom said. "You said she's single. You're single. Sounds like she's got you right in her crosshairs."

"Not a chance," Brett said emphatically. "She's useful to the bureau, but I don't need to get any closer to her. Besides, she's skinny and severe."

"What do you mean, 'severe'?"

Brett thought for a moment. "How do I explain it? She's kind of edgy. Exhausting really. Even the way she dresses. Always just black and white. She looks like an anorexic Dalmatian." Dom burst out laughing. "Actually," Brett said, "I was thinking of shifting her contact info into your inbox."

"Forget it. I've got enough to worry about. Now, back to the embassies. What about the Russians?" Dom asked.

"Last I heard they were talking about someone from the Russian Embassy getting permission from State to go beyond their twenty-five mile travel limit." Brett checked his watch, refilled his coffee mug, and started for the door. "Come to think of it, I should check with Nori to see if she's got anything new from last night. See you later."

Brett walked down the hall to Nori's office and knocked on the door. He looked forward to his conversations with this agent. She was smart, concise, and didn't waste anybody's time. "Hey,

Nori. Just taking a break and thought I'd check in with you. Anything new from our Russian friends? Any more conference calls with Moscow?"

Nori looked up and adjusted her glasses. "Glad you stopped by. I just finished translating some notes, and I was about to come find you." She glanced down at her computer. "Remember when they were talking about conferences and a Russian banker named Alexander Tepanov?"

"Sure," Brett said, walking to her desk and taking another sip of his coffee.

"Well, Tepanov is going to a conference. And since an official from the Russian Embassy got the okay from State for a travel waiver, it sounds like they are going to the same meeting. And both have talked about security."

"Sounds pretty standard. I can check with State, but did you hear them mention the name of the conference?"

"They talked about *finansists* in *Dahakson.*"

"What does that mean?"

"I'm sure it means the financiers going to the Federal Reserve conference in Jackson, Wyoming," Nori said with a confident wave toward her computer.

"That's where Samantha Reid is going, along with a lot of people from Treasury and just about every other central banker and finance minister from every important country. It doesn't seem strange that Russians would be going too. Everyone else is," Brett said.

"Maybe so. But here's where we need to take action."

"*We* need to take action? Treasury has its own security people."

"I know, I know," she said. "But I also heard conversation fragments about Tepanov and rumors he's heard. Things that could affect the international markets. I don't know what he means, but I wonder if somebody is planning to disrupt the conference in some way that could spook the markets."

Brett stared at her. "Affect the markets?" His eyes darted to the floor and then back to Nori. "Can you print out your notes right now and email them to me as well?"

"Of course," Nori said, quickly hitting a few keys and then reaching over to retrieve the pages from her printer. "Here you go."

Brett grabbed her report. "Thanks. Good work." He turned and raced down the hall.

He barged into Trevor's office. The boss was on the phone. He gave Brett an irritated look and held up his hand for silence. Brett waved the report in front of Trevor's desk and pointed to his watch.

"Looks like something's come up. I'll have to get back to you," Trevor said into the receiver and quickly hung up. "What's so damned important that you have to interrupt me?"

Brett thrust Nori's notes into his boss's hand and said, "Something's up in Jackson. The Fed conference. That's where Samantha Reid and the Treasury Secretary are going. Later today. I want to head out there. Now."

"Hold your damn horses," Trevor said, glancing at the notes. "If she's right, and there's something off, first we alert Treasury, and then I call our Denver office. They have jurisdiction out there. Their agents will cover the conference and coordinate with the other security teams. There will be a lot of big names involved, so it'll be a big job. But it's not *your* job."

"Dammit it, Trevor. Samantha Reid *is* my job. You just said so. There have been several attempts on her life. And there's been a lot of publicity about this conference and how she's been invited to give a speech. Who's to say she wouldn't be a special target, especially if someone's planning something? In fact, I want to see if I can persuade her *not* to go."

"Oh, so now you're the scheduling director for senior White House officials?" Trevor said in a gruff voice.

"No, I'm not. But I do feel responsible for *protecting* her," Brett said. "I—*we* have been doing that all along."

"Well, Denver can take over. At least while she's in *their* territory."

"Okay, so Denver takes over. I want to be there too."

Trevor eyed Brett and cocked his head to the side. "Are you sure you're not being *too* protective of this particular person? This particular *female* person?"

Brett didn't answer the question. "I've been on this case from the get-go, and I'm not about to give up now. I've been tracking this Otto guy. I've memorized his features, researched our data-bases, and I *know* Samantha Reid, her habits, her traits, her fears."

"What fears? Besides being the target of an assassin, that is," Trevor said.

Brett hesitated. He didn't want to divulge too many personal observations to his boss, like Samantha's fear of heights. Better to keep it professional. "That's what I mean. You'd be anxious too if you were afraid some crazed gunman was going to run you down or try and take another shot at you every time you left your office."

"I understand that," Trevor muttered. "But you've got too much going on here in D.C. There's absolutely no evidence, no reason to believe that some kid is going to follow Samantha Reid all the way out to a Federal Reserve conference, or that some banker in Moscow is tied in to anything that would threaten her. You need to stay right here where that waiter was last seen. Denver will handle any possible threat at that conference."

Brett stared at his boss. What now? His gut kept telling him something was wrong. Very wrong. Even though he knew the Denver agents and other security teams would be out there to protect all the other delegates, he still wanted to get special protection for Samantha.

I've got to call her and talk her into cancelling this trip.

He turned and walked back to his office to contact her. He knew it would be a tough sell. She'd say that the program was set, her schedule was set, and her boss was set. Set on her going out there to sweet-talk all those delegates into cooperating with her money-laundering investigations. Besides, she probably would feel safer out of town than in D.C. where that shooter could still be at large.

As he dialed the number, he felt apprehensive, even helpless. He couldn't remember the last time those kinds of emotions had churned inside him. He reached for his coffee. Cold now. He drank some anyway and held his breath until the call was answered.

THIRTY-EIGHT

"IT'D BE NICE IF THEY'D LET US FLY FIRST class once in a while," Homer said, shoving his carry-on into an overhead bin. "At least our seats are somewhat close to the front. Here, let me help you with that," he said, hoisting Samantha's black bag up in one quick move.

"Thanks," she said. "Let's just hope that nobody has the middle seat on this flight. It'll be a good opportunity to go over our notes for the Secretary. At least *he*'s in first class."

"That's because Treasury security says so. They've got two guys up there with him. Guess they don't care what happens to us back here in steerage. But they should. Especially with that last FBI warning you mentioned on the way over," Homer said. "What do you make of it?"

"I'm not sure. I got that call from a friend, I mean, from the FBI. He's one of the agents on my protective detail. As I said, they picked up a possible threat tied to the conference, and he told me not to go. I tried to explain that I couldn't just back out because

237

of some rumor. When I told him I had to do this, he finally con-
ceded that their Denver bureau would be in Jackson and they
would check everything out. So we should be okay."

She looked around as the cabin filled up with teenagers haul-
ing backpacks, young mothers carrying babies, and a few elderly
people hobbling down the aisle with canes at their side. "I guess
it doesn't really matter to me which class I fly. However, it would
be nice to see something on the menu other than peanuts and
pretzels. Thanks for getting some sandwiches to bring onboard."
She glanced at her watch. "Too bad there aren't any nonstop
flights from D.C. to Jackson Hole. At least the layover in Salt
Lake isn't too long."

"With the time difference, we'll land in Jackson with plenty
of time to drive to the lodge and get a good dinner. Plus, a lot of
the other delegates will probably be there already. Maybe we can
meet some. I was looking at the list and noticed there's a new
central banker from Russia coming. Alexander Tepanov. Ever
heard of him?"

"Brett, my FBI contact, mentioned his name once," she said,
shoving her purse under the seat and fastening her seat belt. "Do
you know anything about him?"

"Not too much. But since certain Russian banks are on our
target list, I did a quick background check. Didn't find out a lot
because before he got this appointment, he was in the SVR. Evidently handled some money issues there. I peg him as some kind
of well-connected accountant."

"Aha, their foreign intelligence service. Formerly KGB," she
said, raising her eyebrows. "Interesting that they'd take someone
out of there and put him in the bank."

"Not too amazing when you consider how Putin promotes
his buddies to everything from state-owned mining companies

to the highest government positions. Tepenov and Putin came out of the same outfit. We always see that the closer they are to the president, the higher level their job is. And competence doesn't seem to factor into the equation. Since this is a pretty recent move for the guy, he was never high profile enough to make the sanctions lists. We have no idea how much influence he might have now, but who knows? With all the tension between us and them, he may want to curry some favor as insurance against any future sanctions. So, if you play your cards right, we might get him to cooperate with us on tracking a few accounts."

"Maybe you're right," she said. "We'll try to get to know him if we can. We could use a little cooperation over there. I'm afraid they've got a lot of secret accounts that we'll never be able to penetrate, especially when it comes to arms dealers."

"While they're dealing, we keep digging," he said.

Samantha started to read a copy of the *Wall Street Journal* she had packed into her purse. She pointed to a column in the Business/Technology section. "Here's another story about how several virtual currencies are moving more billions all over the world, especially in Estonia and Asia. They're even using it for dowries in Africa. I'm sure money launderers are using it."

"That's kind of a tough one for us. Anyone with a cryptocurrency account can be anonymous. And with a lot of legitimate businesses accepting them for payment now, that leaves us in a bit of a quandary."

"I see what you mean. Maybe you can put some sort of controls on them. Ask for more transparency or something," she suggested.

"It's not that easy. No one knows exactly who started it by creating those complicated algorithms."

The captain announced they were ready for takeoff. Samantha was glad that the middle seat remained empty. She never wanted to look down from a window seat, which is why she had requested one on the aisle. While her fear of heights caused her problems in many areas of life, she never had to worry about it on airplanes as long as she didn't look out a window.

Riding up the side of a mountain in a big tram was a different story. She knew she'd have to face that reality when she gave her luncheon speech, but she didn't want to think about that right now. Instead, she settled back in her seat, picked up her copy of the *Journal* again, and read the editorial page.

The cabin attendant came through with a cart and asked if they wanted a beverage. Homer requested a Diet Coke while Samantha settled for a bottle of water. They enjoyed their sandwiches, chatted about Samantha's speech, and discussed the notes they had both submitted to Secretary Pickering.

They flew west against a strong headwind and then changed planes. Finally, they prepared to land in Jackson Hole, the only airport located in a national park. "Take a look at those mountains," Homer said, pointing out the window at the Grand Teton.

"If you don't mind, I'd rather not look," Samantha said.

"Oh right. Sorry. Hopefully, we'll be on the ground soon. Do you know how far away the hotel is?"

"Yes. The Jackson Lake Lodge is a bit of a drive from the airport. We have to go a long way through the park. Then it all depends on how many moose breaks there are."

"Moose breaks?" Homer asked.

"My assistant gave me a whole list of things that happen out there. Whenever there are moose around, the tourists stop their cars, get out, and take pictures. It can tie up traffic for a while. That's why the locals call them 'moose breaks'."

He rolled his eyes. "What else do I need to know?"

"Let's see," she said. "You have to stop at a checkpoint where a ranger charges everyone a fee to drive through the park. Well, except for the senior citizens who have lifetime passes."

Homer chuckled. "Why would anyone need a lifetime pass? How many times would you want to go there anyway?"

"Well, it's how you drive to Yellowstone. There aren't many other roads out of Jackson. Three really. Anyway, I don't think we'll have time to hit Yellowstone with our schedule. We're not here to sightsee."

"I know. I got my orders from the secretary: meet the delegates, drum up support for our initiatives, help you in any way I can—including security. I'll stay on my toes, especially now that the FBI has tipped us off to a possible threat," he said.

"Thank you. I'm sure the Treasury people can handle whatever it is, so let's not worry about it," she said.

Homer looked at her across the middle seat and said, "I don't know how you do that."

"Do what?"

"Compartmentalize everything."

"What do you mean?"

"Well, a guy took a shot at you at your apartment, you have FBI protection, and now there's talk about something else going on out here. And you just sit there, calm and collected. How do you do that?"

Samantha sighed and finally answered, "What other choice do I have?"

THIRTY-NINE

"OLEG, WHAT HAVE YOU DONE?" JOLENE WAS practically weeping into the phone.

"What do you mean, what have I done?" Otto asked, clutching his cell.

"An FBI agent was just here. He showed me a drawing of someone they're looking for, and it looked just like you. They had a different name. Otto. But that's so close to Oleg! Is it really you they're after?" she asked, sounding desperate.

Oh no. They must be checking every hotel in Washington.

He took a deep breath and asked, "What did you tell them?"

"I told them I didn't know anybody like that," she said. "But tell me the truth. Are they looking for you?"

What can I tell her? I need her help, but I don't want her to get in trouble too.

Otto finally said, "Look, there's something going on, and I need to talk to you."

243

"Something *is* going on?" she echoed. "What is it? You're scaring me."

"I don't mean to scare you. I just need to *talk* to you. There are some things I want to explain. Really. When can I see you?"

She hesitated. "Oleg, listen to me. Every time we've been together, you've evaded my questions and never told me why you're really here. And now it looks like you're caught up in something bad. You may have been nice to me, but I'm not about to see you now. Maybe not ever. So, I am going to ask you again, what have you done?"

"Look, Jolene, I'll explain everything when I can tell you in person."

"No. Tell me now. If the FBI comes back, I swear I'll tell them I've thought about that drawing and how similar it looks to someone I know."

"No!" he shouted into the phone. "Stop. Remember I told you I was working for my uncles?" When she didn't respond, he went on. "I don't know about all of their businesses, but I'm pretty sure they're involved in something bad."

"So, you're saying it's your uncles the FBI really wants, not you?" she pressed.

"Well, sort of," he said. "It's complicated, okay?" He glanced at his watch and added, "I'm leaving. Obviously, I can't stay here any longer."

"I still don't like it. Maybe your uncles are bad, but it sounds like you're involved with them. And that means I can't be involved with you. My shift is over now. I'm leaving too."

"Wait, wait," he said. "I'll work it out, and then I'll call you and explain everything. You're the only friend I have here."

There was a long pause. Jolene finally sighed and said, "Oleg, I thought you were smart. Whatever is going on definitely isn't smart, and I want no part of it."

"If I can work it out, can't I call and fill you in?"

"I don't know." She clicked off.

Otto frantically started packing. He had to get out of the hotel and find someplace else to hide. The agents might come back and talk to other employees, maybe one of the maids or somebody in the restaurant downstairs. Any of those people might figure out that *he* was the guy in the drawing.

He yanked open the bureau drawers and piled his jeans, pants, shirts, and socks into his suitcase on top of the Glock that was still wrapped in a T-shirt. He grabbed his slacks off hangers, folded them haphazardly, and shoved them in. He grabbed his extra pair of running shoes, pushed them into the suitcase, and then went into the bathroom to gather up his razor, toothbrush, toothpaste, and some extra soap and shampoo the maid had left.

He quickly checked a couple of news sites on his iPhone. Nothing about Samantha Reid. Except for one article about a speech she was giving out west, there hadn't been any news about her since that night he took a shot at her. Maybe he had missed her. But they could be hiding her real condition if she had been hit. He had no idea. But at this point, he didn't care.

He only cared about getting away and Jolene.

Not long after they moved her into her new apartment, they spent the night together. She had been spectacular in bed, and he had never known any girl like her. She was fresh, nice, and turned out to be a pretty good cook. Kind of like his mother.

Now he would lose her. He couldn't blame her for being scared. Who wouldn't be? Their little affair had happened so fast, she was probably berating herself and thinking he was some kind of demon. Was he?

Yes.

Yes, he had agreed to plant that bomb in Naples.

He remembered what they had told him before they sent him there. Vadim had said that the C-4 would cause some damage and might take out the White House woman, someone he said was their real enemy. Otto knew how enemies of the oligarchs were treated in Moscow. They were simply eliminated, and nobody raised much of a fuss except for a few reporters.

Even though Vadim insisted that Samantha Reid was in a position to ruin their businesses, Otto was incredibly relieved when no one was hurt in Naples. He never wanted to become a murderer.

He dashed to the desk, turned off his computer, and unplugged the charger. As he put both items into his suitcase, he wondered how his mom was doing out on the farm. He knew she would be shocked if she learned everything he had done.

He checked his wallet. He still had some cash as well as the credit cards. He glanced around the room to see if he had forgotten anything, flipped off the lights, and hustled to the elevator. In the lobby he saw that Jolene had left the desk and been replaced by other staff. He pulled down his hoodie, walked over, put his room key card on the counter, and said, "Checking out."

"Certainly, sir," the clerk said. "Would you like your receipt?"

"I guess so. Just put it all on the credit card."

"Of course, sir." The woman hit a few computer keys, reached for the printer, handed him the receipt, and said, "Hope you enjoyed your stay. Come back and see us again."

"Don't think I can. I'm flying to Chicago," Otto said, hoping that would send any other inquiring agent in a different direction.

"Safe travels," she said and then turned to answer a ringing phone.

Otto quickly walked out the door, dragged his luggage to the rental car, shoved the bag into the trunk, drove onto Wisconsin

Avenue, and turned left. He steered down to M Street, turned right, and then took a left to cross Key Bridge. As he drove, he glanced back toward the Whitehurst Freeway. That's where the Reid woman lived. Otto swore never to drive by there again.

He accelerated and headed south on 395. Where was he going? He had absolutely no clue.

FORTY

BRETT WAS WORKING LATE. SAMANTHA WAS in Jackson, so he didn't have the evening protective detail, though he wished he did. He was still upset about their last conversation. He had practically begged her to cancel the trip. Didn't she realize that there could be real danger at this conference? What was more important? Giving a speech to a bunch of economists or protecting her life? He pondered that thought as he scrolled through reports and recent searches on his computer.

By now, most of the agents had gone home to their families. Just the overnight crew and one or two other specialists were still working. Maybe they didn't have families to go home to. Brett didn't have anyone except his mother back in Indiana. When was the last time he had called her? He pushed that thought to the back of his mind with a mental reminder to contact her over the weekend.

Even though he had many other files to work on, he wanted to examine the search for the shooter again. How many times had he gone through the data? Had he missed something? Was

249

the guy still in the city? He couldn't believe they still hadn't found this kid.

The suspect had set off an explosion in a hotel and made two attempts on Samantha Reid's life. But every time Brett tried to analyze the kid's actions, he couldn't figure out a motive. And every time Brett repeated that process, he almost seized up with a personal fear for Samantha's safety. Now that Samantha was in Jackson, Brett should have felt relieved. With all the Treasury security and the Denver agents in town, he should feel better. But he didn't.

He grabbed a sheaf of Nori's translations and reviewed them again. Russians going to the conference. Russians talking about security and rumors of a problem with the markets.

Brett checked his watch: 9:00 p.m. A lot of his work days seemed to extend to 9:00 p.m. or later. He thought about taking a break and going out for coffee and a sandwich down the street, but he wasn't really hungry. In fact, his gut was telling him to get the hell out of his office and out to Wyoming.

During his FBI training, he had been told to pay attention to details. And when those details added up to too many questions, a perverse reaction to a suspect, a plot, or a target, you took action. And that's precisely what he wanted to do. The only roadblock was Trevor.

He had to get a hold of his boss, convince him to change his mind, and then see if there was a plane on standby at Dulles. He'd also have to talk to the Denver agents. He looked at his watch again.

They're two hours behind. I'll ask them to double-check the tram and the restaurant and everything else on that goddamn mountain tonight. But I want to get out there to double-check everything myself.

Brett picked up his phone and dialed Trevor at home.

"Trevor Mason here," said a gruff voice.

"Trevor, it's Brett."

"This better be good. Did you find the kid?"

"No, not yet. But I need your help," Brett said.

"You need *my* help? Well, that's a first," his boss said. "What is it?"

"I've been going over Nori's Russian translations about the Jackson conference and their concerns about security and rumors. And damn it, Trevor, I have to get out there myself. Before you say anything, just let me say that it's a hunch. But with all those officials out there, they need all the help they can get. And I need to be on the ground, working with Denver, with Treasury, with everyone."

Trevor heaved a long sigh. "You really are a persistent son-of-a-bitch, aren't you?" He paused and then said, "Well, I have to admit you came to us with an excellent record, and I know you've been working your ass off on all these issues." He stopped again for a long moment. "What the hell. If I don't okay the travel, I'll probably never hear the end of it. Get your gear together, and I'll call in the order to transportation at Dulles. Keep me posted on everything. I want a tick-tock on this entire trip. Is that clear?"

"Absolutely clear, sir. Thank you."

Now he needed to confirm that he could get a flight on one of the FBI's private jets. He waited a few minutes to give his boss time to make the first call. When he finally got through and explained his mission, the dispatcher said they had just heard from Trevor Mason. The only plane that would be available was due to land at 7:00 a.m., and they couldn't be certain it would be on time. They would also need an hour to refuel and get a new crew in place.

Brett had no choice but to say he would be at Dulles and ready for takeoff at 8:00 a.m. With the time difference, the three and a half hour flight would get him to Jackson at ten o'clock in the morning local time, if they didn't hit strong headwinds. It would be close to the time of Samantha's luncheon speech. Way too close. But he had no choice.

Just to be sure, he checked the schedule for commercial flights. There was nothing that would get him there any faster.

Since he couldn't leave D.C. until tomorrow, all he could do was gather up his things, head home to try to get some sleep, and then drive to the airport in the morning. But first, he had to talk to the Denver agents.

Brett called their bureau and got through to the man in charge of the Fed conference. The agent assured him that they were covering the Jackson Lake Lodge and other meeting sites. He had even assigned agents to monitor activities like fishing, raft trips, and golf. He also told Brett that several of his men were already in Teton Village and would take the tram up the mountain. They would search the restaurant where the luncheon speech would be as well as the surrounding area. They would also carefully investigate each tram car and ride back down on the last tram of the night with the restaurant workers. In the morning, only restaurant staff and other necessary personnel would be allowed to board the tram until the conference delegates arrived.

When the agent asked Brett why he thought it was necessary to fly to Jackson, Brett quickly explained that he had headed up the investigation so far and simply wanted to be on site. Not wanting to get into an argument, Brett left it at that, thanked the agent for his help, and hung up.

So, they would have to let restaurant workers up the mountain before Samantha and the others.

He thought back to the waiter in Naples and felt his pulse race.

He glanced at his watch again, packed up his computer, put his gun in his shoulder holster, turned out the lights, and headed for the door. When he passed Dom's cubicle, he looked in and saw that some of the sample listening devices and bomb detectors were on his desk.

On a whim, he walked in and shoved the small, experimental bomb pre-emptor in his pocket. He knew it was a prototype and nobody knew if it would actually work in the field. But it was small, so why not take it along? He also decided to *borrow* the other detector that was the size of a briefcase. Then he made another decision. He picked up Dom's desk phone and called his home number.

"Turiano," the voice said.

"Hey, Dom, it's Brett. I'm still at the office, and I just talked to Trevor. I made my case again about flying out to Jackson, and he finally gave in."

"You actually got Trevor to *agree* to something?" Dom asked in a somewhat incredulous voice.

"Yes. I've scheduled a ride out of Dulles. Leaves at 8:00 a.m. Any chance you could come with me?"

"Did Trevor okay that too?" Dom asked.

"Not exactly," Brett said hesitantly.

"Well, there's no time for requisitions and paperwork, but I'd really like to go with you on this one. Besides," he added with a chuckle, "I'm sitting here trying to find a decent movie to watch and I'm deciding between *Killer Tomatoes Eat France* and *Mega Shark versus Giant Octopus*."

Brett gave short laugh. "Okay, stash the remote, grab some shut-eye, and meet me at Landmark Aviation at Dulles a little before 8:00 a.m. As for Trevor, I promised I'd give him regular updates. I'm going to send him an email right now. I'll tell him when I'm leaving and that I've analyzed the situation and would like you to be there with me for backup. If he checks his email and says no, I'll call you ASAP. Otherwise, throw some gear together, and I'll see you at our FBO. Oh, speaking of gear. I just appropriated a couple of your toys."

"Which toys?"

"Some of the stuff on your desk. You never know what we might need once we get there," Brett said.

"You're really focused on this conference, aren't you? Or is it Samantha Reid that you're focused on?" Dom asked.

"All of the above."

"What about the Denver bureau? Thought they were in charge out there."

"They are. I talked to the lead agent. He said they were doing all the usual checks and that he *hoped* any threat or rumor would turn out to be a hoax. Hope is *not* a very compelling strategy in my book."

"Agreed. See you in a few hours," Dom said and hung up.

Brett had one more idea. He texted Samantha to tell her he was coming and would arrive before her speech. He had no idea what her reaction would be. Would it make her feel more secure to know he was close by? Or would it make her feel that there really was a threat he was worried about and that she should be doubly concerned about it too? He'd have to deal with all of that tomorrow.

He walked out of Dom's office, took the elevator to the garage, and retrieved his car. As he drove home, he wondered if he would make it there in time to prevent a disaster, or if this truly was all in his head.

FORTY-ONE

TOURISTS, HIKERS, AND LOCALS LINED UP ON the tram platform at the base of one of the tallest ski runs in Teton Village. Even though early evening shadows streaked across the landscape, there was still time to ride to the top of Rendezvous Mountain, wander around the summit for a while, check out the view, and then come back down on the last ride of the day.

Lubov and Stas were standing off to the side watching the crowd when they noticed several men who were much better dressed than everyone else. One of them held a German Shepherd on a leash. Stas pointed to them and whispered, "Looks like they're undercover. What do you think?"

Lubov scrutinized the men now boarding the tram car. He leaned in and replied, "I'll bet they're working the conference and checking out the restaurant at the top because of tomorrow's lunch. I'm glad we protected our supplies."

Stas nodded. "Best thing to do is hang back and let them go first."

"Exactly what I was thinking. Once they're up there, we'll give them space while we take a hike, just like we planned."

"Yah. We've got plenty of time," Stas said, surveying the crowd.

They had carefully packed supplies into their backpacks and sprayed their most important cargo with Deer Off to dispel any lingering scent that might be picked up by dogs. Lubov figured they would have to wait a while for the next cable car, so he pointed to a restaurant off to the left. "Let's grab coffee and a sandwich while we kill time."

They ambled over to the Mangy Moose. Inside, they walked up to the bar, placed their order, and grabbed a handful of cookies from a basket. When their food was ready, they paid the bartender, and headed out to a small table on a long porch.

"You know, if we weren't in this town to do a job, we could have a pretty good time out here," Stas said, eyeing a trio of twenty-something girls in shorts and colorful T-shirts at the next table.

"Yah, maybe. But remember, we're leaving immediately after we finish. Then we collect our money first from Vadim and later from all those brilliant trades we made."

Stas laughed. "I know. The short sales. I can't wait to tell the partners back in Moscow about the profits we make betting the organization's accounts. We'll be able to expand our operations all over the place."

When they finished their sandwiches, Lubov shoved a cookie in his mouth, washed it down with a gulp of coffee, and then glanced at the tram. It was nearing the top of the mountain, so he gave Stas a thumbs up.

Back on the tram platform, Stas handed his ticket to the operator and stepped on board the next red and black cable car. It was emblazoned with the words "Jackson Hole" along the bottom, and white silhouettes of a cowboy on a bucking bronco were painted on some of the windows. Lubov followed, and they pushed through the crowd to take a spot at the wide front window where they held onto railings that extended around the periphery. Though the tram could hold up to one hundred people, only a third of it was filled at this time of day. That was fine with Lubov. He wasn't sure how steady it would be with a full load. Now it just held a bunch of aging tourists with cameras, a gaggle of teenagers huddled together, and several couples who looked dressed for dinner.

The doors closed, and the car began its fifteen minute trek up the side of the mountain. A woman standing nearby was holding a leaflet. She started reading to the guy next to her. Lubov assumed they were headed to dinner at the summit restaurant. Together, they easily took up enough space for three or four hikers.

Lubov could hear her saying, "Larry, it says here that this cable goes up 4,129 vertical feet, and we'll be able to see all of Jackson Hole, the Snake River, Grand Teton National Park, and even the summit of the Grand Teton. That's the biggest mountain in the range." Lubov wondered if they'd be the biggest couple *on* the range.

The other man didn't look too interested as he kept flicking through texts on his iPhone. She was undeterred as she continued reading, "Says here that you can hike and see wild flowers up there." Lubov thought hiking would be a good idea for them, but he doubted if he and Stas would bump into them in the mountains. They wouldn't survive an overnight hike.

As the car hauled its human cargo along the cables, Lubov said, "It's quite a sight up here. Jagged peaks over there, and looks like deer or something down by those trees."

"Those are elk," Stas said. "Might see some moose wandering around too. I heard that you shouldn't approach a female moose if she has babies, even though they're the size of a horse."

"They're dangerous? I thought they were just slow and ugly."

"Nope. They can kill you. Just like bears."

"Do you think any will be near the restaurant?" Lubov asked, raising his bushy eyebrows.

"I doubt it. I'm sure they want to keep the tourists happy, so the management probably watches for them," Stas said. "Maybe they put repellent around to keep them away. Not sure if it would be like our Deer Off spray, but there has to be something."

When the cable car slowly crept to a halt, the doors opened, and the passengers scrambled out, clutching purses and backpacks. Lubov and Stas let the others go first and then finally emerged onto the upper platform.

They looked around and saw two of the well-dressed men from the previous tram leaving the restaurant. The men nodded as if they had finished something, then they headed over to the bottom of the tram tower that stretched up several stories. They were examining the base, walking around, kneeling down, and rummaging through the underbrush. The German Shepherd nosed around and finally backed off. The men patted the dog and nodded to each other again.

"Don't get off until they leave," Lubov warned as he and Stas hung back to let the other passengers walk out the door.

"Looks like you were right," Stas whispered. "They checked everything around here. But now they're going back to the restaurant. I think we can get off now. We need to hit the trails for a while."

Once off the tram, they walked toward the back of the ridge. Lubov pulled out a little map showing some pathways around the summit and others leading all the way back down. He doubted if many people would attempt that sort of hike. In fact, he was counting on it.

Stas shifted his backpack and joined Lubov on one of the trails. They hiked away from the tower and down behind the restaurant, stopping occasionally to look over their shoulders. They were alone on this part of the mountain. They continued walking until they stumbled over some rocks and crevices and entered a small clearing where they sat down on the ground to rest.

They pulled out water bottles, leaned against a tree, and talked about what they would do with all the money they were going to make. If not tomorrow, they were certain the profits would start rolling in by next week.

The sun gradually receded behind the mountains, and the temperature started to plummet. "Glad we brought jackets. It's summer, and I'm already getting cold," Lubov said.

"Gets down to about forty in the valley. Of course, we're much higher, so it'll be pretty frigid soon."

"Too bad we can't build a fire or something," Lubov ventured.

"If anybody can handle being cold, we can. We're Russians," Stas said. "Put on your gloves. It'll only be another hour or two before that restaurant closes. The security guys will probably wait until everyone is out of there, take another look around, and then head down on the last tram of the night."

"Yah, that sounds about right. They didn't look like the hiking type to me," Lubov said with a shrug.

"I never thought I'd be the hiking type either," Stas said. "Then again, it's a pretty brilliant idea."

"Thanks," Lubov said.

The two men hunkered down and talked in low voices for the next few hours. They reviewed their plans, speculated about how fast Vadim would pay them, and considered how long they should stay in the states before heading back to Moscow.

Lubov kept looking around for a stray moose or elk. He hoped they would stay farther down the mountain or even in the valley. They certainly were in no position to deal with predatory wildlife. All they had with them for protection was a can of bear spray.

Stas and Lubov were looking through the trees when they saw the restaurant's lights finally shut off. They waited another half hour and then gingerly picked their way back up the trail to the top. There, they didn't see a soul, but they did see what must have been the last tram car slowly chugging its way down the mountain.

They watched it for a few seconds and then split up. Lubov headed to the restaurant. They had already scoped out the area during their last trip, so he knew exactly where to place his first cache of C-4. It would be shoved under a broad windowsill at the back of the building. Two others would be nestled behind the gutters, and another would rest against a side wall that was covered by a bush.

He leaned his backpack against the back wall and took out a small lump that looked like modeling clay. It always reminded him of Ivory soap in a plain brown wrapper. He was glad that his associates had shipped them their supply of *Czech Plastique* on time. It was perfect for this job and pretty cheap too. They only needed about five thousand dollars' worth to complete their job. Five thousand dollars to make millions. How great was that?

When he had taped the lump under the windowsill, he hooked up the initiator that would be triggered by a cell phone call. Basic, but effective. While he placed the rest of his charges,

Stas planted his own C-4 lumps at the base of the tram tower, covering them up with loose rocks.

Lubov finished first and walked over to the base to help Stas. "How's it coming?"

"Almost done with this one. It took me a while to gather enough rocks and brush to hide it, but I think it looks pretty good. I want to try one more thing, though. See that box up there on top of that tower ledge? I think it's a weather monitor or something."

"How are you going to get up there?" Lubov asked, craning his neck.

"Not sure. I can't reach it. But you're lighter than I am. I'll get the package ready, then you can climb on my shoulders and try to get it on top of that box," Stas said. "No one will see it if you shove it toward the back."

Stas steadied himself while Lubov finally placed the last explosive with the blasting cap carefully inserted. Then he jumped down. "We did it," Stas exclaimed. They gave each other high fives and then sat down to reassemble their backpacks.

"Time to get the hell out of here," Lubov said. "Think we can make it down the mountain when it's so dark?"

"No problem," Stas said. "I brought flashlights, and there's a half moon that'll help."

"I hope we don't run into any animals up here. You got the bear spray, right?"

"Bears only roam around at dusk and in the early morning," Stas said. "I read that somewhere."

Lubov stared at him and said, "Well, let's just hope we get to the bottom before dawn."

"I'm sure we will. Then I want a long, hot shower. I'm freezing my ass off up here."

FORTY-TWO

THURSDAY MIDMORNING: JACKSON, WYOMING

"PRETTY SIGHT DOWN THERE," DOM SAID, peering out the window of the Learjet as it banked toward the Jackson airport.

"Sure is," Brett said. "I just hope it stays pretty." He checked his watch. "Damn. It's 10:30. I knew we'd hit a bad headwind. The Denver office better have a car waiting for us like they promised. I told them we didn't need a driver. I figure we can drive faster ourselves. They said we can keep the car as long as we need it."

"Do you know the way to Teton Village?"

"Sure. Shouldn't take too long to get there. Maybe twenty minutes or so." Brett spent the rest of the flight watching the valley and its surrounding jagged peaks.

Once the plane landed and taxied to the Jackson Authority FBO, Brett and Dom grabbed their luggage and briefcases and hurried down the steps to the tarmac.

"Your car is here," one of the pilots said, pointing to a black sedan next to the wing. "Have a good one."

"Thanks for the ride," Brett said. "And nice job on the landing. Not the longest runway I've ever seen, but you handled it perfectly."

"Thanks. Let us know when you need to head back to D.C. We have orders to stay here for two days. But keep in touch with dispatch in case we get called for another mission."

"Will do," Brett said and hustled over to the car. Dom tossed their luggage in the trunk and then stepped into the passenger seat.

As he buckled his seat belt, Brett pulled out his cell phone, activated its Bluetooth, and dialed Samantha's number. He put the car in gear and drove away from the plane. Voicemail again.

Is there something wrong with cell phones here?

"Damn! Samantha isn't answering her cell," Brett said, already feeling agitated.

"Maybe she's in the dining room or something," Dom ventured. "Why don't we call the lodge? I'll get the number." He called information, asked for Samantha Reid, and handed his cell to Brett when the desk clerk finally tracked her down.

"Hello?" Samantha said.

"Samantha, it's Brett. I'm using Dom's phone. We've just landed in Jackson."

"It's good to talk to you. I really appreciate your concern. But I think you've made your trip for nothing. The local FBI briefed us late last night. They said they combed the entire area, and everything was fine."

"Let me be the judge of that," Brett said. "Look, I'm heading to Teton Village. What's your schedule?"

"We're all in the lobby. They don't have very good cell service here. Glad you called the desk. At least it got through on this end."

"Have you noticed anything out of the ordinary at the conference? Anything at all that you would call suspicious?"

"Not really. I had breakfast with a charming Russian, Alexander Tepanov. He's the one you asked me about. Turns out, he's quite nice, even if he does come on a little strong. Anyway, we're pushing the Russians to be more vigilant about money laundering. But it's tough with all the mafia gangs and with so much corruption at almost every level of their government."

"I'll bet," Brett said. "When is everyone coming to the village for your speech?"

"We'll be leaving here shortly. They have buses waiting outside. Should be going up the tram around noon," she said. "I'm not looking forward to it."

"The whole heights thing, right?" Brett said.

"Yes," Samantha admitted. "I don't know how it'll go. I'll just have to close my eyes."

"Well, I'll keep *my* eyes open. I don't want to miss anything. I'll see you there."

"Okay. And, Brett, I didn't mean to sound ungrateful earlier. I know that you're just being cautious, and I just want you to know that I appreciate it. See you later." When she hung up, Brett pictured her brushing some of her long brown hair off her lovely face.

What if there really are people who are out to get her here?

Brett shuddered and drove on.

"Is she all right?" Dom asked.

"God, I hope so," Brett said. "We'll know soon enough."

Brett maneuvered around a building, drove through a gate in a chain-link fence, and then continued onto the access road leading to the highway. He suddenly pointed to a rough, wooden sign on the right. "What does it say?"

Dom read the words: "'Howdy stranger. Yonder is Jackson Hole. The last of the Old West.'" He chuckled. "Forgot my cowboy boots. But at least we've got our guns," he said, patting his shoulder holster.

Brett nodded and turned onto the highway, the first place he could really cut the engine loose. "As soon as we get there, we've got to locate the agent in charge, get briefed, and then head up the mountain before Samantha and the others get there. I know he said it's all clear, but I've got to check everything at that restaurant. It's the most logical place to target. Now that we're here, I keep thinking, what if the Denver agents missed something? Some hidden explosive like the one in Naples?"

"I hear you," Dom said. "It may turn out that everything's fine, but I follow my instincts like you."

Brett checked his watch. "While I go up the mountain, you stay on the ground with the other agents. You should be surveying every single person anywhere near the tram. I want you to take pictures of everyone. And I mean everyone."

Holding up his cell, Dom said, "We'll get good shots if we can. And then we've got to make sure no one tries to use their cells for calls. Except our guys, of course. I brought our own VHF radios, which can't be jammed, in case the locals disrupt something. We need to be in touch. On the ground and up at the restaurant."

"Right," Brett said. "Wish we could just confiscate every cell phone in the area or shut down the cell towers. But last time I talked to them, Denver said we can't do that. Too many muckety-mucks in town for the conference that we need to protect, not irritate."

"It sucks," Dom said. "If there are any problems at the res-taurant, cell phones are always the triggers of choice, unless there are timers involved. What are the odds?"

"Cell phones work better. If somebody set a timer, there could be delays. The ministers could take longer to show up, the lunch could start later—who the hell knows? No, I'd opt for a cell phone. That's why it's vital that you take pictures and watch every person trying to make a call. Confiscate those phones if you can. I know it's going to be tough because we can't just cor-don off the entire area. This is high season for tourists, and word is that even the Fed hosts say they are here as guests, not intrud-ers. Not the way I'd do a protective detail, but we've got no choice."

"Right," Dom said. "This is going to be a bitch of a problem. But if Denver has as many agents as they say they do, we should be able to cover the territory pretty well."

"Well, 'Hope springs eternal' and all that," Brett said. He was speeding down the highway, hoping there weren't any sher-iffs around, when he spotted their turnoff to the right. "We'll take this road to Spring Gulch."

"Sounds like a flooded pot hole," Dom said.

"There's actually another way from the airport to the village that looked shorter. But part of it goes through some park, and it's not even paved, so I decided to take this route," Brett explained.

"Hey, look ahead. Looks like this road isn't paved either. But there's a truck up there that's going pretty fast, so maybe we'll be okay," Dom said.

They passed cow pastures and signs pointing to ranches along the way. Then they took a right onto Route 22 and another right at a sign that said, "Teton Village, 7 miles."

After a few more minutes Brett said, "There it is. Up on the left." He sped toward the village, past the Snake River Lodge and the Alpenhof, and found a place to park near the Jackson Hole Aerial Tram entrance.

They opened the trunk, grabbed their gear, and ran up to the platform. There they spotted several agents who pointed out the man in charge. He was stationed near the ticket taker. Brett walked over and offered his hand. "Brett Keating, D.C. office. This is Special Agent Turiano. Can you fill us in on the latest?"

"Oh yes, Agent Keating." The Denver director shook Brett's hand with a smile. "Stuart Pierce. Good to finally put a face to a name. As I said on the phone, I believe we have this area under control. We had people up at the restaurant until closing last night. They went over every inch of the place and came down with the kitchen staff on the last tram. No one except the cooks and waiters have been allowed to go up there this morning. And we already finished our background checks on the restaurant staff. Took some time, but they all cooperated."

Stuart continued, "We've been double-checking tram cars this morning for any sign of explosives, even chemical discharge, and we've found nothing. You can trust me when I say there's nothing to worry about here."

Brett vaguely remembered something President Reagan once said about trust. He'd have to look it up. Right now, he was surveying the tram cables as Stuart continued to talk.

"As soon as the buses arrive with the delegates, which should be around—" Stuart paused and glanced at his watch—"forty minutes or so, we'll have agents on the cars with them when they ride up to the top. Right now, the tram is stopped."

"I want it started again," Brett said.

"Why?" Stuart asked.

"I need to get up there *before* the delegates. I'm not saying your people didn't do a good job, I just want to be there in advance. Okay?"

The agent shook his head. "I know you've been heading up the investigation in D.C., but this is our territory. And I told you, we've got it covered."

Dom intervened. "Look, it can't be too much trouble to get the operator to send up one tram. I'll stay here on the ground and work with you and your agents while Brett helps with security at the restaurant. After all, we *are* here now, and we want to help," he said in a friendly tone.

The agent sighed and finally said, "Fine. Just don't do anything stupid up there. The restaurant manager is nervous enough trying to get this luncheon together for all the officials, including our own Treasury Secretary."

"Got it," Brett said.

Stuart walked over to the tram booth but was told that the operator was on a break. He gave the order to restart the tram, but the girl standing there said it would be a while. Brett watched the exchange and shook his head as he checked his watch again: 11:30 a.m. Samantha and the others would be here in less than thirty minutes.

Where the hell is the operator?

Brett stood there as his panic started to build. Finally, a young guy in jeans and a "Teton Valley Rocks" T-shirt approached the booth. Stuart pointed to the tram car and the guy nodded slowly. After several more minutes, Brett heard motors running, and the cables started to move.

The tram car skirted the edge of the platform and stopped so that Brett could board. He waved to Dom and hopped inside. Leaning against the window, he turned on his VHS radio, clipped it to his belt, felt in his pocket for the little bomb pre-emptor, and held onto the briefcase he had also filched from Dom's office.

Fifteen minutes felt like forty as the car made its way up the side of the mountain. Maybe Stuart was right. Maybe there was no threat at all. Maybe he had been too involved with Samantha Reid to think straight. But he didn't settle for maybes. He got facts.

The car halted at the top, and the door opened. Brett thanked the operator and raced to the restaurant. Inside, he saw long tables set for about a hundred people, complete with colorful cloths and wildflower arrangements in small vases lining the centers. He noticed waiters placing water glasses and napkins at each place. Others were moving a lectern and microphone to the front of the room.

He asked a server where the manager was and watched him point to a swinging door. Brett entered the kitchen and found a rather harried looking man.

"Sir? You're the manager?"

The man nodded. "Who are you? I thought nobody was allowed up until noon."

"Brett Keating, FBI." He offered his hand. "Just want to take one last look around if you don't mind."

The manager nervously shook his hand and said. "Be my guest. We're awfully busy here, but do what you have to do." He hurried off.

Brett began by scanning the room, but he had a hunch that he wouldn't find anything in the middle of the lunch preparations where it might easily be discovered. Besides, the restaurant must have been locked overnight. If anyone were going to sabotage the meeting, they wouldn't want to leave some tell-sign of a break in.

He went to the porch area, set the small briefcase on a wooden chair, and opened it. He took out the square detection device that looked like a flashlight and started to walk around the perimeter of the building.

Brett studied the small screen on the side as he slowly moved forward. Right now it was showing .50. He remembered Dom telling him .60 was a zone of uncertainty. He kept checking the number as he walked. It started to inch up a bit. Brett held his breath and cautiously stepped toward a set of windows in the back. He looked again. The read-out registered .90.

"Shit!" he muttered as he felt along one of the windows and looked under each sill. He inhaled sharply as the reading hit .99.

There it was. An explosive pack of C-4.

He examined it, noticed how it was taped in place, and finally located the trigger. He yanked it out and disconnected it from the payload. Then he released a huge breath, grabbed his radio, and called Dom. "You there?" he demanded. He waited until he heard Dom's voice.

"Here with the Denver guys taking photos. The delegates arrived while you were on your way up. They're all on board, and the tram is starting to move."

"They can't come up!" Brett yelled. "You've got to stop the tram."

"Why? It's already on the way," Dom said. "It doesn't go backwards. It has to loop around to come down again."

"They've *got* to get off," Brett shouted. "Evacuate. Do something."

"We can't. The tram is over a gorge right now. What the hell is going on up there?"

"I just found a piece of C-4 under a window. But I don't know how many more are up here. I only found it because I used your new briefcase device," Brett said while rushing around the side of the building and feeling along the edge.

"How the hell did it get there?" Dom yelled. "They covered the whole building last night."

"Someone must have come up here and stayed late," Brett said into the two-way strapped to his belt.

"Can you disarm the one you found?"

"Did that," Brett said, rounding a corner. "It was way too easy. I think it was a decoy." He thought about telling the manager to evacuate the building, but he couldn't afford to stop searching. Whoever planted the C-4 probably planned to detonate it as soon as the delegates arrived. At least that bought him time. But what if they also sabotaged the tram cables or the tower? He'd have to check them too. Brett started to sweat.

As he reached under another window sill, he found more C-4. "Shit, there's more. I don't know if I can find it all in time," he said and disconnected the trigger. "Dom, try again to stop the goddamned tram. Wait. No. Alert the Denver agents and cover every frigging inch down there at the base. Somebody is going to try to trigger this stuff, and we don't know if most of it is up here or down there. And I need Denver's bomb squad ASAP. Where are they?"

"I don't know if they have team here in the village. They may have been checking other locations, but I'll find out."

Brett clicked off and frantically went back to work.

FORTY-THREE

"IT'S BEEN SUCH A PLEASURE GETTING TO
know you, Miss Reid," the Russian banker said with a broad
grin. "We are all looking forward to your remarks."

"Thank you, Mr. Tepanov," Samantha said, glancing at the
man standing between her and the tram window. "I just started
reviewing my notes."

"I'll leave you to your preparations, but perhaps we could sit
together at the luncheon and continue our discussion?"

"If they don't have a seating chart, we may be able to do that.
Thanks," she said and tried to smile, but she was nervous. The
tram car was jerking upward and swaying in the wind. She
turned to Homer, who was standing next to her, and said in a
low voice, "I know we need Russia's help on a lot of things, but
that guy has been all over me since we got here."

"It's pretty obvious he's a ladies' man," Homer whispered.
"But knowing you, you'll figure out how to charm and co-opt
him at the same time."

273

"Charm and co-opt?" Samantha asked, trying not to think about where she was, but about what she had to do.

"How else could you survive in a job where you're surrounded by men who bank on Kissinger's old line, 'Power is the ultimate aphrodisiac?'"

Samantha sighed. "I'll see what I can do with the Russians in the next few hours. But first, I need to get through this speech," she said, trying to look down at her notes and ignore the nearby windows.

"Want to go over your main points again?" Homer asked.

"I don't think so. Those four things we worked on are already written down on these cards. Still, I've never just *read* a speech."

"You'll be great. Some of the speakers at the morning sessions were so unbelievably boring with their prepared remarks," Homer said. "Whoever writes their speeches should be fired. Did you catch that nonsense about M-1 and M-2, velocity and convergence?"

"Sure did, though I sort of needed subtitles," Samantha said. She knew Homer was trying to distract her from thinking about heights, so she tried to continue their conversation as the car lurched higher. "That word 'convergence' is actually pretty important, but I'm using the idea in a completely different context."

"I know. It's more like the word 'combination' we talked about last night."

"Exactly. I've worked that into my pitch about the threat of global trafficking routes combining with narco-terrorism. When we've got trillions of bucks in cybercrimes every year, and when you combine that with money-laundering, it all leads to the weapons trade, drug trade, and even WMD. And that leads to gigantic threats and problems."

"Right. They combine the servers, routers, and hackers with the big money guys, and it becomes a real mess," Homer said. "We make a little progress here and there, but I can see why they wanted you out here to make our case." He glanced at the Russian who was staring out his window. "If you can get guys like Tepanov to cooperate with us, along with some of their former republics, that would be a huge deal."

"I'm trying," she said, tucking her notes back into her purse. Samantha edged toward the center, farther away from the windows. She didn't want to be anywhere near them, and she prayed that she wouldn't freak out before they reached the top.

"Doing okay?" Homer asked gently.

She stared at the floor. "I'll make it if I can stop thinking about the last time I was out here with my husband."

"I know," Homer said, taking her arm. "They said it'll only take fifteen minutes. When we get to the top, we can head straight into the restaurant and not look down anywhere. Just focus on your speech and the dinner we're going to have tonight in town. I think the Treasury guys booked us into a place called the Snake River Grill. It's right on the square, and it's supposed to be pretty good."

He stayed close to her as the car vibrated on its trek upward. She closed her eyes and mentally counted off the minutes.

FORTY-FOUR

FRIDAY NOON:
RENDEZVOUS MOUNTAIN

"STUART IS APOPLECTIC ABOUT WHAT YOU found up there. He's screaming at his agents and asking everyone how the hell any sort of explosive was overlooked. Have you found anything else?" Dom asked.

"Yeah. Three more small packs of C-4 around the building," Brett said nervously. "One was right behind a bush for god's sake. But there are no more readings here, so I think the restaurant is secure. I'm running to the tower now. It would take a helluva cache to bring it down, but I want to make sure it's clean. Did you ever get a hold of their bomb squad? They need to dispose of this stuff immediately."

"We're trying to round them up. After last night, they went back to the lodge to double-check security there. They're on their way here, but it looks like they'll be too late to do you any good," Dom said.

"Well, what about the agents on the ground? See anything suspicious down there? Getting pictures I hope," Brett said as he rushed to the tower.

"We're all over it. There were several guys in cars parked nearby. They might just be waiting for someone, but we got photos just in case." He hesitated and then said, "I don't want to alarm you, but the tram will be there in less than ten minutes."

"Damn! The tower is on a ridge far from the restaurant. Maybe I should have checked that first. If I were a criminal, I'd include the tower in my shit scheme. Gotta go."

As he careened away from the restaurant and ran toward the tall tower's base, he thanked God that he'd brought along Dom's new detection system. He checked his watch. Not much time before the car containing the most important financial gurus in the world would be here. Them and Samantha. Christ! What if there were more explosives?

———

"See those guys over there with the cell phones?" Dom called to a Denver agent.

"I got them covered," the man replied as he raced over to talk to the group. Dom saw him argue with the quartet of tourists standing near the tram platform. Eventually, the group nodded, and the agent handed them cards and pocketed their phones.

Dom scanned the rest of the crowd. A young woman wearing a bulky jacket looked like she was taking pictures of the tram. Dom walked over and grabbed her iPhone.

"What are you doing?" she cried out.

He turned off her phone and said, "FBI. We're running a security sweep. No cell phones."

"I thought this was a free country," she countered. "Give me back my phone."

Dom took out his own cell and snapped a picture of her. Wearing a jacket on a warm day made him think she might have a weapon on her. All the agents were constantly briefed about home-grown terrorist plots. He couldn't take any chances.

"You have no right—" she protested.

"I have every right," he said. Then he pocketed her cell. "Open your jacket."

"What?" she said.

"Do it," he demanded.

She stared at him, hesitated, then unzipped it. Nothing suspicious was inside. No suicide packs. No weapons of any kind.

Dom nodded and handed her a business card. "Later today, call this number and leave your address. We'll send your phone back."

She glared at him with contempt. "I still say you have no right," she muttered and stalked off.

He saw that the other agents were fanned out, taking more photos and confiscating cell phones amidst shouting and swearing about being in a public park and needing to make a call. Dom couldn't care less if some tourists were upset.

This isn't Parks and Recreation. This is national security.

Brett was circling the tower. He stared at the read-out again. It was starting to climb. As he scanned the base, it suddenly hit .90. "No!" Brett shouted. He held it closer and studied the entire area around the huge edifice.

Where the hell is it? If something blows up here, it could sever the cables.

He glanced down and saw that the tram car was hanging from the cable over the deepest crevices of the mountain.

God help me! I've got to find it.

Brett kept walking around the tower's base. When the read-out hit .99, he looked down and saw a pile of stones and brush. He knelt down and began throwing the rocks aside. Then he saw it.

This time it was a huge chunk.

This could blow the pilings to dust.

He searched for the trigger mechanism. It would be about the size of a fat cigar. He finally felt it and yanked it out. Was that the only one? He checked his device again as he stood up and walked to another girder.

As he examined the rest of the base, he realized that the explosive he had just disarmed had been placed in the most easily accessible spot on the base. The remaining legs of the tower were thickly wrapped with underbrush, bushes, and other coverings.

Suddenly, the read-out dropped to .70. That meant there could still be something nearby. He felt he had covered the base as best he could. Now he scanned the upper girders. Nothing up there. No place to hide anything.

What the hell is that?

He moved around to get a better view. It looked like it might be a weather monitor. He aimed the detector in its direction and the read-out jumped to .85.

Another one?

He didn't know what to do. It was too high to reach without a ladder, and he had no time to search for something to stand on. He glanced toward the restaurant some distance away. The tram car was still wending its way over a final deep gorge, but it was getting closer. He didn't have time to run to the restaurant manager or the staff and explain the threat, which would cause a panic. What could he do about this new read-out?

Had Dom and the other agents confiscated enough cell phones to keep the culprits, whoever they were, from detonating whatever might be on that tower ledge? His heart was pounding as he stared up at the weather monitor and swore out loud.

FORTY-FIVE

THURSDAY NOON; TETON VILLAGE, WYOMING

"THE CABLE CAR IS ALMOST IN THE PERFECT spot," Lubov said, looking through a pair of binoculars from his perch on the passenger seat of their car. They were parked on the exit road in Teton Village. They had checked out of their hotel, stowed their luggage in the trunk, rechecked the conference schedule—though they practically had it memorized by now— and told Vadim and Maksim to do the same.

As soon as the explosives went off, they would all drive out of the village, follow the road toward Wilson, turn right, and then head over the pass to the Idaho Falls FBO where a jet was already waiting. Lubov handed the binoculars to Stas and pulled out his cell phone.

"Let me see," Stas said, looking through the binoculars. "Some of those security people are still on the platform. Looks like they're arguing or something. Idiots. They're still taking pictures of the tourists, though. Remember that one guy who got close a while ago? They were scanning all the cars around here. I think he might have even taken a picture of us."

"Who cares?" Lubov said. "They don't know us, and we don't look like we're doing anything. We're just taking in the view. Besides, no one has seen us with cell phones. That's why we hid them until now." He punched in a series of numbers. "Ready?" he turned to Stas with a smile.

Stas nodded, and Lubov hit the connect button. They heard it ring. And ring.

After a minute, Stas yelled, "What the hell happened?" He refocused the binoculars on the tower. "Fuck! There's someone up there. I knew I saw someone. He's getting up, but I can't see what he's doing."

"The real question is, what the hell did *you* do?" Lubov demanded. "You placed the stuff at the bottom of the tower. Did you screw up the trigger?"

"I don't know," Stas shouted. "I placed it perfectly at the base. And I covered it up with rocks. You saw that."

"Wait," Lubov said. "Maybe I dialed wrong." He re-entered the prescribed set of numbers. His cell rang again. But again, there was no answer. No connection.

"Do you think those security people killed cell phone service here in the village?" Stas asked.

"They could have. Those people can do anything they want. I'm gonna try another number, just to see."

"What other number? You can't call Vadim. Not yet."

"No, I'm calling the hotel. I just want to see if it goes through."

"Well, hurry up," Stas said.

Lubov hit some numbers and mumbled, "If we don't get the tower, don't freak out. I set all those bricks around the restaurant, and I know I did *my* job right." He put the cell on speaker as it began to ring.

"Teton Mountain Lodge. How may I direct your call?" a chipper voice answered.

Lubov quickly hit the end button. "Damn. Cell's still working. Something's wrong."

Stas trained the binoculars on the tram again. "They've only got a minute or two to get to the top. Quick, try the number for the weather station."

"Give me a second. I want to make sure I have the right number for that trigger." He looked down at a list he had placed in the cup holder, studied it for a minute, nodded, and grabbed his cell again. "This time it'll go through. Now watch. That cable car is gonna look like it's in the middle of a Chinese New Year."

FORTY-SIX

THURSDAY NOON: RENDEZVOUS MOUNTAIN

AS BRETT STARED UP AT THE WEATHER monitor, he suddenly remembered the miniature bomb preemptor in his pocket. He pulled it out and quickly studied it, remembering what Dom had said about activating it. Pull the pin, toss the thing into a suspicious area, and let its electrons disrupt communication channels and render any explosive immune to a charge. He also remembered it had never been tested.

Left with no other alternative, Brett stood back, pulled the pin, and lobbed the BPE toward the box. It smacked the edge, bounced off, hit the ground, and rolled away.

Brett cursed and scrambled after it.

I already pulled the pin. How long will it work?

He had no idea. He looked back up at the weather box with renewed determination. Brett stepped back and took careful aim once again. This time, he threw with an underhand motion and watched it land.

It seemed like the BPE had actually settled right on top of the box. It was just sitting there. He heaved a sigh of relief and tried to slow his breathing. He turned around and saw that the tram had just arrived. The Denver agents were the first to exit the car and fan out. The delegates began to spill out while Brett took one last walk around the base of the tower.

Safe, I think. Safe, I pray.

He saw Samantha step out along with Secretary Pickering and a few others. They hadn't been warned. What would have been the point except to cause massive hysteria on board a moving tram car? His first impulse was to rush over and tell them everything. But he thought for a second and decided he shouldn't do that.

Brett felt confident that the restaurant was completely disarmed and Samantha, along with all the delegates, would be safe. For now. She had to give her big speech, and she must have fought pretty hard to keep her equilibrium on the trek up the mountain. He fought the urge to reassure her that everything was going to be okay. Later. He'd do that later.

Once she was inside the restaurant door, he walked over to a group of Denver agents. "I'm sure you'll want to see the evidence," Brett said.

"Show us everything," one demanded. "Chief reported that you found explosives. We had to keep it quiet on the tram, or we would have started a panic. I can't believe this."

"Come over here first," Brett said, leading the way to the tower.

"Where the hell did this come from?" One of the agents said, examining the lump of C-4 surrounded by loose rocks at the base of the structure. "We scoured this place last night. We checked the tower. There were no piles of rocks, no indication that anybody had been near this area."

"See up there?" Brett pointed to the weather box. "Another big problem."

"What?" an agent asked, peering up.

"I used a biologically based bomb sensor that reacted to something up there. I couldn't climb up myself, so I threw a bomb pre-emptor on top of it."

"You threw it?" the agent asked, astonished. "How did it work?"

"It's new. Never been tested until now," Brett said. "It uses electrons to disrupt cell signals. Very clever contraption. Shaped like a hand grenade. It's sitting up there on top of the box. You'd better hurry up and disarm whatever explosive is up there. I have no idea how long the pre-emptor's batteries will last."

"Shit, he's right," an agent said. He turned to one of his team members. "Boost me up."

While they tried to reach the box, Brett said to the others, "Let's head over to the restaurant. I'll show you the rest."

Brett led the way and carefully pointed out every location where explosives had been set. The Denver agents stared, argued, asked questions, and carefully examined each cache to be certain it was inert. They finally retreated to the side of the restaurant to radio their boss.

After Brett completed the tour, he stepped away and contacted Dom. "Bomb squad ever show up? We need them to clear everything away."

"They're here now," Dom replied. "I'm sending them up. We closed the tram after Samantha and the others left. I got the operator to start it again, but only to send up the bomb guys."

"Do they have their retrieval sacks?"

"Yes. Think you found everything?" Dom asked.

"I sure as hell hope so. I've been showing the other agents all the handiwork. They freaked out. But what about you? Did you spot any suspects? Anything that could point us in the right direction? Our window of opportunity to find whoever did this is closing."

"I'm talking to local enforcement about roadblocks. They should be done setting them up soon. There aren't that many roads out of town," Dom said. "Find Pickering, and get him to work on closing the airport. If anyone involved left after trying to trigger those explosives, it will take them a while to drive to Jackson, get through security, and wait for a flight. Oh, and what about Trevor and the director?"

"I'll call D.C. in a few minutes," Brett said breathlessly. "What about cell phones?"

"We didn't see anyone near the platform using a cell while the group went up. But there were a lot of cars in the lot and on the access roads. We tried to cover them, but they're all over the place. Just like the tourists. We stopped a bunch of people before the tram went up, but anyone could have been sitting in a coffee shop or on a deck or in a parked car trying to use a trigger."

"We'll wait for the bomb experts. They may be able to help us narrow our search for trigger sources. In the meantime, we'll clear everything out and come down after the lunch. But first, I want to talk to Samantha and Pickering. He's got to be informed about everything. And I want to update Trevor. He'll want to notify the director and the president. If these explosives had detonated...I can't even *think* about the fallout. We'll have a ton of work to do on the evidence. I'll go inside in a minute to find the Secretary."

"Treasury's security people are going to lose it," Dom said. "Then there's the public. Jeez!"

"You're right," Brett said. "We can't keep a lid on this. But hang tight. I'm going to call Trevor right now. I'm sure he'll want us to set up a command center with Denver. That is, if he trusts them after this debacle. We'll have to analyze all the photos, cross-check with our databases, and see if we get any matches."

"On it," Dom said and clicked off.

Brett punched in Trevor's private line.

"That you, Brett? Recognized the number. What's going on out there? I was just about to return an urgent call from the Denver office, but saw your call first."

Brett took a deep breath. "Denver is going ape-shit. I found some C-4 on the mountain. Planted all around the restaurant and even at the base of the tower." He quickly explained the entire situation, his efforts to disarm the explosives, Dom's work on the ground, the expected roadblocks, and his plan to ask Pickering to handle the airport shutdown. For once, Trevor was silent, though Brett heard the man inhale and almost choke.

When Brett finished his summary, his boss said, "Unbelievable. Damn glad I sent you out there. Could have been an international catastrophe. I've got to get this to the director. He'll take it to the White House. You coordinate with Pickering. He's senior on site. You said the bomb squad is coming up to deal with the C-4?"

"Yes. On their way. And Dom is handling the local sheriff."

"As for Denver," Trevor said, "that office will be in a shambles for weeks picking up the pieces. But I'm sure they'll fall all over themselves to help search for the suspects. As for you, good job, Keating. Actually, make that an excellent job. Keep me posted." Trevor clicked off.

Brett shook his head and pondered the rare compliment as he headed inside the restaurant.

———

"Ladies and gentlemen, friends and colleagues, as I've outlined today, the cost of illegal money transfers is monumental, and it impacts our legitimate private and government operations, to say nothing of the continuing threat to our collective societies posed by illicit arms sales, drug and human trafficking, and the further development and proliferation of WMD," Samantha said, making her final points. "So, we welcome your cooperation to track and shut down these accounts and these systems wherever they may be. Thank you for listening, and thank you in advance for working with us. . . for working together."

All the delegates stood up, and some called out, "Bravo!" Everyone took a drink and applauded. Alexander Tepanov was the first to rush up and try to hug her. She stood back and shook his hand instead.

"You were marvelous, Miss Reid. I wish I had you on my staff in Moscow."

"Thank you, sir." She smiled and turned to others who were crowding around, complimenting her, offering help, and suggesting the creation of working groups. She was detained for several minutes while others filed out and headed to the tram for the ride down.

Brett was inside looking for Pickering. He heard Samantha's final words and was amazed by her composure and the way she won over the delegates. He caught himself wondering if *he* could win *her* over. He pushed the idea out of his mind as he looked around for the Treasury Secretary. Spotting him, Brett moved across the room.

"Excuse me, sir. Brett Keating. FBI. May I speak with you privately?"

"Of course," Phil Pickering said. "Come over here." They headed to a corner, and Brett saw that Samantha was freeing herself from the crowd.

"I believe Samantha should hear this too," Brett said.

The Secretary motioned to Samantha who grabbed her purse and approached them. "Great job," the Secretary said. "You really got their attention. Couldn't have done it better myself."

"I doubt that, but thanks," Samantha said. She turned to Brett. "So great to see you again. Obviously, everything turned out to be just fine."

"Not really," Brett said somberly. "I came up just before you all arrived, and I located six caches of C-4 ready to be triggered by cell phone calls."

"What?" Samantha gasped.

"Are you sure?" Pickering asked severely.

"I'll show you. But first, agents on the ground are searching for the culprits. The sheriff is in the process of setting up road-blocks. Can you shut down the airport?"

"Of course. Wait a minute." Shaking off his initial shock, the secretary pulled out his cell, was quickly connected to the FAA, and gave the order. He pocketed his phone and turned to Brett. "They'll handle Jackson. It's a small airport. We'll decide later how long to keep it closed. Now, about finding that C-4. You were alone? No other agents were with you?" Pickering asked.

"Denver had scoured the area last night, and they were sure it was clear," Brett explained. "I wanted to double-check, so I came up by myself."

"But how could someone plant C-4 without those other agents finding it?" Pickering asked.

"That's what we have to find out," Brett said. "Looks to me like someone was up here and *stayed* up here after everyone else left last night. I don't know how they got back down, but they obviously meant to destroy this whole area. And everyone in it."

Samantha was listening carefully to every word. She grabbed Brett's arm as if to steady herself. "You disarmed *six* packs of C-4 before we got up here? In such a short period of time? This is incredible," she said in a weak voice.

"I had some new detection equipment with me. The bomb squad will be here pretty soon. They have to get the material out of here and safely off the mountain. Come with me, and I'll show it all to you."

Samantha began to shake. She couldn't help herself. Six bombs ready to go off? Brett could have been killed. They all could have been killed. Once again, the man had saved her life and countless others. She still couldn't breathe right. She reached over to a nearby table, grabbed a glass of water, and took a gulp. She held onto a chair and tried to take deep breaths.

As the Secretary discussed the airport shutdown with Brett, her mind raced. Who in the world had planned to massacre so many people? And why? Turning to Pickering, she asked, "How long can you keep the airport closed? Word will get out pretty fast that there is something wrong."

"We'll have to make a public statement but not until we have more facts. For now, they can blame it on a system failure. There are so many government and private planes; we can't stop those from leaving. But we've shut down commercial traffic so that security people can check every single person scheduled to fly out of Jackson for the rest of the day," the Treasury Secretary said.

"And the sheriff will get the three main roads out of town covered," Brett said. "Roadblocks are already going up. Of course, whoever is responsible for this may already be on their way out of town."

Secretary Pickering was on his cell again, consulting with his Chief of Security. Samantha couldn't stop herself. She moved closer to Brett and put her arms around him. "You did it again," she whispered. "You saved my life."

He held her close, and she reveled in the feeling of warm safety. But she knew they couldn't hold onto each other much longer in front of Secretary Pickering and other delegates who were still in the room.

"Samantha, I think you're shaking. Natural reaction," Brett said softly. He loosened his arms, looked into her eyes, and gently touched her cheek.

She gazed up at him with gratitude. "How can I ever thank you?"

"We'll think of something," he murmured. "Let me show Pickering the evidence, then let's get off this damn mountain."

FORTY-SEVEN

THURSDAY EARLY AFTERNOON: TETON VILLAGE, WYOMING

"DURAKS! HOW STUPID ARE YOU?" VADIM blared into the phone. "We watch the mountain, the tower, the restaurant, the tram. We wait. Now everyone is leaving lunch and getting back on the cable car. Nothing has happened. No explosions. No fires. Nothing. You make plans. You tell us they're perfect. We pay you millions. We come here. And we see absolutely no results."

Stas had his cell on speaker. He and Lubov let Vadim shout for a full minute before Stas tried answering. "We don't know what happened. We placed all the charges in exactly the right places. We don't know how anyone could have found them. We've done this kind of work before. You know that. We are just as upset as you are." He conveniently forgot to mention that they had seen one guy ride up the tram and snoop around the base of the tower before the lunch attendees arrived. Vadim didn't have to know about that.

Stas was worried that their call might be monitored, though he had no idea how anyone would have found his number. He couldn't think too much about that right now. He had to focus on calming Vadim down and getting out of Teton Village.

"Wait," Lubov called out. "Now that they're going down on the tram, I'm going to try to set off a charge again. The one we put on the tower. Stand by." He grabbed his own cell, re-entered the number connected to the weather station, and hit the green call button.

"That damn tram is still going down the mountain. Safely." Vadim yelled.

After a long pause, Lubov stared at his ringing cell. He finally said, "That should have worked. It should have taken down the whole damn tower. I don't know what went wrong, but we're just as upset as you are."

"How could you *possibly* be as upset as we are?" Vadim demanded. "Where did you get your C-4?"

"We told you. It's *Czech Plastique*. Always worked before."

"Are you sure it was from the Czechs and not the Chechens?" Vadim yelled.

"Of course, I'm sure," Stas said. "Where are you now?"

"We were parked on the access road with a clear view of the entire mountain. Now we're driving to Idaho Falls."

"We're heading that way too. We don't want to draw any attention, so we won't be driving fast. But we *will* meet you at the airport and talk more there. Maybe we can salvage this."

"How?" Vadim demanded.

"Lubov and I will discuss it on the drive over," Stas said. "Right now, we have to get over the pass before any of those security people set up roadblocks. That's the first thing they'll do if they find anything on the mountain."

"That's the first thing you've been right about all day," Vadim said. "Do you have *any* idea how much we had riding on this?"

"Yes, we do," Stas said. "And we lose too, especially our commission on the deal," he mumbled to Lubov as he shifted gears and headed out of the village as quickly as he could maneuver around several parked cars and trucks.

"Fine. I dealt with the plane order yesterday. I'll deal with you two later." Vadim abruptly ended the call.

As Stas pocketed his cell, Lubov started to chuckle.

"What could you possibly be laughing at?" Stas asked.

"Vadim loses everything, except for that five million he was going to pay us. But we don't have to lose anything. Except that five mill."

"What do you mean? You said you shorted our accounts too."

"Yes, but not the way he did. He told me he went on margin to buy puts. Those are contracts he purchased. He can't get out of them. He has no money to do that. It's all tied up. But we shorted exchange traded funds. They're just like regular stocks. I'll call Moscow and give the order to sell them. Then our accounts will be more or less back to normal. So you see, we weren't such 'stupid *duraks*' after all."

FORTY-EIGHT

THURSDAY LATE AFTERNOON: JACKSON, WYOMING

"THE DIRECTOR IS BRIEFING THE PRESIDENT right now," Brett announced as he stepped into the makeshift crisis center they had set up inside the local sheriff's office on South King Street in the heart of Jackson. "Last time I updated Trevor, he said he'd give me instructions as soon as the Director is done in the Oval."

"Is he finally taking your calls right away?" Dom asked.

"Yes. Guess I'm no longer the interloper from Chicago," Brett said, pulling up a gray metal chair to sit across from Dom's desk.

"That's what happens when you become a hero. The boss takes interest," Dom said.

"Definitely not a hero. Just doing my job. I will say Trevor's been preening a bit since our team got the drop on Denver and saved the whole damn situation. He says we all have to work together as fast as we can to find these terrorists, militants, or whatever the hell they are."

301

"We are," Dom said, waving his arm to indicate other agents and sheriff's deputies who were pounding computer keys, checking on roadblocks, and talking on countless phones. "What about Secretary Pickering and Samantha? Where are they?"

"They'll be here pretty soon. Trevor told me that since Pickering is on site with details, the Director may decide to have him announce what happened. They want *any* leads we've got from the photos or interviews at the hotels and airports. So, what do we have so far?"

"We've been analyzing all the photos Denver and I took. A few are already getting extra scrutiny," Dom said, pointing to several pictures spread out on the large desk.

"Who's this?" Brett asked, pointing to a scowling woman in a large jacket.

"She was trying to take pictures of the tram with her cell. I stopped her, and she got angry. As far as we can tell, she left the area before Samantha's tram went up. Her photo's not in our database. No criminal background or affiliations."

Dom pointed to another group of pictures. "This is a group of four guys I argued with. Turns out they're all students from Northwestern. One of the clerks at the Pink Buffalo Motel told a Denver agent she recognized them. Said they were friendly. Not exactly terrorist types. Anyway, the agents tracked them down and are talking to them right now, showing them some of the other photos, seeing if they saw anything suspicious."

"Who are those men?" Brett asked, pointing to two other images.

Dom grabbed two photos and held them up. "These two were sitting in a car close to the tram platform. I was trying to cover as many people in the area as I could, so I took these on the run. They came out pretty clear, though."

Brett stared at the men. One had bushy eyebrows, the other was rather thin with a long nose. "Look foreign. Of course, there are a ton of foreign tourists around here. These could be Eastern European. Maybe Russian. Any hits?"

"We're running them now. The agents searching the hotels have their pictures, along with a bunch of others. They should be calling in any minute with a report. We're doing background checks on other photos too, but these two guys...there's something about them. Maybe I've seen them somewhere before. It's bugging me," Dom said, scratching his head.

"They could be on some watch list," Brett said. "Let's try to find out if they're still in town. What about the airport?"

"Some Denver agents are all over it. There's a lot of griping about delayed flights. People are pretty steamed. They want to know why. The airlines have been told to make it sound like a computer problem until further notice. We'll have to make a public announcement pretty soon. As for the rest of the Denver team, you should see how they've been scrambling for clues. Makes Poirot look like a piker. Pretty obvious they're trying to save face for totally missing the C-4 and endangering the entire place."

"I've been thinking about that," Brett said. "I told Pickering that whoever planted it must have been on the mountain and stayed up there after the Denver guys and everybody else left. I just asked the sheriff about that possibility, and he said that there are trails down Rendezvous. So, they could have hiked back down after midnight. The trails are dangerous, but they're necessary. If the tram ever had a mechanical problem and the ski patrol had to rescue someone, that's the way they'd go."

Dom's cell rang. He answered, "Turiano." Then he listened for a moment. "No shit. Face recognition matches? Email the files ASAP. This is huge. Thanks a ton." He turned to Brett. "D.C. got a match of those two. Turns out they're Russian mafia. They use a lot of different last names, but Lubov and Stas cropped up twice. They're checking visas to see if they can find out when they came into the country. And they're contacting airlines too."

Brett grabbed the photos and studied them again. "You did a good job with these. Obviously, we don't have any evidence that ties them to the C-4, but I'll show them to Pickering and see if he wants to use them in his press conference. If he and the Director decide to circulate the photos, they'll be everywhere in a matter of seconds."

"I think we should go for it. They should never have been let into the country. Probably had a bunch of fake passports and visas. If not the C-4, they could have been up to something else," Dom said.

"I have to agree with you."

"We should know pretty soon when they landed in Jackson, where they stayed, and if they're still here," Dom said. "The locals have all been extremely helpful. They don't have much crime out here, and they want to keep it that way. I get the sense that they mostly deal with search and rescue during ski season and the occasional tourist who tries to outrun a bear. After all, this is a concealed-carry state. You don't even need a permit to own a gun in Wyoming. So, with every carpenter, electrician, and rancher carrying a shotgun, especially during hunting season, who's gonna hold 'em up?"

"I get your point," Brett said. "Right now, we'll wait for Pickering. He's meeting with his people, but he said he would come here right after to get an update. The other delegates haven't been told about the explosives yet. Samantha is the only other one who knows right now."

"Well, with agents asking questions all over town, word will get out in nanoseconds," Dom said.

"I know. But Pickering still wants to do this right—get all the facts out, post pictures, do everything in an orderly way. He doesn't want to scare the public. He just wants to reassure them we stopped a threat but need their help to track down the suspects."

"You know what I don't get?" Dom said. "If this were a straight-up terrorist plot to blow up all these important financial people, that would be one thing. But if these Russians are involved, the mafia is involved. What the hell would the mafia be doing trying to blow up an economic conference? Especially since there were other Russians on the delegate list. It just doesn't make any sense to me."

Brett thought for a moment and replied, "You're right. Looks like terrorists, but it may not be. What kind of motive would the mafia have?" He looked up as the Secretary of the Treasury strode in with Samantha by his side.

FORTY-NINE

OTTO SAT ON THE BED IN HIS BEST WESTERN motel room with his laptop balanced on his knees.

When he left Georgetown and drove down 395 toward Richmond, he had spotted the motel sign, saw that the parking lot was pretty full, and figured no one there would notice him if they already had a lot of guests. He had checked in, kept his hoodie on, and stayed in his room, trying to decide what to do next.

He rechecked his inbox, but no new emails from Vadim had come through. At least his uncles weren't paying attention to him either.

Otto closed his laptop and slid it onto the bed. Then he clicked on the TV, tuned to CNN, and saw the Breaking News bar appear as the anchor came on to announce a bombing attempt that had been thwarted in Jackson, Wyoming. The man announced, "Treasury Secretary Philip Pickering is asking anyone with information as to the whereabouts of these two persons of interest to contact the FBI immediately."

Photographs of Lubov and Stas flashed on the screen. "These two individuals are believed to be members of the Russian mafia and were identified as being at the scene of the event under investigation. The number to call is 1-800-CALL-FBI. Again, that's 1-800-CALL-FBI. Details of the plan to attack the Annual Federal Reserve Conference in Jackson Hole, Wyoming, are now coming in. Here is our local reporter, Celinda Lopez, live from Jackson."

"We have just spoken to a number of finance ministers from Europe as well as central bankers from Asia and Russia," the correspondent explained. "All have thanked the FBI agent who discovered and disarmed the explosive devices, just before everyone arrived at the top of Rendezvous Mountain for a luncheon speech by Director of the White House Office of Homeland Security Samantha Reid."

Otto stared at the screen and tried to process what he just heard. Samantha Reid? *His* assigned target was in Jackson, not D.C.? Is that why Lubov and Stas were there? Did Vadim tell them to take her out along with all those other important people? He sat transfixed as he continued to listen to the report.

The camera panned to a wide shot of the mountain behind the reporter. "I am here with one delegate from Russia, central banker Alexander Tepanov."

Vadim mentioned that name. Something about changing accounts. Why was Tepanov there too?

Tepanov spoke in a measured tone. "I am astounded by the news of this threat. I cannot imagine what sick minds engineered it. I know I speak for all the conference attendees when I say we are supremely grateful to America's FBI for stopping this attack and saving all of our lives."

"But, Mr. Tepanov, photos of two of your countrymen are being circulated. Men who were at the base of the mountain and who could have been involved," the reporter said. "Do you have any idea who they are or where they might be?"

Tepanov looked at the reporter. He seemed shaken by her question. "I have no idea. However, I'm sure that Russia's security forces are working closely with U.S. officials to track them down and discern *if* there is any connection to this threat. If you will excuse me, I have to get back to my delegation."

As he turned away from her microphone, the reporter wrapped up. "We have word that FBI agents from the Denver and Washington, D.C., offices are interviewing witnesses, hotel employees, and rental car companies. The Jackson Airport remains closed, and roadblocks are set up to screen any vehicles attempting to leave the area. Reporting from Jackson, Wyoming, I'm Celinda Lopez."

Otto hit the mute button and put his head in his hands. Were Vadim, Maksim, Lubov, and Stas behind a plan to bomb a whole conference of international financial leaders? He knew Vadim was a bastard, and he hadn't liked Stas and Lubov. But how could they come up with something so horrible?

He started to shake. This was the worst day of his life. He looked back up at the TV and saw the FBI number plastered across the screen. His wanted to call the number and confess to everything. But if he did that, he would end up in jail along with his uncles.

When people went to jail in Russia, some never came out. He started to breathe heavily.

He looked at his cell phone charging on the side table and had an idea. He didn't know if she would even take his call, but he had to try. He grabbed the phone.

"Oleg? I saw your number. You know I don't want to talk to you," Jolene said in a firm voice.

"Wait! Don't hang up," he pleaded. "I have some new information. I need help, and I don't know anyone else I can call."

"What new information?" she asked cautiously.

"Have you heard about the bomb threat the FBI stopped out West?"

"The one in Jackson? You have information about that?" she practically shrieked. "If you had something to do with a terrorist plot, get out of my life. Now!"

"No, wait. I had nothing to do with that. Please believe me. Nothing. But I might know who did."

"You know terrorists? What are you? Part of ISIS? My God, Oleg. How could you be so totally screwed up? I thought you were a smart guy. If I knew where you were, I'd turn you in. In a heartbeat."

"No, listen. I'm not a terrorist. I don't know anything about ISIS, but I do know about the Russian mafia."

"You're a member of the Russian mafia?" she asked, raising her voice another decibel.

"No, I'm not. I said I *knew* about it. Everyone in Russia knows about it. Here's the thing. I just saw a news report about two Russians they're looking for, guys they say were in Jackson. I think I know who they are."

"If you know anything you have to call the police! Or the FBI. Somebody," she implored.

"I know. I want to."

"Then do it," she said emphatically.

"I'm afraid."

"Afraid of what? Because the FBI is looking for you too?"

"Yes. But that has nothing to do with what happened in Jackson." There was a long pause. He held his breath.

Finally, she sighed. "If those men had anything to do with this, and if you can help get them arrested, you *have* to turn yourself in."

"How do I do that? Just walk into a police station and get myself arrested too? Nobody does that in Russia. They get a lawyer or somebody to front for them first."

"Then that's it. You get a lawyer, and he represents you."

"I don't know any lawyers," Otto said.

Another long pause. Then Jolene said, "There are lawyers all over Washington. Look up criminal defense attorneys. Good-bye, Oleg." She clicked off.

FIFTY

FRIDAY AFTERNOON: JACKSON, WYOMING

"TAKING THE FBI'S LEARJET BACK TO D.C. IS the way to go," Phil Pickering said, strapping himself in. "I'm glad we can fly back without changing planes. I think we've done all we can do here, and with the Denver contingent staying in town to tie up loose ends, we all need to get back."

"I'm with you. I can't wait to get out of here," Samantha said, "This is the second time I've been in Jackson, and the second time something terrible has happened."

"Oh? I didn't know," the Secretary replied. "What was it?"

Samantha gave him a summary of the hiking trip she and her late husband had taken several years ago. "It left me with a fear of heights, among other things."

"I'm sure that tram ride didn't help," Pickering said.

"It didn't. But I kept my eyes closed," she said with a faint smile.

"Well, you recovered wonderfully and gave a bang-up speech. It was the one highlight of this whole affair," he said.

"I caught the tail end of it," Brett said from the seat behind them. "Great job."

"You're the one who did a great—no, make that spectacular—job," Samantha said, turning around to face him.

"I agree," Dom said.

The four of them talked about next steps in the investigation, the search for the culprits, announcements that should be made to the press, and how quickly they thought they could solve the case.

None of the other photos had triggered anything in the databases, but two of the interviews had given them leads. One was from a hotel clerk who worked at the Teton Mountain Lodge. She recognized the two Russians since they had stayed there the previous week. The second was from a clerk who said they checked into her hotel a few days before the conference began. Her records showed the men had checked out the morning of the planned attack.

That bit of news made it even more likely that Lubov and Stas were involved. They must have come to Jackson to scope out the area, made their plans, and then returned to execute them.

"First thing I need to do when we get back is talk to the Russian Ambassador," Secretary Pickering said. "We need their help tracking down these men, especially any connections they have here in the states. After all, one of their officials was at the conference along with Alexander Tepanov. I spoke with him at the lodge, and he said he'd see what he could do with the authorities back home. So far, the Kremlin isn't talking."

"Shades of Snowden. They don't talk about him either," Brett muttered. "Whoever they are, I'm sure they haven't left the country. We got the Interpol Red Notice out so damn fast, they'll be stopped if they try to fly anywhere."

"You're right. I'm sure they're waiting it out somewhere. We should get some reliable hits on them soon, though. Those pictures are on every newscast and social media outlet, and your press conference, Mr. Secretary, is all over the internet, thanks to YouTube. The bureau has already receive tons of calls from people who thought they might have seen them. They're checking everything now," Dom said.

"After that news conference," Pickering said, "the media kept asking to interview you, Brett. Of course, we didn't let them. We always protect our agents and their identities."

"Thanks. Appreciate staying anonymous if I can," Brett said.

"They still want to know exactly *how* you disarmed all of the explosives, though. I wasn't about to tell them. I want to get that detection device and the bomb pre-emptor over to the SecDef. After you proved how effective they were, I believe the Pentagon should begin their own tests."

"That's what I thought when we first got those demos," Dom said.

"I doubt if I could have found all six packs of C-4 without them. Not with the little time I had," Brett said.

Samantha turned to face Brett again. "You were amazing. You might have found some of them, but tossing that BPE on the tower was the best move I've ever heard."

"Just trying to channel LeBron I guess. Actually, it was a lucky shot," Brett said.

"Everyone was lucky to have you two out there," the Secretary said. "I know you worked late trying to come up with a list of suspects, and you haven't had much rest. So, I'm going to leave you two alone and let you catch some shut-eye."

"Okay, thanks," Dom said. "We'll go over everything again before we land."

When the jet began its descent to Dulles Airport, they buckled their seat belts. Once on the ground, they turned their cell phones back on. Brett saw he had an urgent text from Trevor. He called his boss as they taxied to the FBO.

"You're not going to believe this," Trevor said, answering on the first ring.

"What?" Brett said. "We're landing at Dulles right now."

"I just finished a meeting with a lawyer who says he represents a client named Otto. Ring any bells?"

"The Naples waiter?" Brett shouted. Samantha looked back at him, and he put up his hand in a "wait-a-second" gesture as he listened to Trevor.

"The kid is in D.C. Been here for a while. He wants to come in and cut a deal."

"What kind of deal would we possibly give him?" Brett asked.

"A deal where he tells us where he thinks Lubov and Nickolai are right now."

"He knows their location? Was he involved in the bomb threat?"

"Nope. Says he heard them talking about a plan, but he had no part in it. The lawyer says the kid will explain everything if we grant him immunity. Turns out that when he saw their pictures on TV, he recognized them as friends of his uncles, who evidently told him to follow Samantha Reid."

"Incredible," Brett said breathlessly. "What are you going to do?"

"I've got a meeting lined up with the Director in an hour," Trevor said. "We'll go over the details and sort it out. But we're going to make a decision fast. Those guys could be on the move."

"We just pulled up to the FBO. We have a car waiting. I'll be back in the office in less than an hour. Can I come with you to see the Director?" Brett asked.

"Sure. Get your ass in here, and we'll figure it out with the Director," Trevor said and clicked off.

Brett turned to the others. "I don't know how much of that you heard, but the Naples waiter has offered to cut a deal and tell us where the Russians are. They have a connection to his uncles who could be the real culprits."

"That's fantastic," Samantha exclaimed, unfastening her seat belt and standing up.

"Now *this* is an incredibly lucky break," the Treasury Secretary said. "I need to get back to my office, and I'm sure Samantha wants to get to the White House, but let's have the driver drop you at FBI headquarters first."

"Are you sure?" Brett and Dom both said at the same time.

"Absolutely."

FIFTY-ONE

"HI, BRETT, COME ON IN," SAMANTHA SAID, opening the door to her apartment. "I'm so glad you can take a quick break for dinner. All I've been able to think about for the last forty-eight hours is what you did for me and everybody else on that mountain."

Brett walked in and handed her a bottle of pinot noir. "This one okay?"

"Perfect," she said, leading the way to her tiny kitchen. "You're in good company, by the way. Even though it's Sunday, I just got home. I don't think the word 'weekend' is in the White House's vocabulary. Can't be helped, though. Things have been absolutely insane with all the news coverage, but probably not as crazy as what's going on at the FBI."

"I'll fill you in," Brett said, opening a drawer to get the wine opener. "We've all been pulling the late shift to track down every bit of evidence we can find to build the case against those Russians."

"How did your second meeting with the lawyer go? Are you going to bring Otto in?"

"Yes," Brett said, pouring some wine and handing her a glass. "I'll tell you all about it over dinner. Can I help you with that?"

She pointed to plates of sliced tomatoes and mozzarella. "You can take those to the table. I'll get the veal parmesan. I picked it up at a deli on the way home since I didn't have time to cook anything. Hope it's all right."

"Whatever you have will be great," he said with a grin.

She lit some candles on the dining table and sat down. "Now, tell me about the meeting."

He joined her at the table and sampled the tomatoes. "As you know, Trevor and I met with the Director on Friday and Saturday. We all decided that the gravity and scale of the bombing attempt outweighed the actions of that kid. So, we agreed to negotiate with the lawyer. We haven't started the negotiations yet, but the attorney has already convinced us that we made the right decision. During our meeting with him today, he gave us even more details about Otto's story and how much he could help us."

"What details?" she asked, tasting the wine. "This is good, by the way. Thanks."

"Otto is ready to tell us what he knows about his uncles' so-called businesses, which include arms trafficking to certain groups. He also overheard his uncles talking to the Russian mafia guys—he calls them Lubov and Stas—about a plan to make a ton of money. It sounds like the kid knows what he's talking about, and we're going to need his testimony when we arrest these guys and bring them to trial."

"Do you really think he'll testify against his own uncles?"

"Only if we give him immunity, disguise his voice, let him stay here, and put him in our witness protection program. It's all pretty involved, but it'll be worth it."

"What about the Naples explosion, the hit-and-run, and the gunshot?"

"That's all part of the negotiation. There are a ton of things we could charge him with under section eighteen of the criminal code. Our legal staff is working on that right now."

"Well, I hope they hurry. Those Russians could be moving around," she ventured as she finished her tomato salad.

"Apparently, Otto thinks they're hiding out somewhere they feel fairly safe. If we can get a quick read from legal, we're going to bring him in first thing tomorrow and try to cut the deal."

"Do you think I should see him at some point? Maybe make an ID or something?" she asked.

"I thought about that. But I wasn't sure if you'd want to face him after everything he put you through."

"Trailing me around D.C. and even taking a shot at me is absolutely nothing compared to placing explosives that could have killed the most important financial leaders in the world. I can't even imagine what would have happened to world markets if those bombs had gone off," she said.

"You all could have been killed, and you're thinking about how that would have impacted the stock market?" he asked.

"Wait a minute. Could *that* have been the motive? Crashing the markets so that the Russians could benefit somehow?" Samantha said with a startled look.

He put his fork down and stared at her. He suddenly remembered talking to Nori about her hearing references to the markets. "That's it. We've been grappling with motives from the get-go. When it didn't look like terrorism, we knew it had to be bigger than just getting rid of you and your investigations. But we hadn't really analyzed the financial meltdown angle." He picked up his water glass. "Samantha, you're brilliant." He touched it to her wine glass in mock salute and took a drink.

"The more I think about it, it's the one thing that makes sense," she said. "If those guys had shorted the market, they would have made a killing. Anyone who knew about their plan could have made a bunch of trades, like shorting the Dow or the S&P. We would just need to find their broker and see if they really *did* do that. Then we'd have a huge piece of evidence right there." She took a bite of veal and then stopped. "I have an idea."

"Another one?" Brett asked. "You're on a roll."

"Remember Alexander Tepanov?"

"Yeah. I saw a clip of him saying he didn't know the two Russians."

"I saw the same clip. He looked extremely uncomfortable, which makes sense. I did a bit of research on him earlier to see if we might be able to convince him to help us close down some of the money laundering accounts we're tracking. He looks pretty corrupt to me."

"So, what are you saying?" Brett asked.

"What if I could get through to him? Find out if he knows *anything* about those guys or Otto's uncles. Or maybe he could help us figure out where and how those men made their trades. If they made any, that is."

Brett pulled out his cell and called Trevor. He quickly went over Samantha's theory about the bombing motive and her idea about getting to Tepanov. He listened for a moment, gave her a thumbs up, and then pocketed the phone. "He's on board. He says that if you can sound out Tepanov, we can send our people over to take his deposition."

"I need to run this by the NSC Advisor. Do we need to get the FBI director on board too?"

"Trevor will handle that."

"Okay, then I'll get on it first thing tomorrow," Samantha said. "Now, back to the markets. They haven't moved much in the past few days. But if we can actually arrest and convict those Russians and reassure the public, I'll bet the DOW will shoot up."

"Could happen," Brett said.

"And, depending on how much they had riding on this, they might be pretty wiped out," Samantha said with a wide smile.

"If we can prove all of this, in addition to nailing them and getting convictions, their organizations will have nothing left to buy arms and drugs with," Brett said. "Talk about a collapse. The best part is, if your theory pans out, they did it to themselves."

"When do you think you can arrest them?" she asked.

"If Otto confirms any of this tomorrow and gives us an address, we'll move as quickly as possible."

Brett poured more wine for Samantha and finished his veal. For the first time in over a week, he felt optimistic. This nightmare of an investigation was finally coming to a close, and he was having dinner with a beautiful woman. A smart woman who was also helping him solve the case better than any partner the FBI could have assigned him.

It was hard not to think of her as a colleague. He felt like he knew her better than people he had spent years working with. While he had been her bodyguard, she had told him about growing up in Texas and about all the life lessons her father had taught her. She also shared some of her experiences managing the countless threats that came to her directorate. But no matter how difficult or distressing those stories were to tell, she never lost her calm or subtle sense of humor. And that floored him.

The more he learned about her, the more he wanted to be with her. Sure, she was easy on the eyes, but there were a lot of gorgeous women in D.C. He saw them every day, but none of them affected him the way she did.

Samantha got up to clear the table. "Would you like some coffee? I also picked up chocolate chip cookies."

Brett carried the rest of the plates to the kitchen. "Coffee and cookies would be great. I'll have to go back to work after that, though." He was standing close to her, inhaling her scent. She must use special shampoo or something. Whatever it was, he liked it. When she straightened up, she paused and looked at him. Was that an invitation to come closer? He didn't know, but he hoped it was.

Suddenly, her buzzer sounded. "Who would come here at this hour?" Samantha muttered as she walked to the intercom. "Yes?"

A girl's voice said, "Flowers for Samantha Reid."

"On a Sunday? It must be a special delivery or something. Just a moment."

"I'll get them," Brett said. "Be right back."

As Samantha poured the coffee, Brett walked back in her apartment carrying a large vase filled with roses. "Girl said they had a lot of weekend orders, so she decided to work overtime to make all of their deliveries. Here you go," he said, setting the vase on the kitchen counter.

Samantha looked at the beautiful arrangement and grabbed the card. She opened the tiny envelope and read the message: So glad you are safe. Love, Tripp.

FIFTY-TWO

MONDAY MORNING:
SAN FRANCISCO, CALIFORNIA

"FBI. OPEN UP!"

"What the hell," Vadim said in a low voice, grabbing his pistol from a drawer in his desk.

Maksim, Lubov, and Stas rushed in from their rooms. "What's happening?" Stas asked.

"Quiet," Vadim hissed. "This has to be another one of your screw-ups," he added, aiming the barb at Lubov and Stas. "You got your stupid faces splattered all over TV. Someone around here must have spotted you and called the feds. We should have kicked you out of here as soon as we got back from Jackson."

Maksim walked slowly toward his brother. "But remember we talked about feeling safe here. I'm sure they're watching all the airports. Besides, we had to be sure Lubov and Stas didn't implicate us if they were picked up separately." He motioned to the others. "There's a service exit in the kitchen. Maybe we can get out that way."

325

The foursome moved cautiously, trying not to make any noise while the pounding continued.

"Maybe they'll think we left town," Lubov said.

"They'll still come in," Vadim mumbled.

Just before they reached the exit, a platoon of agents crashed through the door and burst into the room. Vadim spun around and fired his pistol while the others hid behind the kitchen door. The bullet tore through the front door, and an agent returned fire, hitting Vadim in the leg. He yelled, dropped his gun, tried to grab his leg, and fell backwards, knocking over a floor lamp.

"Don't shoot," Maksim shouted, peering out from behind the door. "I'm not armed."

Another agent bolted to Vadim's gun and kicked it out of reach. "Where are the others?" he demanded. Maksim glanced nervously to the left. The agent called out, "Come out. Now!"

Stas inched his way out of the kitchen and raised his hands. An agent rushed up, turned him around, and quickly snapped a pair of handcuffs on him. Another was already cuffing Vadim and Maksim.

"One more," the lead agent said. "Where is he?"

"I don't know," Stas said.

The lead moved cautiously toward the kitchen. When he stepped inside it, he saw the other door. He yanked it open, revealing stairs leading down. "Trying to get away," he said.

"He won't get far. Building's surrounded," one of his colleagues replied.

"You shot me!" Vadim shouted. "I need a doctor."

"You'll get one soon enough," an agent said, peering at the leg wound. "Unfortunately, you'll live."

"Why are you here?" Vadim said, raising his voice. "I own this apartment. I am a citizen of Russia. I have a valid visa. We all do. You have no right—"

"We have every right," the lead agent said. "You are all under arrest for conspiracy, the attempted murder of over one hundred people in Jackson, Wyoming, resisting arrest, firing on an agent—probably with an unregistered weapon. And that's just the start of it. Read them their rights," he said to an agent standing next to him, who performed the perfunctory notice.

"Search the place," the special agent in charge said over his shoulder. "Take computers, cell phones, and everything else you find while we escort them outside. Look for bills, accounts, travel documents. You know what to bag."

Several agents fanned out through the apartment. One went into the bedroom, another walked to the kitchen, and a third started to search Vadim's desk in the corner of the living room. He set the computer aside and rifled through several drawers. In the bottom of one, he found an envelope delivered from Moscow by DHL. He opened it and pulled out several pages covered with numbers.

"This could be important. It's all in Russian, but looks like it might be a list of stock trades. I recognize a couple of the symbols. We'll bag everything and get it to D.C. for analysis."

"Oh shit," Vadim mumbled. "You've got nothing on us," he barked, hobbling forward. "Show me a warrant."

"Got it right here," the special agent said, pulling a piece of paper out of his pocket. "You can read it in the van on your way to jail."

FIFTY-THREE

"WE GOT THEM!" TREVOR ANNOUNCED, hurrying into Brett's office. Brett was sitting at his desk, and Dom was leaning against the wall.

"Where? When?" Dom shouted.

"Right where the kid said they'd be?" Brett asked.

"Exactly. Just happened. Perfect take down," Trevor said with a note of triumph. "One of the uncles, Vadim Baltiev, managed to get off a shot. Our guys weren't hurt, but they returned fire and shot him in the leg. Nothing serious. He'll live. One of the other Russians tried to escape down a back stairway. Nailed him too. Now they're all in jail in San Francisco, waiting for us to finish the paperwork to bring them back here."

"That's incredible," Dom said. "I was just getting briefed on everything else the kid said this morning."

"I'll leave you to go over that," Trevor said. "Just wanted you to know about San Francisco. The Director is going to announce the arrest pretty soon. Watch Fox News."

"Thanks," Brett said, leaning over and flicking on the TV remote. He put it on mute.

"Oh, before you leave," Dom said to Trevor, "we just got an analysis of the C-4 used in Jackson. The lab also worked on the remnants of the material they found in Naples. Guess what? Same source," Dom said handing over a report.

"*Czech Plastique*," Trevor read. "Pretty common."

"It was probably shielded and sent through the mail," Dom said. "The Denver agents found an employee in a Wilson, Wyoming, post office who remembered one of the suspects in the photos. The one named Lubov. Said he rented a box and got several packages. He remembered because the guy sounded foreign and was rather rude."

"That all ties in. Case is building pretty fast," Brett said.

"Keep at it," Trevor said before turning and walking back down the hall.

"So, back to this morning's meeting," Brett said. "The kid sang like a choir boy after we agreed to immunity and protection. He said that if he testified, the perpetrators would know it was him, and he would never be able to go back to Russia. The mafia would kill him for being a snitch.

"His attorney reminded us that he's concerned about his mother," Brett continued. "She lives on a little farm outside of Moscow. Our embassy is trying to see if we can move her over here. After we finished discussing his mother, we pressed him on Samantha Reid, and he broke down. Said he was only following his uncle's orders and that he didn't really want to hurt her, just keep her scared and sidelined for a while."

"Wish I had been in that meeting," Dom said. "What else?"

"A treasure trove," Brett said. "Turns out his uncles had all sorts of clients for their weapons' deals. One is Lashkar-e-Taiba, the militant outfit operating in Kashmir that likes to attack cities in India. Otto also remembered the name FARC in South America. Samantha was excited to hear about that connection. It all ties into a major investigation at the White House, Treasury, and DOD."

"A real home run," Dom said.

"And there's a lot more. Otto said that Vadim and Maksim talked about how much money they lost in Cyprus and Malta, and even more because of the sanctions. Then when Lubov and Stas—that's what he called them—were staying at his uncles' penthouse, he overheard them talk about a plan to crash the stock market and make back their money while he was playing video games in his room."

"All of that supports Samantha's theory," Dom said. "So far, it looks like we've got motive, means, and opportunity."

"Yep."

"So, what's next?"

"The analysts will go through everything they found in that penthouse—computers, cell phones, bank records. I didn't get a full read-out of what they hauled out of there, but I'm sure we'll get a report soon," Brett said. "Oh, and Samantha told me she contacted that Russian banker, Alexander Tepanov. You'll never guess what she pried out of him," Brett said.

"What?"

"He agreed to give a deposition. Turns out Vadim, one of Otto's uncles, actually asked him to execute a lot of contracts to short the market. Tepanov warned Vadim that if the market went up, he could lose everything. But Vadim seemed sure of himself, so the order went through. Tepanov also placed a few shorts for the two mafia members."

"Why did he deny knowing them before?" Dom asked.

"Didn't want to get involved. And he told Samantha that he was still shaken by the news of the explosives when he said that. He also admitted that after the shock wore off, it became very clear to him that shorting the market through a massacre had always been Vadim's plan. And that's exactly what Samantha predicted."

"Pretty amazing woman to figure all that out," Dom said.

"Amazing for sure," Brett said with a smile. "We've been feeding all of this up through channels to the Director as we get it." He glanced at his computer when he heard the ding that announced a new email. "Oh boy."

"What is it?" Dom asked, leaning over.

"It's from Eleanor, the real estate agent."

"After your bod again, huh?"

Brett shrugged, read the short note, and started to chuckle. "Says she's sorry she has to cancel her previous invitation to the Kennedy Center. While I was out of town, she met a lobbyist who is taking up all her free time. She hopes I understand, and she'll be glad to continue to work with the bureau to protect national security."

Dom burst out laughing. Then he pointed to the TV as the FBI director stepped up to a microphone. "Turn it up." Brett hit the button as dozens of reporters and cameramen jockeyed for a position in front or to the side of the Director as he read a prepared statement.

"Good afternoon. I want to announce that FBI Special Agents have just arrested four suspects in the attempted bombing of the Federal Reserve Conference in Jackson, Wyoming. They are Russian citizens who were arrested at a penthouse apartment in San Francisco owned by two of the suspects. They are brothers, Vadim and Maksim Baltiev. The other two suspects are known members of a Russian mafia organization.

"While there is an ongoing investigation, it does not appear that the incident had any connection to terrorist organizations, such as Al Qaeda, ISIS, or other militant groups. The suspects' motives appear to be related to the financial markets.

"I want to assure the American people that every delegate who attended the conference is safe and that the markets are operating as smoothly as usual. I would also like to thank the FBI agents who worked tirelessly to discover and prevent this unthinkable crime. It is a tribute to their dedication and constant vigilance to keep our country safe.

"Finally, I cannot take any questions at this point, but as we continue our investigation and uncover more facts, we will keep the American people informed." He folded his notes and prepared to leave the podium, ignoring the shouted questions.

"How did you know about the threat?"

"Were you monitoring cell phones and emails?"

"Why were the suspects in San Francisco?"

"How did you find them?"

The Director waved his hand and quickly left the room.

"What do you think?" Brett asked, clicking off the TV.

"He was talking about you, you know," Dom said.

"Not just me. You were there. We never would have found those suspects without your photos."

"I guess. Can't wait to question them. Once we get them here and separate them, it'll be interesting to see if one of them rats on the others."

"They all seem pretty tight-lipped to me, but we'll see," Brett said.

Dom nodded, took his coffee mug, and headed back to his cubicle.

Brett spent the next couple of hours reviewing data on the four suspects and exchanging ideas with other agents about the Russians' connections to the arms trade. They analyzed visas, fake passports, and travel itineraries while they waited for the delivery of the computers, cell phones, and other items collected in San Francisco.

He checked his watch and saw that it was almost time for the closing bell on Wall Street. He turned on CNBC where an anchor was finishing her wrap-up of the trading day. "As you can see, the S&P, NASDAQ, and Dow Jones industrial average have all posted major gains with the Dow up just over three hundred points."

Brett leaned back in his chair and grinned.

FIFTY-FOUR

"*FINALLY, WE GET TO DO SOMETHING OUTSIDE* together. Something without bodyguards," Angela said, leaning back to stretch her calves. She looked across the street and saw the sign for Montrose Park. "After hearing you and Brett talk about how beautiful the park is, I'm looking forward to seeing it myself."

Samantha tossed her friend a water bottle, grabbed one of her own, and started to jog across the street. "You'll like it. There's a nice path that goes for miles."

They entered the park, and Samantha continued. "Speaking of Brett, he has been so great lately. He's been keeping me up to speed on how the case is building. And I'm trying to keep up with Treasury and Defense on the efforts to close a lot of illicit accounts and stop a ton of arms shipments. We're all working late these days."

"The press has been all over the court case," Angela said. "The reporters have been going nuts on the North Lawn."

"Yes, it's all happening pretty fast compared to other cases. The grand jury has already written the indictments. I'm glad I don't have to help prepare for the trial."

They started to jog down the path at a leisurely, warm-up pace, passing picnic tables and monkey bars as they continued into the woods.

"Every time we talk about the Jackson case, I get goosebumps big enough to hang a hat on," Angela said with a nervous laugh.

"Me too. I was nervous and in bad shape during the entire trip. But I don't really want to relive it right now."

"Oh, sorry. It's just all so wild. But we won't talk about it anymore," Angela said, stopping to take a sip of water. They both paused to catch their breath.

"So, what's new in your shop? Every time I hear about the crazy petitions you have to handle, it makes me laugh. Lately, it's been nice to do that once in a while," Samantha said.

"Well, if a laugh is what you wanted…on my way over here, I drove past a building with a newly installed drug rehab center. There was a sign out front that said 'Keep Off The Grass.'"

"Love it," Samantha said, grinning at her friend.

"As for my shop, let's see. Oh, we keep getting requests for White House meetings from a tax simplification group. They want members of Congress and the administration to sign a pledge to fill out their own tax returns."

"Fat chance. Congress would never take that kind of pledge," Samantha said.

"Why shouldn't those members follow all the laws and rules they make the rest of us follow?" Angela countered. "Anyway, when I tried to get the support of the political affairs shop, they laughed me out of the room. Should have just flown a kite before they told me to," Angela said.

They started to run again. After another twenty minutes, Samantha said, "Wait until you see where I like to cool down. Follow me."

They jogged back to the entrance of the park, reached the sidewalk, and turned left toward the cemetery's iron gates. When Samantha got inside, she looked to her right, and there he was.

"Wilkinson," she shouted and ran over to him. She sat down on the bench next to him and threw her arms around his neck. "How *are* you? I haven't seen you in ages."

"I'm just fine, Samantha. It's wonderful to see you again. When I read about your ordeal out west, I couldn't believe my eyes."

She patted his arm, leaned down, and petted Roosevelt. "Well, I'm fine now too. I want to introduce you to my best friend, Angela Marconi. We work together in the White House."

Angela took the gentleman's hand in hers and gave him a big smile. "Great to meet you, sir. You remind me of an old quote I heard once. It was from President Reagan. He said, 'There are three stages of life: youth, middle age, and you look terrific.'"

Wilkinson broke into a hearty laugh and gestured for Angela to sit down. "My favorite quote from him used to be on a little plaque he kept on his desk. It said, 'There is no limit to what a man can do or where he can go if he doesn't mind who gets the credit.' And that reminds me, who found all those explosives on that mountain? The FBI never mentioned any names in the news reports I've seen."

"They don't like to name their agents," Samantha said. "You never know who might want to retaliate for something they do. But I know I can tell you."

Wilkinson leaned forward as she said, "Remember Brett?"

"Of course. *He's* with the FBI? Was he out there in Jackson?"

"Yes." Samantha's face suddenly lit up. "He found all the caches of C-4 by the tower and around the restaurant where we were having lunch. It was incredible." She quickly stretched her left calf and then continued. "So, now you know. I'm sure you can keep it to yourself."

"Absolutely," Wilkinson said. "I remember another quote from long ago, before you ladies were born. I believe it was Harry Truman who said, 'Never miss a good chance to shut up'."

Both women laughed. Samantha took a drink of water and checked her watch. "We should get going. I have some errands. But now that you're out and about, maybe we could have dinner sometime?"

"I'd be delighted," he said. "Whenever you have a free evening, you just let me know. It would be an honor to squire a young lady like you around town," he said with a mischievous smile. "You girls take care of yourselves."

"Will do," Samantha said. As they headed back to her car, she turned to Angela. "Speaking of dinner dates, I'd like to set one up for you."

"What do you mean?" Angela asked.

"Remember the FBI agent you met at Chadwick's? The one who walked you to your car?"

"Sure. He was with Brett. He's the one you said took great photos of the suspects."

"Yes, he's very good at what he does. He's also a really great guy. And his last name is Turiano. I'll bet your mother would approve," Samantha said with a grin.

FIFTY-FIVE

"WHAT'S THIS ABOUT?" BRETT ASKED, straightening his navy tie.

"I have no clue," Samantha replied. "I usually don't get summoned to the Oval Office unless there's something really big going on in my shop. It does seem strange, especially since you were asked to come too."

"The President will see you now," the ever-efficient secretary said. "Just follow the military aide please."

The young uniformed officer walked out of his glass-walled cubicle, opened a door, and led them into the well-lit room. Sunlight streamed through a trio of windows behind the traditional Rutherford B. Hayes desk, and photos of the President's family adorned a table just behind it. Two small bronze Remington statues stood on a side chest. The president was talking with the Chief of Staff, the NSC Advisor, and the Director of the FBI. A portrait of Abraham Lincoln observed the small gathering from the wall.

"What are our bosses doing here?" Brett whispered.

Samantha shook her head and walked forward. "Good morning, Mr. President. It's nice to see you today. This is Special Agent Brett Keating."

Brett stepped onto the white, oval rug with the presidential seal in its center and shook hands with the President. "It's an honor to meet you, sir," Brett said.

The President picked up his phone and said, "Kathy, would you please send in the White House photographer?" He motioned toward the fireplace across the room. "Let's stand over there."

The group moved to the appointed spot as Samantha exchanged a quizzical glance with Brett. A young woman with two cameras slung around her neck walked in and stood in front of them.

The President joined them and said, "I asked the director to invite you here, Agent Keating, because I know all about your actions in Jackson Hole. I also wanted Samantha here to witness our little ceremony."

"Ceremony, sir?" Brett asked, raising his eyebrows.

"I'll let the director take it from here."

The FBI Director stepped forward and pulled a notecard and a small box out of his pocket. "Agent Keating, as you know, we do not publicize the names of individual agents who have performed in specific ways, especially when a court proceeding involving their assignment is currently taking place. Since this threat against the Federal Reserve Conference is such a high-profile case that involved officials from all over the world, the President requested that we arrange this special tribute for you here at the White House. Please step forward."

Brett looked at Samantha who was beaming. She nodded to him as the Director read from the card. "The FBI Medal for Meritorious Achievement is awarded for extraordinary and exceptional service in a duty of extreme challenge and great responsibility, extraordinary achievement in connection with criminal or national security cases, or a decisive, exemplary act that results in the protection of the direct saving of life in severe jeopardy in the line of duty."

He then opened the box, took out a round medal, and handed it to Brett as the photographer snapped a series of photos. "And so, we present this to you, Special Agent Brett Keating."

Brett looked startled and rather overwhelmed as he stared at the medal. "I...I'm honored, sir. But I don't—"

"Yes, you do deserve this," the President said, stepping forward to shake his hand again. The photographer took another picture and quietly exited the room. "What you did to disarm those explosives, alone no less, is truly remarkable. We're all proud of you."

Taking a moment to recover from his shock, Brett took a breath and said, "May I make a comment about that, sir?"

"Of course," the President replied.

"I have to admit that I kind of swiped—I mean *appropriated*. . . Let's just say there were a couple of device prototypes in our office that were untested. I took them with me when I flew to Jackson. I couldn't have done any of that without them."

"What kind of devices?" the NSC Advisor asked.

"One looks a bit like a flashlight. It detects explosive material at close range. Without it, I'm sure I wouldn't have been able to find those caches in time."

"You said a couple?" the Chief of Staff asked.

"Yes. The other looks like a small hand grenade. They call it a BPE, a bomb pre-emptor. It has a pin you pull before tossing the device where you think an IED might be. It uses electrons to interrupt cell detonation signals. I used it when I thought there was a piece of C-4 higher than I could reach. I tossed the BPE where I thought the cache was, and that must have intercepted a signal. Or our agents on the ground stopped somebody from sending a signal. We just don't know."

"These are prototypes?" the President asked.

"Yes, sir," Brett replied.

The President turned to Ken Cosgrove. "Get with the SecDef on this, will you? This is exactly the type of equipment we need in the field. I don't know why our soldiers don't already have these things in their arsenals."

Ken said, "To be honest, Mr. President, there are so many products, weapons, and systems being offered to the Pentagon by defense contractors and small companies that it's hard to test them all in a timely manner. And now with the budget cuts. . ."

"I know about the budget," the President said. "But these are small items, so let's get about it. Imagine how many the Pentagon could purchase compared to another F-35 stealth fighter or a new Apache helicopter."

"Understood, Mr. President," Ken said.

The Director looked at Brett and said, "So, you *appropriated* some equipment without authorization. Is that correct?"

"Yes, sir. I'm afraid I did," Brett said.

"Good job. I'll tell Trevor he's got an agent who takes the initiative."

"Thank you, sir," Brett said, pocketing the medal.

The President turned to the FBI Director and said, "Now that the trial of those Russians is approaching, I trust you have all your evidence in order?"

The FBI Director replied, "We've been working overtime to put it together. We have witnesses lined up from Jackson and San Francisco, and we have the deposition of a Russian banker taken by one of our lawyers at Spasso House in Moscow. The deposition was Samantha's idea," he said, nodding to her.

She smiled in return as he continued. "We have cell phone and computer records, travel documents, stock transactions, photographs, and the testimony of the nephew of two of the perpetrators. He was the key to cracking this entire case. Took a lot of courage to testify against his family. But after everything they put him through, it looks like he's really trying to turn his life around."

"Yes, I've been briefed on that. How is the young man doing?" the President asked.

"Pretty well," Brett answered. "He had a little plastic surgery to change a few of his facial features, but he's recovering quickly. We've had agents with him 24/7, and our lawyers have him prepped for the trial. After that, he'll be in our witness protection program."

"Good work," the President said. "Oh, and Samantha?"

"Yes, Mr. President?" she answered.

"I want you to know that we've received thank you messages from almost every finance minister and central banker who attended that conference. They've sent not only words of gratitude for the FBI but also offers of further cooperation to track and shut down money-laundering accounts. And several working groups have devised new ideas to track and prevent the proliferation of various weapons systems, especially trades between North Korea and Iran. Pickering is especially pleased with this turn of events as I'm sure you've heard."

"Yes, Mr. President. We've made a lot of progress."

"Well, that's it then. We've got another state visit tomorrow, so we all have a busy day ahead of us. Thank you, everyone. And congratulations, Agent Keating."

As they walked out, the Chief of Staff turned left to go into his corner office while the NSC advisor walked straight ahead and opened the door to the Roosevelt Room to attend another meeting. The FBI Director, Samantha, and Brett turned right and walked toward the Cabinet Room. Then they took a left down a corridor leading to the West Wing lobby.

Brett turned to the Director. "Thank you very much for the medal."

"You deserve it. Thank you for your service. And thank you for helping to prepare the evidence and witnesses for the trial. Now that its only two weeks away, I doubt you have time for anything else."

"You are correct, sir. Our whole office is on it. Along with your top prosecutors, of course."

"Well, after we get the convictions—and we *will* get our convictions, thanks to you all—I may have another assignment for you."

Brett jerked his head up. "Already?"

"We'll let you finalize everything, and then you can take a few days off. But after that, I want you to come see me. Could be another major threat."

"A threat, sir?" Samantha asked. "Should my office be involved?"

"Maybe. It's too early to tell. But it's something I'm very concerned about." They reached the front door of the lobby. A uniformed officer opened it, and they stepped out toward the North Lawn. "Depending on how things develop, I might need both of you on *my* team this time."

FIFTY-SIX

"GOOD JOB," AGENT PAUL BORGES SAID AS he led Otto out of the courtroom through a back door. "The way you answered those questions on cross-examination was right on target."

"I was pretty nervous. But I remembered what you said: 'If you tell the truth, you don't have to remember anything.' I'm trying to learn to do that," Otto said with a slight smile.

"Well, you succeeded. All during your testimony, the defendants just sat there like statues."

"I saw that," Otto said. "That was one of the few times I've been in a room with Uncle Vadim when he wasn't shouting. Then again, I was behind that two-way screen, so I'm not sure if it counts."

"I think it does. Even though they couldn't see you, I'm sure the defendants still knew it was you under the voice alterations," Paul said, stepping into the hallway. "At least they haven't seen your new look."

345

"Agreed. Could I ask you a favor?" Otto asked.

"Sure."

"Did you see the girl sitting in the second row? The pretty one with short black hair?"

"Hard to miss her. I think she's been here almost every day of the trial. What about her?"

"Do you think I could see her? Talk to her? She's a friend. *Was* a friend. I've talked about her before. She's the one I went out with in D.C."

Paul hesitated and scrutinized Otto's face. "Do you really want someone from your past seeing what you look like now? The plastic surgery is supposed to change your identity so that no one will recognize you while you're in our witness protection program."

"I know. It's just that. . ." His voice trailed off. Otto took a long breath. "I want to thank her. She's the one who told me to get a lawyer and turn myself in. But she wouldn't talk to me after that."

"She was probably just afraid of being connected to all of this. It's a huge case," Paul said.

"I know, but this might be my last chance to talk to her. What do you think?"

Paul shrugged. "Come into this witness room. I'll go back in the courtroom and see if she's still there. If she gave you advice, it doesn't sound like she'll be a threat to you. What's her name?"

"Jolene," Otto said with an expectant look.

The agent nodded and walked back down the hall.

Otto headed into the sparse room and paced in front of a conference table surrounded by several plastic chairs. Would she agree to see him after everything he had put her through? He knew she was angry about his deception—never telling the truth about his life, his uncles, or the real reason he was in Washington. But he couldn't talk about any of that. Not until now.

Suddenly, the door opened. Otto spun around and saw her take a tentative step into the room, followed by Paul.

"Jolene, you came," Otto said with a rush of relief.

"Oleg?" she said, staring at him. "I hear your voice, but I don't quite recognize you."

"They gave me some plastic surgery to protect me from the *mafya*. Is it that bad?"

"Bad? No. You just look kind of... different," she said, standing very still next to the agent.

"I know I look different and, um, I want you to know that I *am* different. I know I did a lot of dumb things—some were bad things—but after going through all of this, I've changed."

"How have you changed?" she asked cautiously.

He looked over at the agent. "Can I tell her?"

Paul took Jolene's arm and led her to the conference table. "Let's sit down for a minute," he said as he pulled out a chair for her. Otto sat on the other side. He had no idea what he should say.

"First," Paul began, "his name really isn't Oleg. It's Otto. But that doesn't matter. We're changing it. Since he gave a crucial testimony in a case with international and underworld implications, we're also going to protect him."

She nodded as he went on. "He asked to see you, but do you want to see him after today? We try to put our protectees into a whole new life with a new home, a new job, and new contacts."

Jolene looked from Paul to Otto. Her face softened slightly. Finally, she turned to Paul and said, "When I first met him, I thought he was a nice guy. And after listening to his testimony,

I don't think I was wrong about that. It was obvious that he hated living with those sick men. But I never found out why you were looking for him. And not knowing worries me."

Otto held his breath, wondering how much Paul would tell her.

"Let's just say that we had reason to believe he was involved in activities that turned out to be minor compared to his uncles' plans for that conference. Plans that Otto had nothing to do with. So, when he came in to cooperate with us, we decided to start with a clean slate."

A clean slate. Otto really liked the sound of those words. He wondered if he could ever make a clean start with Jolene.

"I see. You really did do a great job at the trial," she said, looking at Otto again.

"Uh, thanks. But it wasn't just me. All those other witnesses were really good," he said.

"Yes," she said. "The case they put together was so compelling, especially that deposition from the Russian banker."

"I thought Vadim was going to have a heart attack when they played it," Otto said.

"And that meek little post office worker they flew in from Wyoming. He was kind of clever," she said. "And the woman from the Snake River Spa was very descriptive when she repeated the conversation she overheard about the tram as she gave Vadim a massage."

"Serves him right. He never treats women well. He treated Lubov and Stas the same way, which is probably why Stas broke down and ratted him out," Otto said.

Jolene looked like she was relaxing now. So was he. Otto carried on the conversation as Paul sat back and listened. "I still can't get used to my face. At least the bruises are almost gone."

"I think you look good. The doctors did a great job. It'll take a while to get used to, though," she said.

"Actually, I think getting used to my new name will be difficult too. That is, if you ever want to see me again." It seemed like a full minute passed before she answered.

"Am I allowed to see him?" she asked, turning to Paul.

"We have protocols to read in certain people if all parties agree. But there are strict rules. We can brief you if there's an agreement here."

She paused and then nodded. "I guess it wouldn't hurt to try and be friends. I trust the FBI."

"All right then. I'll let you two talk while I get some coffee. Want any?" Paul asked.

"Sure, thanks. Just black," Otto said.

"Same for me. Thanks," Jolene said.

When Paul had left the room, Otto said, "Thank you. I was afraid I'd never get to tell you that *you* were the one who gave me the courage to get a lawyer and go to the FBI. You're also what I've been thinking about throughout this whole nightmare. I know I did some bad stuff, but I never really hurt anyone. There are things I'll always regret, but I'll never regret meeting you. In fact, I think you're the best thing that ever happened to me. I hope you believe that."

"I want to," she said. "But it's difficult. I only just learned your real name. Part of me might always worry that I'll never be able to fully trust you."

"I understand. I will do whatever it takes to reassure you that you can. In fact, you'll be the first person I share my new name with. They said I could pick one, and I thought a new name would be easier to get used to if it started with an 'O.' So, I did a bunch of research, but there weren't a lot of names I liked. I looked up 'Oliver' and came up with Oliver Wendell Holmes, who was on the Supreme Court. But I didn't like some of the things he decided. So, I researched some of the other judges on that court, and I came up with Owen Roberts."

"What was he like?"

"He was pretty smart. President Coolidge asked him to investigate a huge scandal."

"Which?" she asked.

"Back then, they called it Teapot Dome. Had something to do with taking bribes. Since my uncles were experts at paying bribes, it kind of struck a chord with me. Anyway, another president, Herbert Hoover, appointed him to the Supreme Court. He also did something else I thought was kind of cool," Otto said with a slight grin.

"What?" she asked.

"Did you ever read about what they did with all the Japanese people who lived here during World War II?"

"They put them in concentration camps because they were afraid they might be working for the enemy."

"Turns out that Owen Roberts was one of the justices who voted against Roosevelt's order to put them into the camps. Since they were Americans and probably not doing anything wrong, I thought that was a good vote. So, I decided to take his name. Besides, I want to become an American citizen."

"Here you are," Paul said, stepping back into the room and handing them each a paper cup. "So, have you made any decisions?"

"Yes," Jolene said. "We're going to keep talking to each other. Where will he be living?"

"I told the FBI I'd like to get a place not too far from D.C. I guess I've always been hoping I could see you again," Otto said.

Jolene gave him a cautious smile.

"We're going to settle him in Maryland," Paul said. "We're already building his new identity."

"And they're bringing my mom over from Russia," Otto said. "I'll be taking care of her once I get a job."

"That's really great," Jolene said. "What kind of job?"

"The agents have been helping me get a lead on one I really want," Otto said. "I've already had an interview, and it looks like I might get it." He turned to Paul. "Can I tell her?"

"It's okay," Paul replied.

Otto smiled at Jolene and said, "I would be the local account manager of a group of small businesses, *legitimate* businesses, who set them up to accept crypto-currencies."

FIFTY-SEVEN

FRIDAY EVENING; WASHINGTON, D.C.

"THE JURY CAME BACK WITH THOSE CONVICTIONS pretty fast," Brett said, taking Samantha's blazer and hanging it in his hall closet.

"Sure, but was there ever any doubt?" she asked.

"Not in my mind. After all these weeks of preparing for the trial, it all panned out. We should celebrate."

"Absolutely," Samantha said. "What can I do to help?"

"You've cooked for me so many times, I thought it was only right that I feed *you* this time."

"I appreciate that. Besides, I'm glad I get to see your apartment. It's nice. You're kind of a neat freak, aren't you?" she said, glancing around at the sleek furniture layout.

"I guess. But it's difficult to mess up when I'm the only one living here. One of these days, I'll probably buy my own place and finally get all my things out of storage. This one came furnished, so I don't have much that's personal in here." He waved his arm toward an empty bookshelf and said, "I've often said it looks like something out of our witness protection program."

"That reminds me. There's something I want to tell you after dinner."

"Okay. Until then, come into the kitchen, and let's get you a drink."

"Let's get *us* a drink, you mean."

"Yes, since I'm finally off duty, I think I'll start with a beer. But I also have wine. I picked up a couple of different kinds. They're over there."

She examined the half dozen bottles in a wine rack in the corner and pulled one out. "How about this?" she asked, handing him a Clos du Bois pinot noir.

"Good choice. Not very expensive, but I remembered you like it." He took out his wine opener, removed the cork, and poured her a glass. He grabbed a beer from the fridge, opened it, and held it up. "Cheers," he said, touching her wine glass with his bottle.

"I think we can expand on that a little," she said. "How about a toast?"

"Let's see." He thought for a moment and then started to laugh. "So, there's this guy who works in my office. He's big on boats, and he said that someone came up with a great toast when they had the bicentennial and brought all those tall ships to New York."

"Do you remember it?" she asked, sampling her wine.

"I think it goes like this: here's to the tall ships and fair ladies of our land. May the first be well-rigged and the latter well-manned." He raised his bottle in a salute.

Samantha laughed and said, "I guess I can drink to that one. Now then, what can I do to help with dinner?"

Brett opened the refrigerator again and took out a package of lamb chops, a jar of mint jelly, a handful of broccoli, and a cantaloupe. "This melon is pretty ripe, so maybe you could cut it up for a salad? I'll start the broiler for the chops. We can cook the broccoli in one of those little pans in that drawer under the stove. Nothing fancy. Is that all right?"

"More than all right," she said, getting to work.

When everything was ready, they took their plates into the dining area and set them down on a table there. Brett took another glass out of a cabinet, refilled Samantha's, and then poured some of the red wine for himself. "Now that the trial's wrapped up and the Russians have been found guilty on all charges, I have to say that it's a bit odd Moscow stayed so quiet throughout the whole ordeal. They haven't asked us to send them back. That should help Otto get a better foothold here. It'll be interesting to see how he makes out with his new identity."

"That's what I wanted to talk to you about. He sent me a letter," she said, reaching for the mint jelly.

"Really? What did he say?"

"It was a handwritten apology for all the trouble he caused me. It was quite heartfelt," Samantha said, cutting a piece of lamb.

"After everything he put you through, he should have sent you the world's biggest gift basket or at least flowers." That reminded Brett of the last time he saw Samantha receive flowers. "Remember that night I was at your house for dinner? We were standing in your kitchen when you got that flower delivery."

"Yes. What about it?"

"It was from Tripp. The guy you used to date."

"Yes. I showed you the card. He said he was glad I was safe. It was a nice gesture," she said.

"I remember the card. He signed it with 'Love.'" Brett said, studying her face. "So, if you don't mind me asking, is he still in love with you? Or maybe my question should be are you still in love with him?"

Samantha looked at him, paused for moment, and replied, "First, it's okay to ask me about him. And no, I don't believe he's in love with me. He moved away, hasn't come back to see me, hasn't invited me to Dallas, and has only been in touch sporadically. I wouldn't say that's a man in love, would you?"

"Doesn't sound like it. But that doesn't mean you don't still love him," Brett ventured. "Not that it's any of my business."

"I'm not in love with him. I guess I still care about him as a friend. He's a good person, and we did a lot together. I told you about some of it," she said.

"Yes, you did. And since you were so involved for such a long time, I just wondered if it might mean you'd get back together at some point."

She took another sip of wine, sat back, and studied him. "I've thought about it. But the more I've analyzed it, the louder my dad's voice gets in my head. He used to say that I shouldn't just pay attention to what people *say,* I should watch what they *do.* Tripp said a lot of things, but he did other things.

"And we were both busy," she went on. "We both had tough jobs. Mine kept me up at night, and his kept him on the road most of the time. And he always seemed as happy to be traveling as he was in his Arlington apartment."

"And that didn't sit well with you? You didn't like him being away so much?" Brett asked.

"It wasn't exactly that," she said. "It was more of an attitude about living here. This may sound strange, but Tripp was a man of the world. I'm just a home-town type. I love it here. Traveling is fine, but I love this country. I want to stay here. I love working here. I love the White House, though I realize I'll probably only work there for the current administration. With Tripp and me, I'm not sure I ever trusted that we were on the same page. Does that make any sense?"

Brett stared at her and said, "It does. I feel the same way about being here, working here, the country, all of it. Besides, traveling is such a hassle these days." He glanced down at their nearly empty plates. "Let's get some dessert."

He got up from the table and took both of their plates to the kitchen. Samantha grabbed their wine glasses and followed him.

"Would you like coffee? I also have some ice cream." He opened the freezer and peered inside. "All I've got is chocolate, though."

"Perfect. Just one more thing we have in common," she said with a warm smile.

"Speaking of having things in common, have you thought about what the FBI Director said to us after that ceremony in the Oval Office?"

"Yes. It sounded like he might want us to work together again."

"I agree," Brett said, opening the ice cream carton and scooping its contents into bowls. He handed her one along with a spoon. "I wonder what he has in mind. I've been so slammed with this trial, I haven't had time to delve into much else. At least Trevor hasn't said anything about a new case. Have you heard about any new threats recently?"

She tasted a spoonful of ice cream. "Mmm. This is my favorite. Thanks. We get notices about new threats from the agencies all the time. But besides the usual things we've been tracking, nothing big and actionable has cropped up. We haven't elevated anything recently. Guess we'll just have to wait to hear from the Director."

Brett and Samantha were both leaning against the kitchen counter when he caught the intoxicating scent of her hair again. He turned toward her. She was looking up at him with what seemed like anticipation. Was that another invitation? If it was, he wasn't about to miss it this time.

He took the dish out of her hand, put it aside, pulled her toward him, and lowered his head. The kiss was gentle at first. When she opened to him, he deepened it and held her close. She wound her arms around his neck as he pressed his body against hers. He heard a slight moan as he cradled her head and ran his tongue over her lips.

"I've been waiting to do this for a long time," he whispered.

"Me too," she answered. "It took you a while."

He leaned back just a bit, glanced down at her, and said, "I was just trying to read the signals."

"Maybe I wasn't sending them on the right frequency," she murmured with a smile. "Trust me, from now on, I'll be sending them loud and clear."

There was the word "trust" again. As he kissed her once more and felt her warm response, he knew he could trust Samantha Reid. And he wouldn't have to verify that at all.

ACKNOWLEDGMENTS

THE INSPIRATION FOR THIS STORY CAME from several quarters. First was the phrase used by President Ronald Reagan when he referred to agreements with the Soviet Union. He said we must *Trust but Verify*. And when I wanted to write about devious Russians plotting against our own interests, those words came to mind.

As for the locations in Jackson, Wyoming—we had a home there for many years and had visited all of those places. The names of restaurants, parks, and hotels are accurate with one exception. I did take one bit of "literary license" when I placed the restaurant where the attempted attack took place at the top of Rendezvous mountain, when it is actually on top of a nearby peak, accessed by a different set of smaller gondolas.

The dialogue between Samantha Reid and her friend, Angela Marconi included many references to groups and organizations who tried to secure meetings with our government. All are true (crazy as they might sound). In writing a thriller, I do like to take a break from the action to insert a bit of humor every once in a while.

Finally, I'd like to thank John Kubricky, former Pentagon official, for information on newly developed listening devices and bomb pre-emptors and I want to thank Jim Chiate and Gordon Dale for their advice on the best ways to "short" the markets, along with schedule information from the staff of the Federal Reserve Bank of Kansas City, which hosts the annual meeting in Jackson Hole. Of course, I pray that this tale will not give anyone "ideas" about future conferences out in that beautiful section of our country. Besides, all of the official meetings take place at the quite secure Jackson Lake Lodge, not on top of a mountain in Teton Village. (At least they do now, and I trust they will keep it that way).

Now, I hope you enjoyed reading about the adventures of Samantha Reid and Brett Keating as I look forward to the publication of their next challenge in the months to come.